Jayne Ann Krentz, who also writes under the names Amanda Quick and Jayne Castle, has more than forty *New York Times* bestsellers under   wenty-five million copies of   the Pacific Northwest.

The futuristic   form the Harmony series. S   ompelling and critically-acclaimed Arcane Society world of Amanda Quick historical and Jayne Ann Krentz contemporary novels, which all feature her customary irresistible mix of passion and mystery, and also have a strong psychic/paranormal twist.

History of the Arcane Society:

The Arcane Society was founded in the late 1600s by a brilliant, reclusive, paranoid alchemist named Sylvester Jones. Jones possessed some unusual paranormal talents and he devoted his life to secret research in the field. He conducted experiments and recorded the results in a hidden fortress-like laboratory that eventually became his tomb.

The laboratory-tomb of Sylvester the Alchemist was eventually discovered and excavated in the Late Victorian era by two of his descendents, Gabriel and Caleb Jones. Inside they discovered the alchemist's most dangerous secret: a formula that Sylvester believed could enhance a person's natural psychic abilities and make the user extremely powerful. The stuff worked – but it produced some terrifying side effects. Over the years the Arcane Society has gone to great lengths to conceal Sylvester's formula but it haunts the Society and the Jones family to this day.

Each Arcane Society novel can be read as a standalone but each one will provide new information about the Society and its members that will be of interest to those who follow the entire series.

To learn more about the Arcane Society world visit www.jayneannkrentz.com

Midnight Crystal

Jayne Ann Krentz
writing as
Jayne Castle

PIATKUS

First published in the US in 2010 by The Berkley Publishing Group,
A member of Penguin Group (USA) Inc., New York
First published as a paperback original in Great Britain in 2010 by Piatkus

A CIP catalogue record for this book
is available from the British Library.

ISBN 978-0-7499-5242-6

Printed and bound in Great Britain by CPI Mackays, Chatham ME5 8TD

Papers used by Piatkus are natural, renewable and recyclable
products sourced from well-managed forests and certified
in accordance with the rules of the Forest Stewardship Council.

Mixed Sources
Product group from well-managed
forests and other controlled sources
www.fsc.org Cert no. SGS-COC-004081
© 1996 Forest Stewardship Council
FSC

Piatkus
An imprint of
Little, Brown Book Group
100 Victoria Embankment
London EC4Y 0DY

An Hachette UK Company
www.hachette.co.uk

www.piatkus.co.uk

For my brother, Jim Castle,
with love and thanks for the background info
on Dream and for Gibson's name.
Ride safe.

The Dreamlight Trilogy

Dear Reader:

Welcome to my other world, Harmony, and the conclusion of the Dreamlight Trilogy.

The legend of the Burning Lamp goes back to the earliest days of the Arcane Society. Nicholas Winters and Sylvester Jones started out as friends and eventually became deadly adversaries. Each sought the same goal: a way to enhance psychic talents. Sylvester chose the path of chemistry and plunged into illicit experiments with strange herbs and plants. Ultimately he concocted the flawed formula that bedevils the Society to this day.

Nicholas took the engineering approach and forged the Burning Lamp, a device with unknown powers. Radiation from the lamp produced a twist in his DNA, creating a psychic genetic "curse" destined to be passed down through the males of his bloodline.

The Winters Curse strikes very rarely, but when it does, the Arcane Society has good reason for grave concern. It is said that the Winters man who inherits

Nicholas's genetically altered talent is destined to become a Cerberus—Arcane slang for an insane psychic who possesses multiple lethal abilities. Jones & Jones and the Governing Council are convinced that such human monsters must be hunted down and terminated as swiftly as possible.

There is only one hope for the men of the Burning Lamp. Each must find the artifact and a woman who can work the dreamlight energy that the relic generates in order to reverse the dangerous psychic changes brought on by the curse.

Some of the secrets of the artifact were revealed in the first two books of the trilogy, *Fired Up* and *Burning Lamp*. Now, far in the future, on a world called Harmony, the lamp's final mystery—the secret of the Midnight Crystal—will be revealed. The destinies of both the Jones and the Winters families hang in the balance.

I hope you enjoy the trilogy.

Sincerely,
Jayne

Midnight Crystal

From the Journal of Nicholas Winters
April 14, 1694

I shall not long survive, but I will have my revenge, if not in this generation, then in some future time and place. For I am certain now that the three talents are locked into the blood and will descend down through my line.

Each talent comes at a great price. It is ever thus with power.

The first talent fills the mind with a rising tide of restlessness that cannot be assuaged by endless hours in the laboratory or soothed with strong drink or the milk of the poppy.

The second talent is accompanied by dark dreams and terrible visions.

The third talent is the most powerful and the most dangerous. If the key is not turned properly in the lock, this last psychical ability will prove lethal, bringing on first insanity and then death.

Grave risk attends the onset of the third and final power. Those of my line who would survive must find the Burning Lamp and a woman who can work dreamlight energy. Only she can turn the key in the lock that opens the door to the last talent. Only such a female can halt or reverse the transformation once it has begun.

But beware; women of power can prove treacherous. I know this now, to my great cost.

From the Journal of Nicholas Winters
April 17, 1694

It is done. My last and greatest creation—the Midnight Crystal—is finished. I have set it into the lamp together with the other crystals. It is a most astonishing stone. I have sealed great forces within it, but even I, who forged it, cannot begin to guess at all of its properties, nor do I know how its light can be unleashed. That discovery must be left to one of the heirs of my blood.

But of this much I am certain: the one who controls the light of the Midnight Crystal will be the agent of my revenge. For I have infused the stone with a psychical command stronger than any act of magic or sorcery. The radiation of the crystal will compel the man who wields its power to destroy the descendants of Sylvester Jones.

Vengeance will be mine.

Chapter 1

THE LADY FROM JONES & JONES LOOKED VERY GOOD in black leather.

Adam Winters waited for Marlowe Jones in the shadows of the ancient ruins. He had heard the trademark growl of the big Raleigh-Stark motorcycle for almost a full minute before the bike rounded the last curve of the narrow, winding road. Sound carried in the mountains.

The nightmares and hallucinations that had struck a few weeks ago had destroyed his sleep. He was living on the edge of exhaustion these days, fighting off the worst of the effects with short bouts of edgy rest, a lot of caffeine, and a little psi. But in spite of the toll the change had taken on him, a surge of exhilaration coursed through him when the newly appointed director of the Frequency City offices of J&J brought the bike to a stop and de-rezzed the engine.

She was close enough now for him to feel the power in her aura. Her energy sang a siren song to his senses. Too bad she was a Jones. He would just have to work around that awkward fact.

She kicked down the stand with a leg clad in leather chaps, planted one booted foot on the ground, and raised the faceplate of the gleaming black helmet.

"Adam Winters," she said.

It was not a question. He was the new boss of the Frequency City Ghost Hunter Guild. Anyone who had bothered to glance at a newspaper or watch the evening news in the past month could recognize him.

"You're late, Miss Jones," he said. He did not move out of the quartz doorway.

"I made a few detours." She unfastened the helmet and removed it. Her hair was the color of dark amber. It was caught in a ponytail at the nape of her neck and secured with a black leather band. "Wanted to be sure I wasn't followed."

He watched her, trying to conceal his fascination. Objectively speaking, she certainly qualified as attractive, but she lacked the bland symmetry of real beauty. Marlowe Jones did not need a cover model's looks to rivet the eye, however. She was striking. There was no other word to describe the strength, intelligence, and passion that illuminated her features. Her eyes were a deep, mysterious shade of blue, almost violet. *The color of midnight,* he thought. *Midnight and dreams.*

And just where in hell had that poetic image come from? He really needed to get more sleep.

She was watching him now with those enthralling, knowing eyes. Energy shivered in the atmosphere. He knew that she was checking him out with her talent. Everything inside him got a little hotter in response to the stimulation of her psi.

When she had called him that morning to request the clandestine meeting, she had explained, in passing, that she was a dreamlight reader. She had no way of knowing just how much that information had stunned him.

A small chortling sound distracted him. For the first time he noticed the passenger on the bike. A small, scruffy-looking creature studied him from the leather saddlebag with a pair of deceptively innocent baby blue eyes. A studded leather collar was draped around its neck, half buried in the fluffy, spiky, cotton-candy fur.

"You brought a dust bunny?" Adam asked.

"This is Gibson," Marlowe said. She held out her arm to the dust bunny.

Gibson chortled again and bounced out of the saddlebag and up the length of her arm to perch on the shoulder of her leather jacket. He blinked his baby blues at Adam.

"Didn't know they made good pets," Adam said.

"They don't. Gibson and I are a team. Different relationship altogether."

"Looks like you've got a collar on him."

"The folks at the gear shop where I buy my leathers made it for him. Gibson likes studs. He takes it off when he wants to play with it."

People, even smart, savvy people like Marlowe Jones, could be downright weird about their pets, Adam reminded himself. Then again, being a Jones, she was bound to be a little different anyway. Not that he had any room to criticize. During the past few weeks he had become pretty damn weird, himself. *Always nice to start off with something in common,* he thought.

"I'll take your word for it," he said. "So, you were worried about being followed?"

"I thought it best not to take any chances," she said, very serious.

He got the feeling that she did very serious a lot. For some reason that amused him. "Sounds like you're as paranoid as all the other Joneses who ever ran a branch of J&J."

"It's a job requirement. But I prefer to think of it as being careful."

Her voice was rich, assured, and infused with a slightly husky quality that heated his senses like a shot of good brandy. The edgy thrill of anticipation that he had experienced when he'd taken her call early that morning became crystalline certainty.

She's the one, he thought.

This was the first time he had met Marlowe Jones in person, but something deep inside him recognized and responded to her. He knew beyond a shadow of a doubt that this was the woman he had been searching for these past few weeks.

As fate would have it, in the end, she had found him. That was probably not a good sign. She was potentially a lot more dangerous than the people who had been trying to kill him lately. But somehow that did not seem to matter much at the moment. Maybe a few weeks of sleep deprivation had started to impact his powers of logic and common sense.

"I wasn't criticizing the paranoia," he said. "I'm a Guild boss. I consider paranoia to be a sterling virtue."

"Right up there with frequent hand washing?"

"I was thinking more along the lines of obsessive suspicion and a chronic inability to trust."

"Which explains why you got here early," she said. She surveyed the heavily wooded forest that surrounded them. "You wanted to check out the terrain. Make sure you weren't walking into a trap."

"It seemed a reasonable precaution under the circumstances. I have to admit, I got nervous after I discovered that these ruins are situated over a vortex."

She looked skeptical. "Can't picture you nervous."

"Everyone knows standard resonating amber doesn't work underground in the vicinity of vortex energy. Even the strongest ghost hunter can't pull any ghost fire when he's standing on top of that kind of storm."

"I am well aware that Guild men don't like to go anywhere near a vortex," she said.

"It's like asking a cop to leave his gun at the door.

After I arrived, it struck me that if I were inclined to take out a ghost hunter, I'd sure like to lure him to a vortex site."

"If you were really that worried, you wouldn't have stuck around."

He smiled. "Guess I'm more trusting than I look."

She eyed his smile with a dubious expression. "Somehow I doubt that."

At that moment Gibson chattered enthusiastically and tumbled down from Marlowe's shoulder to the ground. He hopped up on the toe of Adam's boot and stood on his hind paws. There was more chortling.

"He wants you to pick him up," Marlowe said. "He likes you. That's a good sign."

"Yeah? Of what?"

She gave a small, graceful shrug. "Never mind. Just a figure of speech."

Like hell, he thought. The dust bunny's reaction to him was important to her. When he leaned down to scoop up Gibson, the hair on the nape of his neck stirred. The heightening of energy in the atmosphere was unmistakable.

"See anything interesting?" he asked, straightening.

Marlowe blinked, frowning a little, as though she did not like the fact that he had realized that she was using her talent.

"How did you know?" she asked.

He plopped the dust bunny on his shoulder. "When it comes to talent, it takes one to know one."

She walked toward him, her boots crunching on the rough ground. "When I spoke with you this morning, I explained that I'm a dreamlight reader."

"Yes, you did. Not often I get a call from the head of J&J. Can't remember the last time, in fact."

"Your family hasn't had much connection with Arcane since the Era of Discord," she said.

"According to the legends, things have always been somewhat rocky between our two clans."

"I'm hoping we can put the old history behind us today," she said.

"Hard to do when there's so damn much of it. How did you get the job as the head of Arcane's Frequency office of J&J? Your predecessors at the agency were mostly chaos-theory talents of one kind or another, weren't they?"

To his surprise, she flushed a little, as if she'd taken the comment as a personal affront.

"Yes," she said. "Most of them were chaos-theory talents. But it turns out that the ability to read dreamlight is also a very useful talent for an investigator."

She was definitely on the defensive. Interesting.

"I'm sure it is," he said.

Wistful regret came and went in her expression. "Besides, it's not like the old days. Things have been very quiet for J&J since the Era of Discord. Mostly we handle routine private investigations for members of the Society. I've been on the job for nearly three months, and I haven't had to deal with a single rogue psychic. It's not like there isn't a lot of competition out there. Anyone with a little sensitivity thinks he can go into business as a psychic PI."

"The glory days of J&J are in the past, is that it?"

"That's certainly what everyone in Arcane says."

"You think that's why they put you in charge," he said. "Arcane doesn't need high-end chaos-theory talents running J&J these days, so they went with a dreamlight reader."

Her brows snapped together. "I didn't come here to discuss my career path."

"So why all the secrecy?"

"I'm afraid that you are not going to be happy to hear what I have to tell you."

"Believe it or not, I figured that out about a second and a half after you informed me that you wanted to hold this meeting in the middle of nowhere. Speaking of which, why don't you come inside the gate?"

For the first time she seemed to realize that he had not emerged from the shadows of the narrow opening in the green quartz wall. She looked puzzled, but she walked through the gate and stopped just inside the ancient compound.

The design of the ruins followed the pattern that had characterized most of the other outposts built by the long-vanished aliens. The only feature that distinguished it was the fact that it had been constructed over a vortex. Then, again, Adam thought, unlike humans, the aliens probably hadn't had any problems with vortices. Their paranormal senses had been far more powerful than those of the descendants of the colonists from

Earth. On the other hand, the humans had survived, he reminded himself. The aliens were long gone.

A high, fortresslike wall marked the perimeter of the compound. The handful of graceful towers inside the barricades were windowless. Narrow openings provided access to the various buildings, but it was obvious that the former inhabitants had not been keen on sunlight and fresh air, at least not the kind that was available aboveground.

Like the vast majority of the other ruins left by the long-vanished people who had first colonized Harmony, everything in the compound from the protective outer wall to the smallest building had been constructed of solid psi-green quartz. Even the ground was covered with a thick layer of the stone.

The quartz was impervious to everything the human colonists had thrown at it. Heavy construction equipment could not put a dent in the stone. Fire had no effect. Neither did the most violent storms. A bullet from a mag-rez gun could not even chip it.

Nothing grew on or within the walls or around the outside perimeter. The structures had stood for eons, but there was no moss, no creeping vines, no vegetation on any of the emerald surfaces. The same went for animal life. No insects or snakes had ever invaded the sites that had been discovered to date. Even the rats stayed clear.

The fact that Gibson did not appear to be having any problems with the atmosphere inside the compound was interesting, Adam thought. Like most of the human population, he seemed comfortable in the vicinity of green quartz.

Adam looked at Marlowe. "I think I've had enough suspense for one day. Let's have it. Why did you drag me out here?"

She visibly steeled herself, squaring her shoulders.

"The Burning Lamp was stolen from the Arcane Society vault sometime between midnight and seven AM this morning," she said.

"I'll be damned. Arcane managed to lose the lamp. Again."

She blinked. Her eyes narrowed. "I thought you'd be a little more pissed off. I realize that your family entrusted the lamp to the Society after the Era of Discord."

"Obviously a mistake."

She ignored that. "I went to the scene this morning immediately after I was notified of the breach in security. It took a while to even figure out what was missing."

"No offense, but the museum's cataloging system sounds like it's in need of an overhaul, as well as its security system."

"Yes, it does," she agreed, her tone very neutral. "However, from what I was able to see in the way of dreamprints at the scene, I'm sorry to say that it was evidently an inside job."

"Yeah? I'm amazed that you didn't leap to the conclusion that I was the thief. According to the legend, only a direct descendant of Nicholas Winters can access the energy of the lamp. There's no reason for anyone else to steal it."

"I am aware of that," she said. "The possibility that you were the one who took the lamp did occur to me. Your dreamprints do not match those of the thief, however. As I said, all indications are that whoever took the artifact was a member of the museum staff."

"You're that good?"

"I'm that good." There was a note of professional pride in her voice. "I believe I mentioned that even though I'm not a chaos-theory talent, I do have certain skills that are of use in an investigation."

"Now that you've seen my dreamprints, you can eliminate me from your list of suspects. Is that it?"

She cleared her throat. "There are other possibilities."

"Sure. Maybe I bribed or coerced someone on the museum staff to steal the lamp for me."

"That did occur to me, yes. Which is why you are still at the top of my list of suspects, Mr. Winters."

"I'm honored, of course. But there's one small flaw in your theory of the crime."

She studied him with her midnight eyes. "I'm sure you'll explain that to me."

"The Burning Lamp in the Arcane Museum was a fake."

She looked stricken. He realized that he had managed to shock her. The knowledge bothered him. She shouldn't have been quite so stunned. After all, it wasn't the first time Arcane had found itself with a fake lamp.

"Are you serious?" she said.

"My family has never trusted Arcane to take care of the lamp. When the Era of Discord ended, my multi-great-grandfather, John Cabot Winters, made certain that the Society got a very nice replica for their collection."

"Your ancestors here on Harmony had a fake made?"

"It was one of many my family has been obliged to commission over the years. Whenever the damn thing goes missing, which happens periodically, Arcane starts breathing down our necks. Sooner or later, we give the Society a fake lamp, and that usually satisfies everyone for another century or so."

"You mean until the Winters Curse strikes again," she said.

"Don't tell me you believe in family curses."

"No, but I do believe in genetics. Several centuries ago, Nicholas Winters managed to fry his own DNA with the Burning Lamp, and once in a while the results show up in one of his male descendants."

"That's the legend, all right," he agreed.

"Are you telling me that you have the real lamp in your possession?"

"No," he said. "It's gone missing again."

Comprehension lit her eyes. "Good grief, now I understand. You're looking for it, aren't you? That explains the rumors among the antiquities dealers in the Old Quarter. I've been picking them up for a couple of weeks now. In fact, I was getting set to launch an investigation."

"What rumors?" he asked, trying to buy a little time.

"Some of the dealers have been making very discreet inquiries about an Old World artifact. Word on the street is that a high-ranking Guild man was willing to pay well for it. According to the gossip, the relic possesses paranormal attributes."

"Why were you going to investigate?"

She moved one hand slightly. "Any artifact from Earth that is connected to the paranormal is automatically of interest to Arcane. Combine that with a mysterious collector who is highly placed in the Guild, and you'd better believe that J&J is going to get curious."

He stilled, aware of the extremely treacherous footing beneath his feet.

"What makes you think I'm the one searching for the lamp?" he asked.

"When did the nightmares and the hallucinations start?"

The question blindsided him. She knew about the nightmares and waking dreams.

"What are you talking about?" he said.

"I can see the signs of some ghastly dream energy in your prints," she said. "According to the legend, nightmares and hallucinations are the first signs of the change. I think you've been on the trail of the real lamp a lot longer than I have. Time is running out for you, isn't it?"

"Okay, Marlowe Jones," he said. "Now you've got my full attention."

She walked forward to stand directly behind him.

"If there is one thing about the Winters legend that appears to be true, it's that the Winters male who inherits the problem—"

"We in the Winters clan call it a family curse."

She ignored that. "The descendant of Nicholas Winters who inherits the genetic twist needs a strong dreamlight reader to help him find and work the lamp."

All of his senses were jacked now.

"You know," he said, "this whole scene seems just a little too good to be true. Why don't you tell me what's really going on here, Miss Jones?"

"I've explained. I asked you to meet me here today because I assumed you had arranged for the theft of the lamp. Now I find out that you evidently didn't steal it, which raises all sorts of other problems. But right now we need to concentrate on the first priority."

"Which is?"

"I can see that you need the lamp," she said. "If that's true, then you need me."

"You're from J&J, and you're here to help, is that it?"

"I don't have time to play games, and neither do you. You need me or someone like me." She broke off, frowning a little. "Wait a second, is that it? You've found yourself another dreamlight reader? Do you think she's strong enough to handle the lamp's energy? Because if she isn't, you're both going to be taking a huge risk when you try to fire up the artifact."

Before he could respond, a small spark of light flashed at the very edge of his vision. It came from deep within the dense stand of trees outside, just beyond the barren perimeter that surrounded the quartz walls. He was vaguely aware that Gibson was growling in his ear.

His reflexes took over. He got an arm around Marlowe's waist and propelled them both out of the doorway.

He tried to take the brunt of the hard landing on the stone floor, but he heard a pained *oomph* from Marlowe and knew that she was going to be bruised. Lucky she was wearing a lot of leather, he thought.

The glint of a studded collar flying past his field of vision told him that Gibson had leaped nimbly off his shoulder and alighted nearby.

The bullet seared a path straight through the gate. As soon as it entered the heavy psi environment inside the compound, it became wildly erratic, quickly lost velocity, and dropped harmlessly onto the floor. The crack of the rifle seemed to echo forever in the high mountains around the ruins.

Adam looked down at Marlowe, intensely aware of her soft, sleek body under the leather. Some of her hair had come free. She gazed up at him through a veil of dark amber tendrils.

"You're right," he said. "I do need you, and I need the lamp. But there's this complication."

"Someone is trying to kill you?"

"You noticed. I wasn't too worried about the

problem. Figured it came with the territory when I took over the Frequency Guild. But now I have to wonder if maybe I've been keeping an eye on the wrong people. Maybe Arcane has decided to take me out before I go rogue."

Chapter 2

"I REALIZE HOW THIS MUST LOOK," MARLOWE SAID, careful to keep her voice very even, "but I really, really hope that you don't think that I'm the one who set up this ambush."

She was not in the best position, tactically speaking, she thought. She was flat on her back. Adam sprawled on top of her, shielding her body with his own and simultaneously imprisoning her. His attention was on the slice of forest that could be seen through the gate. A considering expression lit his eyes. Then he shook his head once, decision made.

"Nope, not Arcane style," he said. "The Society is usually a lot more discreet. Gunning down the new Frequency Guild exec would create too much of a stir in the media."

This was not a good time to get pissed off, but she was; very pissed off. She was a Jones, after all.

"Golly, thanks for the vote of confidence," she shot back. "You make Arcane sound like some kind of criminal gang."

"Well, now that you mention it—"

"You're in no position to make that kind of accusation. In case it hasn't come to your notice, in Frequency, it's the Guild that has always been run like a mob, and everyone in town knows it."

"What do you say we save the semantics argument for a more convenient time?"

She took a deep breath and got control of her temper. "Okay."

Both of them were rezzed to the max, their senses elevated by the rush of adrenaline. Being this close to another powerful talent when you were both running hot was always disturbing, but in this case there was something else going on, and whatever it was, disturbing did not begin to cover it, she thought. The feeling of intense, hungry recognition and spiraling excitement that she had experienced when she had arrived a few minutes ago qualified as disturbing. What she was feeling now was nothing less than a stunning psychic shock.

Her senses were running wide-open, and she was in direct physical contact with Adam Winters, who was also rezzed to the max. She should have been fighting off the heavy energy of his nightmares and hallucinations that she had seen in his prints. She never touched others when her talent was at full throttle except in the course of her work at the clinic.

Gibson rumbled ominously in her ear. She turned her head a little and saw that he was no longer a cute ball of fluff. He had gone into full predatory mode: sleeked out, his second pair of eyes—the ones he used for hunting—wide-open. The studded leather collar hung loosely around his neck. He hovered protectively near her but, like Adam, his attention was on the opening in the wall.

Adam rolled to his feet, moving with the same specter-cat grace and power that he had displayed a moment ago, just before the rifle shot. He flattened himself against the green wall and studied the small section of mountainous landscape visible through the narrow opening.

Gibson dashed after him and took up a position near his booted foot, ready to hunt.

Couple of predators, Marlowe thought, getting to her feet. Automatically, she started to dust off the seat of her pants. She stopped when she remembered that there was never any dirt on ground covered with a layer of alien quartz.

She studied Adam's hard profile. In her hasty research that morning, she had located a rare image of Nicholas Winters, the alchemist who had forged the Burning Lamp centuries earlier on Earth. Adam was a mirror image of his ancestor, right down to the arresting green eyes and obsidian-black hair. There was no hint of softness in the implacably determined planes and angles of the features of the man in the portrait and none in Adam's face. Everything about him whispered of power. His enemies might be able to kill this man, she thought, but they would never break him, never shatter his will.

"Stay out of the doorway," Adam ordered.

"I'll certainly try to remember to do that."

He gave her a sharp, assessing look. "You've had some experience in situations like this?"

The doubt in his voice was clear. She wanted to defend her fighting skills. Unfortunately, she did not possess many. Uncle Zeke had taught her how to use a mag-rez gun, but she never carried it. Instead, it was safely tucked away in a hidden floor safe back at the office. A mag-rez wouldn't have done any good in this case, anyway, she reminded herself.

"I've been a J&J agent since I was in college," she said, keeping her tone cool and assured.

"You didn't answer the question."

"My expertise is in reading crime scenes and coming up with a theory of the crime. In essence, I'm a very, very good profiler, but I admit that I do most of my work at my desk."

"In other words, no one has ever tried to kill you."

"No," she admitted. "Like I said, business has been off at J&J for the past few decades. Any idea what this is all about, or is this just Guild politics as usual?"

"Someone tried to take me out shortly after the Chamber made it official that I would be assuming control of the Frequency Guild. Tried again a couple of days ago. This is probably the same guy."

"That's hard to believe."

"What? That someone might want to get rid of me?"

"No, Guild bosses always have enemies. But men in your position are also very high-profile. There was nothing in the papers or on the news about any attempts on your life. That kind of stuff would have made especially splashy headlines. Everyone knows that you were handpicked by the Chamber to take charge of the Frequency organization."

"I didn't hold a press conference. We don't work that way in the Guild."

"Oh, right. The Guild polices its own."

He ignored the sarcasm. "Same policy as Arcane."

She could not argue with that, so she moved to another topic.

"What now? Do you think he might be dumb enough to try coming through the gate with guns blazing? He's got to know how dangerous that would be."

It was common knowledge that the paranormal energy infused in the ancient green quartz had wildly unpredictable effects on high-tech gadgets of all kinds, including guns. A rifle or pistol fired inside the high walls of the compound was more likely to explode in the gunman's face than kill his intended target.

"No," Adam said. "He won't do that. He knows there are only two ways out of these ruins."

"The front gate or the tunnels."

"We're not likely to make a run for it. That would give him a clear shot on open ground. He wasn't trying very hard to hit me a few minutes ago. Just letting me know that he's out there."

"Why would he fire a warning shot and give away his position?"

"Because he doesn't want to shoot me. Like Arcane, he doesn't want a full-scale police and Guild investigation. He's trying to chase us down into the underworld."

She went cold.

"But this is a vortex site," she said, keeping her voice calm. "We can't go down."

"Don't look at me. Wasn't my idea to meet out here."

"Think he knows this is a vortex site?"

"No. He followed me, but there's no way he could have known my destination until we got here. He's been careful to keep his distance. He'd have to get a lot closer, at least as far as the perimeter around the walls, before he could sense the vortex. Even at that range, he'd have to have a lot of talent to pick up that kind of energy."

"For heaven's sake, if you suspected you were being followed, why didn't you shake him today? You must have had plenty of opportunities to lose a tail."

"Why bother? It would only have made him aware that I knew he was hunting me. It's not like a Guild boss can hide, anyway. Not with the media covering every move he makes."

"Got it," she said. "You've been hoping to lure him out of hiding so that you can grab him, right?"

"Yes and no. I'd certainly like to ask him a few questions, but he's not the one I want. I'm after the people who hired him."

"You think that we're dealing with a contract killer? A pro?"

"Well, I'm not sure you could call him a real pro. So far, he's missed twice."

"Probably because you're a very hard man to kill," she said. "No one makes it to the top of the Guild unless he possesses excellent survival skills."

"There is that," Adam agreed. "His objective today is to flush me into the underworld."

"Why would he do that? You're a Guild man. You know how to handle yourself underground."

"The idea is that I go down, but I don't come back up. It's the perfect way to get rid of a Guild boss without leaving any evidence."

"Yes, I know," she said. "The Guilds are notorious for using that method for solving their personnel problems. But for the technique to be effective, you have to strip a man of his tuned amber before you send him down into the underworld. If he's got good amber, he'll be able to use it to find his way back to the surface."

"That guy out there in the woods thinks my amber won't be an issue."

She glanced at the amber ring on his hand. The luminous, dark yellow stone set in black metal was engraved with the seal of his office. There was another chunk of amber in his belt buckle and in his leather bolo tie. She suspected that he carried a lot more elsewhere on his person. And every last bit of it would be tuned.

No Guild man, least of all the boss, would wear untuned amber. It was not just a habit or a safety precaution, it was a matter of pride and tradition. The Guilds were very, very big on tradition, and Adam Winters was descended from one of the oldest, most powerful Guild families. Back in the Era of Discord, John Cabot Winters had helped found the Ghost Hunter Guilds.

To this day the various Guild organizations controlled virtually everything of a commercial or scientific nature that happened down in the ancient alien catacombs and the underworld rain forest. A lot of what happened underground was extremely lucrative.

There were always a few tiny independent operators, fortune hunters, and thrill seekers who managed to sneak below the surface on their own. But large exploration and mining businesses, archaeologists, and researchers had to get their ventures approved and supervised by the Guilds who, in turn, provided security teams for the projects and took a cut of the profits.

The system had its critics, to be sure. A lot of people considered the Guilds to be only about half a step above organized crime mobs. But no one had come up with a viable alternative. The fundamental problem was that there was a lot of dangerous energy underground, and only those with a very special kind of talent could control it. Such individuals were commonly known as ghost hunters. Although there were a few women in the Guilds, the talent was closely linked to the masculine hormone testosterone, which, in turn, guaranteed that most of those who joined the Guilds were male.

Young men who were endowed with the ability to work the alien energy tended to join the organizations early in life, lured by the promise of manly adventure, a steady job, and the fact that young women considered Guild men hot.

"You've got plenty of amber on you, and don't try to tell me it isn't tuned," she said. She looked at the small black leather case securely attached to his belt. "What's more, I'm sure you've got an amber-rez locator in there."

"Sometime within the past forty-eight hours someone de-rezzed all of my standard amber," Adam said.

She was shocked. "That's not possible." She paused. "Unless you took all your amber to a professional tuner who sabotaged it?"

"No one has touched my amber since the last tuning work a month ago. I checked it later, and it was fine. But the frequencies of every piece of standard rez amber that I've got on me are now slightly warped. The disturbance isn't enough to be readily noticeable in casual use, but the damage is more than sufficient to make sure I'd get lost underground."

"How did you discover the sabotage?"

"Let's just say I've been taking a few extra security precautions lately."

"Okay, I can understand why a Guild boss might want to do that, especially after someone tried to kill him. Fine. Someone warped your amber. For crying out loud, why didn't you get it retuned?"

"For the same reason that I didn't try to shake the tail today."

She exhaled slowly. "I see. You didn't want whoever is hunting you to know that you are aware of him."

"Right."

Somewhere in the woods the rifle cracked again. This time the sound was followed immediately by a sharp pop.

She groaned. "Good grief, there goes a tire. That means I'll be buying a new one. Only a fool would patch a tire on a bike."

"Send the bill to the Guild."

"I'll do that," she said. "Why is he shooting at Dream?"

"You named your bike?"

"Of course."

"He wants to be sure we don't make a run for it," Adam said.

"If he's after you, why not go for your car?"

"He probably already took care of the car."

"By the way, where is your car?" she asked.

"Left it in the woods a quarter mile back."

"You say he wants to drive you underground." She touched her amber stud earrings. "But he knows you're not alone in here. Won't he expect me to have some amber?"

"You're a complication I'm sure he would have preferred to do without, but think about it from his point of view. He probably assumes I came here to meet a woman."

"Well, you did." She paused, realizing exactly what he meant. "Oh, geez. He thinks I'm the new Guild boss's secret mistress? That this was some sort of romantic rendezvous?"

"You're the private detective here. What would you conclude if you were in his position?"

She thought about the question. "Damn. You're right. The men at the top of the Guild are notorious womanizers. Your predecessor was infamous in that regard. Yes, I can certainly see why the shooter thinks I'm your mistress. You know, if he didn't have a rifle, I'd be tempted to go out there and tear a strip off him. Talk about insulting."

"The point," Adam said evenly, "is that very few people who don't have a reason to go down into the underworld carry the kind of highly tuned amber needed to navigate down below."

"So he'll assume that I don't have any good amber and that, even if I do, we would rely on yours, not mine." She paused politely. "You being the professional and all."

"He's thinking that we'll stumble into an illusion trap or a big ghost before we even realize we have a problem." Adam's brows rose. "Out of curiosity, do you carry tuned amber?"

"Of course. Some of my investigations take me into the underworld."

His mouth quirked. "You're from J&J. You're a professional, too. That makes three of us. Him, you, and me."

"I can't help but observe that all this talk about amber is beside the point. We can't go underground because of the vortex. Which leaves us with only one option."

"Yeah?" Adam sounded mildly curious. "What's that?"

"We'll have to outwait the shooter. He won't stay in those woods forever. Sooner or later he'll assume his plan has worked, that we've gone underground, and then he'll leave."

"Maybe," Adam said. "But we're not going to risk it. We're going to do exactly what he wants us to do." He turned and started toward one of the green towers. "Let's go."

Gibson chortled and scampered after him, eager for a new adventure.

Marlowe froze. "Where do you think you're going?"

"We're going underground," Adam said.

"But we can't. It's a vortex site."

"I'll deal with it."

"No one can deal with a vortex." She fought to keep her voice from rising. "That's why I chose this site for the meeting."

"I'm aware of that." He kept walking. "But the only reason I stuck around once I realized there was a vortex in the area is because I can handle that kind of energy."

She stared at his back, floored. "You can?"

"You don't have a very high opinion of my intelligence, do you? Did you really think I'd be dumb enough to meet with the head of J&J at a location that would leave me without any defenses or an underground escape route?"

"I just wanted neutral territory."

"I've never been a fan of neutral territory." He stopped at the top of a glowing staircase. "I like territory that I control."

"I did get that impression."

"Come with me, Marlowe Jones. I'll take you on a tour of the underworld."

She looked at him. "You really can handle vortex energy?"

"You're going to have to trust me on this."

"No offense, but how do you deal with it?"

Adam held up his left hand, letting her see the dark face of his watch. "In addition to standard amber, I can work full-spectrum stone. Turns out it can be used to deal with vortex energy."

"That's rainbow amber in your watch?"

"Yes."

"But it's just a dark gray stone. There's no color."

"It doesn't illuminate until I drive energy through it, which I do as rarely as possible."

"Why?"

"There's a major downside."

Another wave of unease fluttered through her. There was no trace of madness in his dreamprints, but she knew that he had been suffering nightmares and hallu-cinations lately. Perhaps he was seeing things that did not exist, things like an exceedingly rare kind of amber in the face of his watch. Maybe the visions had also led him to believe he could work the legendary energy of rainbow amber.

She opened her senses and took another look at his dreamlight.

He was amused. "Don't worry, I'm not hallucinat-ing."

"No, I can see that."

She shut down her senses and walked toward him. "I've never heard of anyone being able to work full-spectrum stone."

"Probably because there aren't a lot of us who can do it."

"What's the downside you mentioned?"

"I have to push a lot of energy through rainbow stone to control a vortex hellhole. It's the equivalent of melting amber. After we get through the vortex, I'll be good for about forty-five minutes, and then I'm going to need to sleep for a couple of hours."

"What's it like?" she asked.

"Going into a vortex? It's like walking into a night-mare. It won't kill you, but it isn't an outing in the park."

She followed him down the eerie green staircase, careful to watch her footing. The quartz steps were wide enough to allow ample room for her feet, but like everything else in the underworld, the proportions seemed slightly skewed to the human eye and sense of balance.

There was no problem seeing where she was going, though. The tunnels were fashioned of the same green quartz that the aliens had used to construct almost everything they had built above- and belowground. And every object made of the mysterious quartz from the smallest tomb mirror to the towering walls of the Dead Cities gave off an eerie, acid green light after dark and underground. Down in the catacombs, the lights were always on.

Like so many things related to the long-vanished aliens, the experts could not explain the luminescence. The working theory was that it was a side effect of the odd paranormal energy given off by the stone.

According to the theory, the energy had been vital to the survival of the aliens. It had become clear to researchers, that, while humans were able to thrive on Harmony, something in the environment had been poisonous to the ancient race that had arrived eons earlier. At some point they had abandoned the attempt to live aboveground. They had gone down below the planet's surface, constructing an endless maze of green quartz tunnels. They had also bioengineered an entire ecosystem, an underground rain forest, to sustain them.

But in the end, they had failed and disappeared.

Gibson bounded down the staircase and vanished into the welling green night. Marlowe wasn't worried about him. He loved to go underground. Unlike humans, dust bunnies did not need amber to navigate in the catacombs or the rain forest.

Marlow followed Adam around another twist in the staircase. "Why didn't you mention earlier that you could handle a vortex?"

"Because it's classified information," Adam said.

"Classified by whom?"

"By me, mostly. But also by the Chamber."

"You worked for the Chamber?"

Chamber was short for the unwieldy Chamber of the Joint Council of Dissonance Energy Para-resonator Guilds, the powerful, overarching governing organization of the Ghost Hunter Guilds.

"I was a Bureau agent for most of my career until I got this cool gig in the Frequency Guild," Adam said over his shoulder.

"I know a little about the Bureau. It's the Chamber's secret black ops agency."

"Sort of like Jones & Jones."

"J&J is not a secret black ops agency," she said coldly. "We just like to keep a low profile."

"So does the Bureau." He stopped on the next to the last step and waited for her. "Careful, the vortex energy starts right about here."

"I remember," she said. "This was as far as I got when I tried to explore these ruins a few months ago. Had to stop and turn back."

The first whispers of vortex energy were drifting around her now, setting all her senses on edge. The ominous sensation of creeping panic would only get worse. There was a reason why Guild men and others who worked in the underworld referred to vortex sites as hellholes.

"You'll probably see things," Adam warned. "Just keep reminding yourself that they aren't real."

"But that's not the worst part, right?"

"No. The real danger in a vortex is that people panic and start running. The energy storm zaps standard amber and locators immediately. When you do finally stumble out of a hellhole, you're lost. There is very little chance that anyone will find you, because your amber is shot."

"But that won't happen to us, because you know what you're doing."

"Right."

"Let's get it over with," she said.

Adam wrapped his fingers around her wrist. "I'm starting to understand why they made you the head of J&J. Here we go. Remember, when you're in the eye of a vortex, you won't be able to trust your vision or your sense of balance. Whatever you do, don't let go of my hand."

"Okay." Not that she had much of an option, she thought. His fingers were clamped around her wrist like a mag-steel manacle.

He went down the last step of the alien staircase, drawing her down with him. She followed him into a slice of hell.

Chapter 3

BETWEEN ONE GLOWING STEP AND THE NEXT, THE staircase and the illuminated quartz walls of the catacombs vanished, only to be immediately replaced by the featureless landscape of a nightmare. Her brain struggled to make sense of the wild energy and produced hallucinations instead. Primordial creatures from the deepest recesses of her unconscious mind rushed at her out of nowhere. They screamed silently.

It's just a dream, she thought. *Only a dream. You can handle this kind of thing. You're a dreamlight talent.*

She summoned her will, and the visions receded. The devastating sense of disorientation did not, however. It was as if she was moving through a psi green thunderstorm. She could not tell up from down, could not even feel the hard quartz under her feet. Ghost lightning crackled around her.

She had expected the vortex winds to grow stronger gradually, allowing time for her senses to adjust to the unnerving effects. Instead, she was instantly swept into the whirling tornado.

A rainbow of energy encircled her wrist, dragging her deeper into the storm. She fought the urge to try to free herself.

"I've got you. You're safe with me."

Adam's voice echoed from somewhere in the stormscape. She focused on it. She realized that she could also see the seething currents of his dreamprints. They should have been invisible in this wild energy field. The fact that she could make them out meant that he was even more powerful than she had thought.

A small monster fluttered toward her through the swirling mists. The creature's fur stood on end. It had four eyes and six paws and it made an anxious, chortling sound.

"Gibson," she whispered.

He stroked through the green storm until he reached her shoulder. He perched there, murmuring in her ear. The fierceness of the storm receded somewhat. She could make out Adam's dark shadow now.

After what seemed an eternity but what was probably no more than a minute or two, she stepped out of the stormscape as suddenly as she had walked into it.

The normal world settled into place around her, at least what passed for normal down in the catacombs.

They were standing in a seemingly endless green quartz hallway. A dizzying maze of identical passageways intersected the corridor at various points. The entrances to an uncountable number of chambers and rooms of various sizes and dimensions were visible as far as the eye could see.

And all of it glowed with the mysterious light that was characteristic of alien quartz.

Gibson chortled on her shoulder. No longer concerned about her, he bounded back down onto the floor and fluttered into a nearby chamber to do a little exploring.

Adam's alchemist eyes were still hot with the remnants of energy he had used to get them through the vortex. He did not release her wrist. She glanced down and saw that the manacle of rainbow psi that he had used to bring her safely through the storm was rapidly fading.

"How are you doing?" he asked. "That was a bad one."

"I'm okay." She took a deep breath and realized that was more or less the truth. "I see what you mean about the disorienting effect, though. No wonder vortices are considered such a hazard down here."

She realized that he was watching her with a thoughtful expression.

"You didn't panic when the hallucinations hit," he said. "I've had some experience taking people through hellholes. No one I've accompanied has ever handled the visual effects as well as you just did."

"Probably a side effect of my talent. I have an affinity for dreamlight, remember?"

"You're strong. You were fully cranked. I could sense your energy field."

His intense, watchful expression was a little unnerving. She did not need any more unnerving stuff. She tugged a little at the wrist he held captive.

He glanced down as though surprised to discover that he was still chaining her.

"Are you sure you're back in the here and now?" he asked.

"I'm sure."

He released her with obvious reluctance and looked down at his watch. The rainbow had disappeared. The stone was once again dark gray. She studied his dreamprints on the quartz floor. The signs of exhaustion were obvious.

"You burned a lot of energy getting us through that thing," she said. "You're right. You are going to need to rest soon."

"Do I look that bad?"

"I can see it in your prints."

He gave her a very unamused smile. "You really are good."

"Hey, they didn't make me the head of J&J because I was only average on the Jones scale. I may not be a chaos-theory talent, but when it comes to reading dreamlight, I'm off the charts." She frowned. "No offense, but you are close to the end of your physical as well as psychical reserves. Are you sure that just a couple of hours of sleep will be enough?"

"I've been living on two hours of sleep at a time for the past month. I can handle it. But like I said earlier, I've only got about forty-five minutes before I crash." He glanced down at his watch. The stone heated a little. "Looks like we've got a four-hour walk to the nearest exit plus an additional two hours for my nap. Let's get moving."

She glanced into the chamber where Gibson had disappeared. "We're leaving, pal."

He chortled, dropped the small quartz tomb mirror he had discovered, and dashed out of the room to join her.

They started along a corridor that curved away into the distance. Marlowe did some calculations in her head. "Six hours before we get out of here. That should put us back in Frequency around six o'clock tonight."

"If we're lucky."

"Why do you say that?"

"No telling what we're going to find in the way of civilization when we finally do get back to the surface. These mountains are sparsely populated and traffic is minimal, especially at night. No cell phone service, either. We're going to have to hitchhike back to the city, which means that we won't get home until we find a ride."

"What about your car?"

"I told you, the guy with the rifle probably made sure it's nonfunctional, like your bike."

She groaned. "I need to get back by the time the office opens or at least call my assistant to let him know I'm okay. If he calls my mother and it turns out no one knows where I am, the whole family is going to panic. Uncle Zeke, being a conspiracy theorist of the first order, will assume the worst. The next thing you know, every member of my family and every J&J agent will be out looking for me. I've only been on the job for two months. It will be humiliating."

"Not a good move for a Guild boss to disappear, either. If I don't show up back in my office pretty damn quick, the rumors will start flying."

"What rumors?"

"That I'm either dead or looking for a wife."

"A wife?"

"It's a Guild boss thing." His watch brightened. "We're in luck."

"What?" she said.

"This indicates that there's a jungle gate not far from here. That means we've got access to all the comforts of the rain forest. You won't have to sit here on the hard quartz floor while I nap."

"What good will that do? It's a heck of a lot harder to trek through the rain forest than it is to walk the catacombs."

"It will make a good rest stop. I'll be able to sleep off the burn, and there will be water. When we leave we'll take some with us. It's never a good idea to get dehydrated in the tunnels. It has a disturbing effect on the senses."

"How do you plan to collect the water?"

He tapped the small black pouch attached to his belt. "Collapsible canteen."

She smiled. "A Guild boss is always prepared?"

"That's the rule."

Chapter 4

HE COULD FEEL THE EXHAUSTION CREEPING THROUGH him like a virus, making it tough to stay alert and aware. It was never a good idea to relax in the catacombs. Illusion traps and the small energy storms known as ghosts were constant threats. The only defense was complete vigilance. If you triggered a trap or blundered into a ghost, it was game over.

The last thing he wanted to do was sleep, especially now. But there was no choice. He had pulled heavily on his already depleted stores of energy when he had taken Marlowe through the vortex. Now he had to use small doses of what little remained to get as far as the jungle gate. By the time he opened it, he would be finished. He had to make certain Marlowe was in a safe place before he went out like a de-rezzed lightbulb.

The slice of full-spectrum on the face of his watch

abruptly darkened to a shade of violet that was almost black. He stopped, unpleasantly aware that it had become a major effort just to stay on his feet, and looked at the featureless green quartz wall. It resembled every other green wall in the tunnel, but the energy that emanated from it was different in some subtle fashion.

"This is it," he said. "The gate."

Sensing a new adventure, Gibson rumbled excitedly and bobbed down from Marlowe's shoulder. He stood on his hind legs in front of the wall for a few seconds. A small opening appeared. He darted through it and disappeared. The dust bunny–sized hole in the wall closed.

"Well, damn," Adam said. "Didn't know the little critters could open gates."

"I think he comes down here to hunt at night with his buddies sometimes," Marlowe said.

"How do you know?"

"He's forever bringing me little presents that could only have come from the rain forest. Flowers, some odd berries and fruit, a shiny pebble. The gifts are always that strange green that exists only in the jungle."

"Psi green."

"Yes." Marlowe studied him with growing concern. "Are you sure you have enough energy left to open a gate?"

"I can handle it."

"I'd offer to do it, but as we know, my amber is shot because of that vortex."

He looked at her, surprised. "You can open gates?"

"I didn't know how until I met Gibson. He taught me."

"How the hell did he do that?"

"I can't describe the process. I just watched him do it a few times with my other vision, and I could see how to manipulate the currents. It's not all that different from handling dreamlight. When you get right down to it, energy is energy. Turns out a lot of alien psi comes from the ultradark end of the spectrum."

"The dreamlight end."

He pulled on his remaining reserves and focused through the spectrum amber of his watch, probing for the pattern of the gate currents.

The quartz wall glowed a hotter shade of green. An opening just large enough for a person to squeeze through took shape, providing a narrow window into the bizarre underground jungle.

Gibson appeared in the gate and chortled a greeting. He had a small stick in one paw.

"I'll go first," Adam said. He moved toward the gate. "Make sure there are no surprises on the other side."

Marlowe followed. "I'm sure there won't be. Gibson would have sounded the alarm if there was anything dangerous waiting for us in there."

"Probably, but, see, in the Guild we have these rules," Adam said.

He squeezed sideways through the opening and moved into the fantastic world of the rain forest. A heavy wave of heat and humidity hit him. In his exhausted condition it was too much. He grabbed a drooping vine cloaked with eerie green orchids to steady himself.

Damn. This is nothing short of embarrassing. Hell of a way to impress a woman, Winters.

Marlowe slipped easily through the gate behind him. When she was clear, he used his last ounce of energy to close the opening. He did a quick survey of the surroundings.

The rain forest grew right up to the walls of the tunnels. The trees, covered in trailing vines, rose toward an artificial green sky lit by artificial green-tinged sunlight. The leaves of the trees formed a thick canopy. Green birds flitted in the branches, and small green creatures rustled in the undergrowth. Nearby, water splashed from a waterfall into a grotto pool. There were several small caves in the rocks at the base of the waterfall.

"This will work," Adam said. "I'll use one of those caves. The water is safe to drink, and the fruit hanging from those trees is edible. There are predators down here, but so far the experts haven't found any that seem inclined to snack on humans."

"Yes, I know," she said.

"Sorry for the lecture. Routine. Whatever you do, don't wander off on your own. Remember, your amber is no good. You'd get lost as soon as you got out of sight."

"Don't worry, I won't be going anywhere without you," she said. "Gibson will warn me if anything dangerous comes along."

"Wake me in two hours if I don't wake up on my own. That should be long enough for me to recover."

"I'm not so sure. You are beyond exhausted."

"Wake me," he ordered. He gathered some thick leaves from a tree and headed into the cave.

"Adam?"

He dumped the leaves on the floor of the cave and sat down yawning. "Yeah?"

"What's the rule about a wife?"

"What?" He checked his watch again. He was so tired now that he could not make out the time.

"A few minutes ago you said that if you didn't show up in your office fairly soon people would assume that you were either dead or looking for a wife. You said it was a Guild boss thing."

"Old Guild tradition."

"I don't understand."

"Civilians," he muttered.

"I think we've established that my family is not Guild," she said. Frost gleamed on each word.

He yawned again. "Haven't you ever noticed that almost all of the heads of the Guilds in just about every city or town are either married when they take the job or get married soon afterward?"

"Hadn't thought about it," she admitted. "But now that you mention it, yes. Generally speaking, they do all seem to have wives. And they often enter formal Covenant Marriages, at that."

"You sound surprised." He lay down on the leafy

pallet. "You think marriage within the Guilds is any different than marriage outside the organizations?"

"Well—" She paused a beat. "I'm sure there are certain similarities."

The doubt in her too-polite tone annoyed him.

"I know you folks in Arcane are real big on the Society's matchmakers," he said. "For your information, Guild families use professionals, too."

"I've always heard that at the top of the Guild marriages are more in the nature of business and social alliances. Love and compatibility are not the primary considerations."

"Are you going to tell me that it's different at the highest levels of Arcane or society in general?"

"No," she conceded. "But it's different in my family. The Joneses have always been very traditional when it comes to marriage."

The rigid social and legal codes set in place by the First Generation colonists had been intended to ensure the stability of the basic building block of the social structure, the family unit. Laws and customs had relaxed somewhat during the two hundred years since the closing of the Curtain, but not all that much. Family was everything on Harmony. Love 'em or hate 'em, you were stuck with your relatives. If you entered a Covenant Marriage, you were also stuck with your spouse.

The loophole for couples who weren't ready to commit was the Marriage of Convenience, otherwise known as shacking up. The arrangements had legal standing, but they were really nothing more than affairs. MCs could be terminated at any time by either party unless there was offspring. A baby changed everything, automatically converting an MC into a full, very permanent Covenant Marriage.

Not everyone approved of MCs. Marlowe's family, for example, Adam thought, along with most of the membership of Arcane. Guild men were infamous for going through a string of Marriages of Convenience before their family and social pressure pushed them into a Covenant Marriage. After that, they settled for a string of mistresses.

"For some reason, I'm really not in the mood to explain Guild marriage traditions," he said. "I'm going to get some sleep."

He closed his eyes and stopped fighting the exhaustion. His last conscious thought was that the sleep that was about to overtake him would be deep and profound. With luck there would be no nightmares.

Chapter 5

MARLOWE SAT ON THE EDGE OF THE GROTTO POOL, eating a round green fruit that tasted of psi sunshine, and watched Gibson surf the grotto pool.

She had found the large piece of deadwood at the edge of the pool and tossed it into the water. After removing Gibson's studded collar so that it wouldn't drag him under, she had plunked him down onto the makeshift raft. He had taken to sailing with his usual exuberance and enthusiasm, just as he did every new game.

After drifting around the pool for a while he had discovered that he could get more speed out of the craft if he caught one of the small waves generated by the splashing waters. Half the time the churning waves toppled him off his surfboard, but he evidently considered the dunking part of the game. Each time he went under he came up chortling.

Marlowe took another bite of the fruit and tossed the remains into the undergrowth. She heard a brief flutter and scurry as something small leaped upon the unexpected meal.

She had removed her leather jacket and chaps in an effort to stay cool, but the heat and humidity were becoming oppressive. She was hot and sticky. Nevertheless, she was feeling better than she had in weeks. The pressure of the prowling restlessness that had plagued her for the past month seemed to have lifted. She felt focused once again. It was as if she had been searching for something and now, at last, she was on the right trail. Maybe all she had needed was an interesting case.

She glanced at Adam sprawled in the shadows on the floor of the cave several feet away. He was asleep, and he was dreaming. She was sitting just beyond the range of the strongest currents of his energy field. In addition, she was taking great care to keep her own senses shut down as tightly as possible.

She never liked to be near a sleeper. Everyone dreamed, and the energy generated in the dream state was intense and disturbingly intimate. She was forced to keep her senses tightly closed down in order to avoid the currents that always surrounded a dreamer.

Dreams were the ultimate personal and private experience, not meant to be shared. Brushing up against another person's dreamlight was always deeply unpleasant for someone who had a strong affinity for that kind of energy.

Adam had been asleep for an hour, but she sensed

that the short rest he'd had so far hadn't even begun to take the edge off the underlying layers of exhaustion. Two hours wasn't going to be nearly enough, either. He was seriously sleep-deprived. What rest he had been getting lately had obviously not been sound.

The fact that he had been able to function at all, let alone take control of the notoriously corrupt Frequency City Guild, was a testament to his power and will. Even so, it was clear that he had literally been running on psi, and no one, no matter how strong, could keep that up for long.

She had time for a swim, she decided. She tugged off her boots and was starting to unbutton her shirt when the first, faint frisson of dark nightmare energy whispered across her senses.

She winced. Her own nightmares were bad enough. Her instinct was to put more distance between herself and the cave where Adam was sleeping, to get out of range of the dark currents lapping at her own aura.

But the very fact that she could sense Adam's dark dream from several feet away with her senses lowered told her just how terrible the nightmare was. Something truly dreadful had clawed its way into his dreamscape. She could not leave him to these private terrors, not when it was within her power to remedy the situation.

"Out of the water, Gibson." She got to her feet and brushed some leafy debris off the back of her jeans. "Time to go to work."

Gibson knew that tone of voice. They had a new mission. He hopped off his surfboard, swam to the edge of the pool, and scampered up onto the rocky rim. Pausing briefly on the rocks, he gave himself a quick shake to fluff out his fur. Then he collected his studded collar and hurried toward her, ready to work.

"I have a feeling that Guild boss dreams are not what anyone would call sweet," Marlowe said. "Understandable, I suppose. The bosses aren't known for being nice guys, after all. Then again, a nice guy would never make it to the top of one of the Guilds."

Together she and Gibson made their way through a mini jungle of exotic, psi-green ferns. By the time they reached the cave, Adam was groaning in response to the scenes of his dreamscape. His muscles were tensed. Sweat beaded his forehead and dampened his shirt. He looked like a man in the grip of a raging fever.

Gibson fluttered close to one clenched hand and made a low, crooning noise. Marlowe braced herself and opened her senses cautiously. The violent energy of the nightmare came at her in relentless waves fueled by the full force of Adam's astonishingly powerful talent. She could perceive his entire dreamlight spectrum now that he was asleep and fully engaged in the nightmare. He was even stronger than she had realized.

She prepared to touch him. Physical contact always enhanced the connection between herself and a dreamer.

She could not actually see another person's dreams. No one could do that, just as no one could read another's thoughts. But her talent, which was directly linked to her intuition, translated the dreamer's energy into images that conveyed the emotional reality of the dream. The result was a disconcertingly accurate impression of what the dreamer experienced.

She put her fingertips on Adam's hot forehead. Midnight lightning lanced across her senses. Adam was lost . . .

. . . lost in an endless maze of mirrors, his senses short-circuited by the violent energy flashing and sparking off the brilliant surfaces. He had to get to her. He was the only one who could save her. The knowledge that he was doomed to fail only served to drive him harder. He was responsible, the man in charge. He could not leave her behind . . .

"Vickie," he mumbled.

The simplest approach would be to awaken him, Marlowe thought. But she was not sure that was possible under the circumstances. He wasn't just asleep; he was almost unconscious because of the psi-burn. It would be another hour, at least, before he could be safely awakened. Even if she succeeded in pulling him to the surface now, he would likely explode out of the druglike sleep, disoriented. People in the grip of a nightmare often reacted violently if they were awakened too quickly. That was especially true of those who were trained to react swiftly to physical and psychical threats. Guild men, for example.

The best option, she concluded, was to dampen the wavelengths of the nightmare.

She set her teeth against the howling gale of nightmare energy and went to work, easing her own currents into the storm.

She was no longer simply aware that Adam was fighting his way through a blaze of brilliant energy in an effort to rescue someone named Vickie. She was in the raging tempest with him.

The disorientation and dread were palpable forces, but Adam's grim determination to get to Vickie was even stronger. He would find her or die trying.

Cautiously Marlowe searched for the pattern in the currents of pounding dreamlight. When she found it, she did not try to alter it or suppress it with the sheer force of her own talent as she would have done with a weaker dreamer. Instead, she applied a gentle counterpoint.

It took a moment, but after a few seconds the hot, dark dreamlight eased into the patterns that she had learned to associate with normal dreaming. Adam stopped groaning. His hand unclenched. His fingers sank into Gibson's thick fur.

Marlowe and Gibson sat quietly for a time, waiting. When Marlowe was certain that the pattern of the dreamlight was stable and calm, she collected Gibson and left the cave.

"He's going to be out for a few more hours," she said to Gibson. "Time for a swim."

Chapter 6

HE CAME AWAKE QUICKLY AND FULLY, THE WAY HE always did underground. That much seemed normal. But something was different this time. He opened his eyes and looked up at the roof of the quartz cave.

What's wrong with this picture?

He felt more rested than he had in weeks. The ghostly images of the nightmare hovered at the fringes of his awareness, but they were already fading just as dreams were meant to fade when the dreamer awakened. The real-world memory of what had happened in the maze of mirrors would never disappear, but that was another issue altogether.

Something was wrong, all right.

He sat up and checked his watch.

"Damn."

Six hours had passed since he'd slid into the deep afterburn sleep state. *Six hours.*

Marlowe appeared at the entrance of the cave. He was pissed, but for some reason that did nothing to stop his senses from stirring at the sight of her. She had removed all the leather she'd had on earlier, stripping down to her white shirt and jeans. Her hair was still in a ponytail, but it was wet. He realized she had taken a dip in the grotto pool. He would have given a great deal to have witnessed her nude swim, he thought. The gliding movement of her breasts beneath the shirt made it clear that she had not put her bra back on after getting out of the water. It occurred to him that a bra would probably be uncomfortable in the humid heat of the jungle.

"Are you all right?" she asked. Her eyes were shadowed with concern.

He reminded himself that he was seriously annoyed. He rolled to his feet.

"I told you to wake me after two hours," he said.

"You needed the rest." Her voice was cool, firm, authoritative, the voice of a woman who was very sure of herself.

"That was not your decision to make." He walked out of the cave and halted directly in front of her. "We've lost a lot of time, thanks to you. We'll be lucky to get back to the city by dawn."

She did not retreat. "Are you always this grouchy when you wake up?"

"Let's get something straight here, Marlowe Jones. You may be the boss at Jones & Jones, but down here in the underworld, I'm the one who gives the orders."

"You needed the sleep."

"I did not need six hours of it. What's more, I didn't need you screwing around with my dream state."

Her eyes widened a little. "You know?"

"I remember having nightmares, and I've had enough of them lately to know that they don't go away on their own. You did something to stop them, didn't you?"

"I just eased the currents a tad. You were having a very bad dream. What was I supposed to do?"

"Believe it or not, I can deal with a few bad dreams."

"That's the real reason you're angry, isn't it? You don't like the idea that I witnessed you in the grip of a nightmare and that I pulled you out of the dreamscape."

"No," he said. "I don't like it at all. My dreams are my business. Stay the hell out of them."

"What about the hallucinations? Handling those just fine on your own, too?"

"I don't know what you're talking about."

"You're lying."

She was right. Usually he was good enough not to get caught at it, though. Clearly his skill set was failing him with this woman.

"From now on, stay out of my dreams," he repeated, mostly because he couldn't come up with anything more brilliant.

He unsnapped the leather case on his belt and took out the collapsible canteens. He stepped around her, heading toward the waterfall.

She turned on her heel, tracking him with a sizzling intensity that sent a thrill of awareness through him.

"You need me, Adam Winters. And I need you."

That stopped him in his tracks. He turned to face her. "What the hell are you talking about?"

"The Burning Lamp. You're searching for it. So am I. I've been doing a lot of thinking during the past six hours. According to the old legend, you require a strong dreamlight reader to find the real artifact. That would be me."

"Even if what you say is true, why would I want to form a partnership with the head of J&J? You'd be the one in charge of hunting me down if I did turn into a damn Cerberus."

"You are not going rogue," she said. "If that was happening to you, I'd be able to see it in your dreamprints. I'm a profiler, remember? I know what crazy looks like."

He went over his options silently. There were not a lot of them. She was right. He needed a strong dreamlight reader, and she fit the bill. In addition, she could access the full resources of Arcane. That might prove useful.

"Something you should know before we leap into this so-called partnership," he said. "I am looking for the lamp, but not because I need it to prevent myself from turning into some kind of psychic monster."

That was very probably a lie. He was changing in ways that could only be explained by the legend. It was entirely possible that the old tales were true. But he had a job to do. He would worry about his own future after he had completed the mission. He had to stay focused.

Marlowe frowned. "If you're not concerned that you might be turning into a Cerberus, why are you so anxious to find the lamp?"

"It's a long story." He checked his watch again. "We sure as hell don't have time to go through it here. I'll tell you on the way to the surface."

A SHORT TIME LATER, EQUIPPED WITH A COUPLE OF canteens filled with water, Gibson riding shotgun on his shoulder, Adam rezzed the gate. Marlowe followed him out into the glowing corridor. She was back in her leathers.

He paused, closed the opening in the wall, took another reading on the full-spectrum amber, and started along the passageway.

Marlowe had to hurry a little to keep up with him. It dawned on him that he had a lot more energy now than he'd had six hours ago. Okay, maybe he had needed the sleep.

"Let's have the whole story," Marlowe said. "Can I assume we're about to talk Guild secrets?"

"Chamber secrets," he said. "Which translates into Bureau secrets. And the Bureau is handling it on a need-to-know basis. A month ago I found something extraordinary in the jungle, even by alien ruin standards."

"What did you find?"

"A vast maze constructed entirely of highly reflective quartz. Imagine walking through these catacombs with every surface covered in mirrors, and you'd have some idea of what it's like."

"I sensed something about mirrors in your dream."

"Damn it to green hell. You can actually see my dreams?"

"Take it easy," she said. "It wasn't a lot of fun for me, either, trust me. And, no, I can't see your dreams, not in the literal sense. But if I have physical contact, my talent allows me to interpret the energy you generate when you are in the dream state. I knew that you were dealing with reflections of some kind. Thousands of them. Everything was too bright. Your senses were blinded. You were searching for someone named Vickie. You called her name."

"Close enough," he said. He glanced at her. "You said it wasn't fun?"

"Getting up close and personal with another person's dreamscape is always a bit nerve-racking." She shuddered. "Nightmares are the worst, of course."

He thought about it. "Yeah, I can understand that. Guess nature intended some things to be private."

"There's the privacy issue, not to mention intimacy issues. But most people are only too happy to tell you about their dreams, detail by boring detail. I don't think that's the real reason why touching a dreamer is so unsettling for someone with my kind of talent."

"What is the reason?"

"Dream energy comes from the deepest end of the spectrum," she said. "It is not meant to combine with the currents from the waking end. When I touched you, I was awake."

"And sensing my dream energy. I can see how that would set up some serious resonance issues."

"My talent allows me to handle the experience but, like I said, I find it very disturbing."

His curiosity was piqued now. "What about when you're asleep?"

"Oh, that's just impossible," she said.

"Hold on, don't tell me you don't sleep at all. Everyone sleeps."

"Of course, I sleep. Alone."

It took him a beat to understand the implications. When he did, he went cold.

"Always?" he asked.

"Always. I can't sleep in the same room with someone who is dreaming, let alone in the same bed. I hate hotels because the beds are always soaked in other people's dream energy. The only way I can sleep in a bed that isn't my own is by wrapping myself in a silk sleeping sack. For some reason silk acts as a barrier of sorts."

"Not to get too personal here, but doesn't that make for a few complications in your private life?"

"I don't have any problems getting a date, if that's what you mean."

"Well, not exactly."

"You'd be amazed by the number of men who think I'm the perfect woman. I'm always gone by morning."

"Huh."

"But it turns out that while men may not always be anxious to commit, they get offended when they realize that I'm not about to commit, either. I've never understood it, but they seem to take it personally."

"No kidding," he said. He wondered why he was getting irritated all over again.

"My mother tells me it has something to do with their rejection issues. But from my family's point of view, the real downside is knowing that I'll probably never marry. Joneses always marry. If I don't marry, I know I'll let down the family. If I do marry, I'll make myself and my husband, poor man, utterly miserable."

"Separate bedrooms?" he offered and then wondered why he was trying to find a solution in the first place. It was her problem, not his. He had enough problems of his own.

"Even if I found someone who would go along with that arrangement—and, believe me, men who think they'd be okay with it aren't as common as one would expect—it wouldn't work. After a while, I'd get resentful. Even though the situation would be my fault, I'd start blaming my husband."

"Why the hell is that?"

"Some part of me would conclude that if he was

really the right man for me, I'd be able to sleep with him." She paused. "I'm getting mad right now just thinking about it."

"Sounds like you've tested your theory."

"Once, shortly after college, I experimented with a Marriage of Convenience. Lasted about five minutes. He got mad when he realized I wasn't going to change. Took the separate bedrooms as proof that I was having an affair. I got angry because he didn't trust me. That's when I realized I was starting to resent him because I couldn't sleep with him. Things went downhill from there."

"Complicated."

"Tell me about it. My family is still embarrassed whenever the subject comes up. The Joneses don't do MCs." She frowned. "And just how did we get off on the subject of my private life? Tell me more about the maze."

He forced himself to focus. It proved surprisingly difficult. For some idiotic reason he wanted to argue about her sleep issues.

"Initially the mirror maze appeared to be just another weird alien ruin," he said. "But there is some kind of energy emanating from the mirrors and bouncing back and forth off the various surfaces."

"Like sunlight on a real mirror?"

"Yes, except that the energy in that quartz comes from the paranormal spectrum. It's not visually blinding the way sun on a mirror is, but it dazzles the para-senses, and that disturbs the normal senses as well. Going into the maze is a very disorienting experience."

"I believe it."

"The standard rez-amber locators don't work inside the ruin, but I discovered that I could navigate with full-spectrum. Two weeks ago I took a small lab team into the maze. We had to turn back because the energy levels were just too much for most of the team. But the para-archaeologist fell behind. She got lost."

"Vickie?"

"Yes. I knew I couldn't risk the whole crew by going back to search for her. So I got the others out."

"And then you went in after her on your own."

"I found her in a small chamber. She was in psychic shock. Awake but nonresponsive. I got her out of the maze, but she never woke up."

"She died?"

"No. She's still in a kind of waking coma in a para-psych ward at a private hospital."

Marlowe studied him with her knowing eyes. "She's not just a member of your team. Who is she?"

"Her name is Vickie Winters. She's my kid sister."

"Dear heaven. Of course, you blame yourself for taking her into the maze."

"Should have known better than to let her talk me into it. But she was right. We needed her talent and expertise to figure out what is going on in that maze. And it wasn't like I had a lot of choice in para-archaeologists."

"Why do you say that? There are dozens of them at the university in Frequency alone, not to mention on the staff at the city museum."

"I needed one I knew I could trust," he said.

Marlowe nodded. "You went with Vickie because she is family."

"Right."

"Why hasn't any of this been in the press?" Marlowe wrinkled her nose. "Forget it. Why do I even bother to ask? Just another Guild secret."

"Bureau secret," he corrected. "I haven't even told the members of my own Council about what's going on."

"Understandable. According to the press, the first thing you did when you took over was fire four members of the Council that you inherited from your predecessor."

"They took early retirement," he said evenly. "With full benefits."

She looked amused. "You mean, you persuaded them to take early retirement. I won't ask how you talked them into it. Given that you haven't yet replaced them, that leaves you with only five remaining Councilmen. I doubt that you trust them any more than you did the four you kicked off the Council."

"That is very insightful of you."

"Why didn't you make them take early retirement, too?"

"You know the old saying: keep your friends close, but keep your enemies closer. At least until you can prove that they're trying to kill you."

"Think it's someone on the Council who is after you?"

"Two someones. Drake and O'Conner."

"Hmm. Before the Chamber pulled its surprise move and put you in charge of the Frequency Guild, rumor had it that Douglas Drake was slated to get the top job."

"That was certainly Drake's plan. Hubert O'Conner was backing his play. The two of them go way back."

"If you know those two are gunning for you, why don't you force them into early retirement?" she asked.

"Because I think they're involved in something more serious."

Her eyes widened. "More serious than trying to murder you?"

"Yeah, and I'd like to find out what they're up to before I get rid of them."

"Does every Guild boss lead such an interesting life?"

"Mine may be a little more interesting than some at the moment."

"I'll say. Back to the mirror maze. You said you discovered it? Do you do archaeological work for the Bureau?"

"No. My expertise is in other areas. I sort of stumbled into the maze."

"Really?" she looked intrigued. "By accident, you mean?"

"Maybe stumbled isn't quite the right word. I was in

the middle of a Bureau investigation that took me deep into the jungle. Drug lab. While I was winding up the case, I sensed the maze energy and went looking for it. Found it several miles away in another sector."

She was watching him very closely now. "Any idea why you might have sensed it?"

"Probably because the energy being generated in that maze is from the ultradark end of the spectrum."

"Dreamlight. Hmm. Your talent emanates from that zone."

"I've got an affinity for that kind of psi, yes. So do you."

"True," she agreed. "But even those of us with a lot of talent can't sense it beyond a radius of fifteen or twenty feet at most. You said you found the maze about a month ago?"

"Yes."

"Right around the time you started suffering the nightmares and hallucinations?"

He hesitated. "Yes."

"And this was at some considerable distance?"

He exhaled slowly. "Like I said, it was miles away in an uncharted sector. That region of the jungle isn't even on the map. Where are you going with this?"

"I can't help but wonder if whatever is happening to you made you more sensitive to the energy in those mirrors."

"That possibility crossed my mind," he admitted. "As I was saying, I reported my findings to Elliott

Fortner, my boss at the Bureau. He notified the Chamber. In the end, it was decided to put the operation under my command. I've locked down the entire project. There's a research team on site working around the clock trying to find out what is happening inside those ruins."

"Why are you so concerned?"

"Because I sensed some instability deep in the maze."

"What's the Burning Lamp got to do with this?"

"Not all of the old family records concerning the lamp got lost during the Era of Discord. I've got John Cabot Winters's journal. He did a lot of research on the lamp. Based on what he concluded and what I experienced within that ruin, I think I might be able to use the lamp to stop whatever is happening in those mirrors."

"If you think the maze is dangerous, just make sure everyone is kept away from it," she said. "Anyone foolish enough to go inside will do so at his or her own risk. It won't be the first time the Guilds have declared certain ruins and sectors of the jungle off-limits for safety reasons."

"I'm not worried about losing a few thrill seekers and indie prospectors, Marlowe. It's the fact that the energy in those mirrors is slowly but surely starting to warp that has me concerned. The resonating pattern is becoming increasingly unstable. The trouble has probably been going on for decades, centuries maybe, but I think the deterioration is accelerating."

"What's the worst that can happen? An explosion?"

"Maybe. Or maybe the maze will just shut down. Either way, I think it's going to be a problem."

"Why?"

"My gut tells me that if that maze goes, it will take the entire underworld—rain forest and catacombs included—with it."

She stopped very suddenly, turning to face him. "What are you saying?"

He stopped, too. "Ever since we discovered the underworld, we've been trying to figure out what powers it."

"Good grief." She waved a hand to indicate the vast stretch of catacombs around them. "You think that maze is the source of the energy that keeps this place going?"

"Yes. What's more, if those mirrors blow, it may take out a lot more than just the underworld. That maze is probably the source of the energy in green quartz aboveground, as well."

"Do you think the Dead Cities and other ruins will just suddenly go dark?"

"That would be the best-case scenario. But this is alien energy we're talking about. Who knows what will happen if the power grid shuts down in an unstable manner? If the energy in the surface ruins suddenly becomes uncontrolled or erratic, there might be massive explosions aboveground as well."

"Frequency and the other big cities like Cadence and Resonance are all built around ruins. So are a lot of the smaller, outlying towns and communities. If all of the quartz explodes, the Old Quarters would probably be destroyed."

"Maybe. There are a lot of *ifs* in this situation. At this juncture, there's too damn much we just don't know. But my intuition tells me it could be very, very bad."

She took a deep breath. "That settles it. This isn't just a Guild problem. You need Arcane's help. You need me."

"Yes," he said. "I believe I do. I think we've got some time. Like I said, the destabilization process has probably been going on for years. I don't want to tell Fortner and the Chamber that the underworld and the Old Quarters in all of the cities will have to be evacuated until I know for certain that there isn't any alternative."

"I understand why you've kept a lid on this situation. If the media picks up on this, there would be instant panic. You definitely need Arcane. The Society has been studying the paranormal for centuries. For starters, we should get an Arcane lab team down to the maze to assist your people immediately. Meanwhile, you and I have to find that lamp."

"The problem with working openly with you and Arcane is that it's bound to start rumors."

She thought about that for a few seconds. "We shouldn't have any trouble keeping a joint research project quiet. Arcane and the Bureau have both had a lot of experience with that sort of highly classified work. But you're right; the media will certainly notice if you and I spend a lot of time together aboveground searching for the lamp. You're a Guild boss. The media loves gossip about high-ranking ghost hunters. We need a cover."

"Got any ideas?"

"I'm the head of J&J. Of course I've got an idea. By the way, I want to meet your sister as soon as possible. Preferably at night."

Chapter 7

❧

SHORTLY BEFORE NOON, WITH GIBSON UNDER ONE arm, Marlowe opened the glass-paned front door of Jones & Jones and walked into the office.

Rick Pratt was at his desk. He fixed her with an accusing look and held up a copy of the *Frequency Beacon*.

"You're having an affair with the new Guild boss, and you didn't tell me, your faithful office manager?" Rick said. "I'm crushed, I tell you. Devastated."

She had hired Rick immediately after taking over the office. He had been the first and only applicant for the job, but one look at his dreamprints had told her he would be perfect. Not only was he intelligent, he had a high level of intuitive talent and a flair for organization.

He was about thirty, red haired and blue eyed. He

wore a pair of gold-framed spectacles and bought his designer jeans and shirts at the trendiest shops in the Quarter. An amber and gold stud gleamed in his ear-lobe. There was an expensive engagement ring on his hand. He and his fiancé, Daniel Fields, a professor at the university, had been formally matched by an Arcane matchmaker. They were in the midst of planning a Covenant Marriage.

Uncle Zeke had been running J&J for years without an assistant, claiming there was no need for one due to the lack of business. It was certainly true that clients were not exactly standing in line out front, but Marlowe had big plans. She intended to make J&J the premier psychic investigation agency in Frequency, once again the first choice for members of the Society who needed the services of a PI.

"Let me see that paper," she said.

She put Gibson down on the desk and picked up the newspaper. The photo on the front page of the *Beacon* showed Adam and her standing on the side of the mountain road at two thirty in the morning. Gibson was perched on Adam's shoulder. The scene was illuminated by the headlights of the pickup that had stopped for them. It had been raining when they had emerged from the catacombs. All three of them were soaked.

The banner headline read, "Guild Boss and Mistress Caught by Storm." Beneath it was another line: "Rain Dampens Secret Rendezvous."

Gibson crossed the desk to the large ceramic cookie

jar and looked hopeful. After replacing three broken lids, Rick had devised a wire closure that thus far had withstood Gibson's attempts to get at the contents of the jar on his own. Marlowe knew that Gibson had not given up, but until he figured out how to undo the wire lock, he was forced to wait for Rick to open the treasure chest for him. Rick had given Marlowe a similar device to lock the cookie jar on her kitchen counter.

"Here you go, little biker dude," Rick said. He unfastened the wire lock and lifted the lid. "You probably need a couple of energy bars. Looks like you had a hard night up there in those mountains."

Gibson chortled agreement and hopped up onto the rim of the jar. He surveyed the mound of High-Rez Energy Bars inside. The bars were identical as far as Marlowe could tell, but Gibson always dithered a bit before making his selection. When he found the perfect bar, he tumbled back down to the desk and began to unwrap it.

Marlowe tossed the *Beacon* aside. "The rain ruined my new leather jacket."

"That's all you've got to say?" Rick demanded. "You're the head of J&J, charged with the noble responsibility of investigating crime. You're having a secret affair with the boss of the most corrupt Guild in the four city-states, and all you're concerned about is your new leather jacket?"

"I suspected the guy who picked us up had taken a couple of shots with his cell phone." Marlowe peeled off her old leather jacket. "He recognized Adam, of course. I didn't realize he would manage to sell the shots to the *Beacon*. Enterprising soul. Wonder how much he got for that picture."

"It's the *Beacon*, and it's an exclusive. Trust me, he got a lot for it. What's more, he took more than one photo." Rick held up another paper. "Sold this one to the *Examiner*. I think Gibson looks especially dashing in it, don't you?

She glanced at the second newspaper and winced at the picture. It showed her getting out of the pickup on a narrow street in the Quarter. She was wrapped in the old, tattered blanket that the driver had given her, and her hair was hanging in damp tangles. The finishing touch was the bright, psi-green sign of the sleazy tavern on the sidewalk behind her. The name of the establishment was Fallen Angel. The headline read, "Bad Date for New Guild Boss?"

"Oh, geez," she muttered. "I knew it was going to be bad, but I didn't realize just how bad."

Rick eyed the picture with a critical eye. "Winters looks good. But then, he's a Guild boss. You, on the other hand, look like a professional dominatrix who fell into a swimming pool. Bet all that leather got tight as it dried, huh?"

She shuddered. "Don't remind me."

"Cheer up," Rick said. "As far as I know, there's no video."

"I'll cling to that." She headed toward the inner office. "Anything from Pete on those alibis he's checking out?"

"Yes, but you're not going to like it." Rick got out of his chair and came to stand in the doorway. "He called this morning to say that everyone on the museum staff can account for his or her whereabouts at the time the artifact was stolen, but he also said that some of the alibis were less than airtight. He's digging deeper as we speak."

She sank down into the old chair behind her desk. It squeaked beneath her weight. The chair had been purchased by Jeremiah Jones at the end of the Era of Discord, one of several items of furniture that had been replaced after the rebels had torched the place. Every Jones who had taken over the Frequency office of J&J following Jeremiah had kept the chair, faithfully sending it out for repair as needed. No one had ever been able to get rid of the squeak.

"Would Dr. Lewis's alibi be one of those that isn't solid?" she asked.

"I'm afraid so," Rick said.

"I just can't believe he took the artifact."

"You're the one who said his dreamprints were the freshest at the scene. You told me they led directly to the cupboard where the lamp was stored."

"I know, but Dr. Lewis loves the museum," she said. "For crying out loud, he has dedicated his life to maintaining the collection. Stealing one of his own precious relics is completely out of character."

"People do things that are out of character all the time."

"Not according to Uncle Zeke," she said. "He claims

that if you look deep enough, you can always find the explanation for an act that seems to come from left field."

"No offense, but your uncle is a chaos-theory talent. By definition, he's always looking for conspiracies and patterns."

The chair squeaked again when she lounged back in it. "I know. Still."

"It's possible that Dr. Lewis has something a little twisted in his psyche that no one knew about until now."

"Maybe."

"You're not buying it, are you?" Rick said.

"Not yet."

"The problem with verifying Lewis's alibi is that he lives alone," Rick said. "He told Pete that he was asleep in his bed when the break-in occurred."

"Well, he does live alone. By the way, I'm expecting a call from my mechanic. Put him through immediately."

"Speaking of which, what the heck happened to your bike? And Winters's car, for that matter? I know the papers said something about both of you having car trouble, but that's a little hard to believe."

"Some idiot hunter mistook Dream for a deer. Flattened one of the tires. Adam sent someone from the Guild to pick it up and drop it off at the bike shop this morning. It's supposed to be ready this afternoon."

"And what about your, uh, date's car?"

"Same hunter got to it. Shot up the tires."

"Right. And if I believe that, you've got a solid-amber bridge you can sell to me."

She made a face. "Okay, okay. Adam has some enemies."

"Of course he does. He just took over the most corrupt Guild in the four city-states." Rick's eyes widened. "Are you saying that someone tried to kill him? While you were with him?"

"Yep. That's why we went underground and ended up hitchhiking."

"Whoa. Whoever it is must be desperate. The Guilds usually keep their political squabbles in-house. They don't like to involve civilians. That's an excellent way to attract the attention of the police, and that's the last thing the organizations want."

"Adam thinks that someone on the Council is very unhappy about being passed over."

"Sure. Douglas Drake. That's no secret." Rick gave her a benign smile. "So, how long have you been seeing *Adam*?"

"Not long." She swiveled the chair to switch on her computer.

"Thought you told me and everyone else that after Tucker Deene, you had sworn off men for six months."

"I changed my mind," she said evenly. "And if you want to keep your job, you will refrain from mentioning Tucker Deene's name in this office."

"Sorry, boss."

Rick sounded contrite, and she knew he was. Tucker

Deene had completely and utterly deceived her. For ten glorious days she had delighted in his company. He had seemed to possess all of the attributes that she had ever hoped to find in a lover: intelligence, humor, an upbeat and positive personality, and complementary worldviews. As an added bonus he had been incredibly good-looking. It had all made for a very sexy package.

Tucker had been perfect. Too perfect.

Discovering the truth had not broken her heart. She was almost certain that her talent made her immune to the kind of deep, abiding bond that her parents and so many others in the Jones family enjoyed. But the experience had done something much worse. It had shattered her faith in her own judgment. She was the head of J&J. She wasn't supposed to make mistakes like the one she had made with Tucker.

"Live and learn," Uncle Zeke had said. *"Chalk it up to experience."*

Attracted by the squeaking chair, Gibson tumbled through the doorway, the wrapper of the High-Rez Energy Bar in one paw. He hopped up onto the window seat and deposited the wrapper in the container Rick had placed there for that purpose.

Marlowe knew that Gibson was not into recycling. He just liked shiny things. Recently he had become especially fond of the bright orange foil wrappers that the High-Rez company used to package the energy bars. He had piles going both in the office and at home. Like all avid collectors, he was obsessed with adding to his collections, hence the new locks on the cookie jars.

When he had added the wrapper to the stash on the window seat, Gibson bounded up onto the desk and from there leaped nimbly to the high back of the chair. It was one of his favorite perches.

Rick folded his arms, propped one shoulder against the doorframe, and looked wise. "Bet your relatives freaked when they heard that you and Winters were seeing each other, hmmm?"

"In case you haven't noticed, I'm a mature adult. I don't take my dates home to be vetted by Mom and Dad." She paused. "But as it happens, they don't know yet that I'm seeing Adam Winters."

"Bet they do now."

"Relax. My parents don't read the *Beacon* or the *Examiner.* I've got plenty of time. I'll give Mom a call later."

The phone rang. Rick looked at it.

"Your mom," he said.

Marlowe sighed and reached for the phone. "Sometimes I forget that she's a high-grade intuitive talent."

TEN MINUTES LATER SHE ENDED THE CALL, THOR-oughly alarmed. She picked up the phone again and punched in the code Adam had given her. To her amazement, he answered personally.

"Hello, Marlowe," he said.

She frowned. "Don't you have an administrative assistant to screen your calls?"

"Of course I've got an administrative assistant. Two

of them. But this is my personal phone. No one screens the calls that come in on this number. It's not usually a problem, because very few people have this number."

"Oh, right." She cleared her throat. "I'm calling to warn you that I just talked to my mother."

"Why is that a problem?"

"She's heard the news. About us. I explained everything, naturally."

"Everything?"

"About how our so-called relationship is just a convenient cover story we're using while we work a joint project involving a major find in the underworld. I told her I'd tell her the details later."

"I'm waiting for the bad news."

"She said she was going to invite your parents and you to dinner. Tonight. Before we go to the clinic to see your sister."

"That's nice of her."

"Adam, pay attention here. I've had one or two other dates in my life. Mom never invited them or their parents to dinner. She knew the relationship wouldn't last long."

"Because your relationships never last long."

"The thing is, she knows now that what you and I have isn't a relationship. I have to ask myself why she's making a big deal about inviting you and your folks to dinner. That's the kind of thing parents do after a couple has been formally matched. Any way you look at this, it makes me very uneasy."

"Maybe this isn't about us, Marlowe."

She paused. "What do you mean?"

"Maybe this is about old times."

"Whose old times? Not mine."

"I just talked to my dad. Turns out thirty-five years ago, your father and my father both worked on a special task force, a joint Bureau-Arcane operation that was set up to track down a gang of rogue talents."

She was stunned into momentary speechlessness.

"My dad and your father?" she finally got out. "Worked a case together?"

"Yes."

"I didn't know that the Bureau and Arcane had ever worked together."

"Evidently the last time was thirty-five years ago," Adam said. "The gang they took down consisted of some powerful ghost hunters and some Arcane talents. The leader was named Gregory LeMasters. Ring a bell?"

"Sure. He was a legendary psi-path of the first order. The LeMasters gang controlled the drug trade from the catacombs. Absolutely ruthless." She paused. "But my father is a businessman."

"So is mine. Now. Doesn't mean they don't have interesting pasts. Dad's got a talent for working an obscure kind of ghost light. Evidently it was the same kind of alien psi that LeMasters used. Very powerful stuff."

She thought about it. "My father is a strat talent. That means he has an ability to think like the opposition."

"Or the bad guys, in this case."

"I can see where your father and mine would have made a good team," she said.

"There was a third member of the team that took down the LeMasters gang: Elliott Fortner."

"The Bureau chief? Small world."

"Especially underground," Adam said. "You know, the older I get, the more mysterious the older generation becomes."

Chapter 8

ELLIOTT FORTNER CRANKED BACK IN HIS CHAIR AND steepled his fingers. He studied Adam with his pale gray eyes. "Why the hell didn't her name pop up when we hacked into Arcane's files to look for a dream reader?"

"Probably because she's a Jones."

"It was a Jones who developed the scale the Society uses to measure talent in the first place. Are you telling me they don't use it to rank themselves?"

Adam almost smiled. As the man in charge of the Frequency City office of the Bureau, Elliott Fortner routinely kept more secrets in a month than most people kept their entire lives. But nothing irritated him quite as much as discovering that others could conceal secrets just as well as he did.

Elliott was a tall, distinguished-looking man in his

mid-fifties. Like a lot of men at the top of the organization, he had started out in the catacombs in his late teens. But when it had become apparent that he had a rare talent for working blue ghost energy, he had been tapped by the Bureau. His intelligence, ambition, and passion for his work had taken him all the way to the executive's office.

It helped, of course, that Elliott had married into one of the most powerful families in the Guild, Adam thought. As with any other large organization, those kinds of connections were an asset to advancement. Nevertheless, within the Guilds, ultimately, it always came down to raw power. No one got to the top unless he possessed a lot of talent.

"The Joneses have always been notoriously secretive when it comes to their own individual talent levels," Adam said.

Elliott exhaled slowly and tapped his fingertips together. "Can't blame them, I suppose. The public has always been wary of those who command a high level of psi. That was true throughout history back on Earth, and it's true here on Harmony."

"Yes."

"Even though the environment on this world has accelerated the development of the paranormal aspects of human physiology, not everyone is comfortable around strong talents. Still a lot of fear and suspicion out there."

"Sometimes for good reason."

Elliott raised his brows. "You say she has agreed to help you find the lamp?"

"Yes," Adam said.

He walked to the window and looked out at the towering wall of the Dead City across the lane. The cramped offices of the Frequency City branch of the Chamber's Bureau of Internal Affairs occupied the third floor of a small, anonymous Colonial-era building located deep in the heart of the Quarter. The ground floor was empty, the windows boarded up. The second floor housed the Bureau's lab.

"Can you trust Marlowe Jones, given the history between your families?" Elliott asked.

"It's old history, most of it based on myths and legends."

"According to what you've told me, the lamp itself is a legend."

"The lamp is real, trust me. It's been in my family, off and on, since the late seventeenth century back on Earth."

"Off and on?"

"This isn't the first time it's gone missing." Adam turned away from the view of the quartz wall and looked at Elliott. "My gut tells me it's our only hope of stopping whatever is happening down there in that maze."

"You're still sure of that?"

"When it comes to those ruins, I can't be certain of anything. But unless and until one of the lab techs comes up with a better idea, the lamp is all we've got."

"I don't like the idea of bringing the Arcane people in on this."

"Marlowe's right. When it comes to the paranormal, Arcane has accumulated more experience than all of the Guilds put together."

"They may be experts in the paranormal, but this is alien energy we're dealing with. When it comes to that kind of psi, we're the experts."

"Energy is energy, and we need all the help we can get. I've already given the orders. The Arcane team will be going underground to join our people later today."

Elliott did not look pleased, but he nodded once. "You're in charge of this project. It's your call. Meanwhile, you and Miss Jones had better get busy and find that damn lamp."

"That's the plan." Adam headed for the door.

"Adam?"

"Yes, sir?" He reminded himself that he no longer reported to Elliott. There was no need to call him sir. But old habits died hard, especially when you were dealing with a legend like Fortner.

"Watch your back," Elliott said. "Judging by what happened at those ruins, you'd better assume that Drake and O'Conner have hired a pro."

Chapter 9

"SHE'S A JONES, AND SHE'S A LITTLE DIFFERENT," ADAM said. "I think you'll like her, Vickie. She's strong. Like you. You've been telling me for years that I need a woman who will stand up to me."

Vickie did not respond. From a distance you wouldn't know that anything was wrong, Adam thought. It wasn't until you got closer that you realized that there was no indication of awareness in her vivid green eyes. Her once-animated face lacked all expression. She sat motionless in the wheelchair, gazing straight ahead at the hospital rose garden.

Her dark hair was cut in a sassy style that suited her. She wore an expensive red cashmere sweater, dark blue trousers, and loafers. Adam knew that his mother made certain that Vickie was always well-groomed. During the day, Vickie always looked as though she was about to dash out the door or go into her office at the university.

At night she wore one of her own nightgowns, not hospital issue. Diana Winters was working on the theory that somehow the element of normalcy in attire would help break through the trancelike state in which Vickie was trapped.

"Marlowe's coming here to meet you tonight," Adam said. "She says dreamlight energy is always strongest around midnight. I know that other dreamlight talents have examined you, but Marlowe is a lot more powerful than the others. Off the charts, I think."

It had been two weeks since he had carried Vickie out of the maze. Officially, the doctors had not given up hope, and the nurses were full of positive stories about miraculous recoveries after serious parapsych trauma. But he knew that the experts had run through all of their options, including the use of one of the strange ruby amber devices that had recently been discovered in the jungle. The ruby amber instruments were alien technology. No one knew how they worked, but some people with an unusual kind of talent were able to use them to treat certain types of psi-trauma. The ruby amber had not worked on Vickie.

The hospital was a private parapsych facility that catered exclusively to members of the Guilds and their families. He and Vickie were sitting at the far end of the serene, elegantly maintained grounds. He had wheeled the chair down here because the roses were in bloom. Vickie had always loved flowers, always loved color.

She looked thinner than ever today, he thought. The experts said there had been no change in her condition, but he sensed that she was getting weaker. The staff had assured him that she was eating properly and she received daily physical therapy. But something inside her was fading. He was losing his kid sister, and he was to blame.

In a few minutes he would urge her out of the wheel-chair and take her for a short walk through the rose garden. He knew from experience that she would not resist, but he also knew that she would show no reaction. Everyone else in the family took her for walks, too, when they visited, which was daily. They got the same lack of results. He wished she would struggle or show some stubbornness. The Winters were all fighters. But it was as if Vickie had given up and gone to sleep.

"The first time I saw Marlowe, she was wearing a lot of leather and riding a Raleigh-Stark," he said. "Got to tell you, there's nothing like the sight of a woman in leather on a high-rez bike to make a man sit up and take notice."

Vickie gazed straight ahead at the roses. He looked at the garden, too. The sundial in the center evolved into a glittering shard of mirror quartz. Nicholas Winters appeared in the face of the dial. His eyes burned psi-green. His mouth opened. He spoke in a voice that came not just from beyond the grave, but from beyond the Curtain.

"You are my true heir, blood of my blood, the one

I have been waiting for all these many centuries. You will find the woman and the lamp. You will unlock the command I have infused into the Midnight Crystal. You will be the agent of my vengeance. You will destroy all that Sylvester Jones hath created. Every last one of his offspring must die. It is my line that shall triumph."

Adam suppressed the hallucination with an act of will. He was getting better at it, he thought. Some days he was almost able to convince himself that the nightmares and the daytime visions were starting to fade.

"You know, Vickie, if any of your shrinks knew that I was having these damned hallucinations, they would suggest that I check in here, too." He got to his feet. "Let's take a walk."

He tugged her gently out of the wheelchair and guided her along the path. When they had completed the circuit, he settled her into the chair and took her back to the private room. He placed a book in her lap, one of her favorite novels of romantic suspense.

"I'll be back later tonight with Marlowe Jones," he said.

Vickie did not respond. He left her sitting in front of the window that looked out over the gardens.

He walked down the hall and went outside to the parking lot, where he had left one of the anonymous cars that he used when he visited Vickie.

He got behind the wheel, rezzed the engine, and drove out of the lot.

His family did not blame him for what had happened. They were Winters. They all understood the risks of working in the underworld. If Vickie was aware on some deep level, he knew that she did not blame him, either. But that did nothing to alleviate the guilt that burned inside him. He alone was responsible for what had happened to her. He would live with that knowledge for the rest of his life.

Chapter 10

AT NINE THIRTY THAT EVENING, ADAM LOOKED around the expansive great room of the Jones home and discovered that he was alone with Marlowe's uncle, Zeke Jones.

Dinner had concluded fifteen minutes ago, and now everyone was marking time until midnight when they would leave to go to the clinic. His father and Ben Jones had retired to Ben's study for a private conversation. His mother and Elizabeth Jones had excused themselves to take a tour of the Joneses' art collection.

Marlowe had said something about going outside onto the terrace for some fresh air. He could see her through the vast wall of windows that overlooked the ruins at the heart of the city. She looked very buttoned up in a black silk turtleneck top, a dark brown calf-length skirt, and high-heeled boots. She lounged against the stone wall, with Gibson perched beside her. Together they appeared to be drinking in the soft night. He wanted to join them, but it didn't take a psychic to know that Zeke Jones had set up this private meeting.

"Marlowe's been on the job for only three months," Zeke said. "Still getting her bearings."

Zeke was nearing eighty. Although he was officially retired, there was no sign of weakness or lack of energy in his posture. He possessed the stern, hard features that were characteristic of the men in the Jones family. A powerful streak of talent ran through the bloodline. You could see it in the eyes.

"She mentioned that she was new on the job," Adam said.

"She's the first Jones to take the helm of J&J in generations—centuries probably—who wasn't a chaos-theory talent. Makes her a little uneasy. Tradition can be a heavy burden to carry."

"I'm aware of that."

Zeke nodded. "You were born and raised inside the Guild. You know all about the weight of tradition. In some ways, Arcane is even more hidebound than the Guilds, though."

"Probably because it's been around a lot longer."

"I suppose so. But in Marlowe's case, there's an added element of family expectations. In addition to being high achievers, Joneses get married and produce large families. Marlowe's convinced that's not going to happen with her."

The last thing that he wanted to talk about was

Marlowe's personal life, Adam thought. He tried to think of something discreet to say.

"She, uh, told me that her talent complicates things," he finally managed.

"Yes, I'm sure she did. She's always very up-front about that sort of thing when she gets involved in a relationship."

Adam took a deep breath. "Marlowe prefers to describe our association as a working partnership."

"Is that what she calls it?" Zeke snorted. "She probably thinks I don't read the tabloid press. Well, it's none of my business. Marlowe is a healthy young woman. Did she also tell you about Tucker Deene?"

"Never mentioned him. Marlowe and I have only known each other for about a day and a half, sir."

"She met Deene earlier this month, and I'm sorry to say, she got badly burned."

Adam watched Marlowe through the window. "She fell in love?"

"According to her, that's not possible," Zeke said. "They only dated for about ten days, but Deene did some damage. She's still trying to recover."

"What kind of damage?"

"The bastard managed to deceive her along with everyone else in the Jones clan who met him. In this family, that's saying something. Hell, I liked him, myself. Deene made Marlowe think that he was the closest thing to Mr. Right that she would ever find. When she learned the truth, it shook her confidence in her own judgment."

"She didn't see anything in his dreamprints that warned her he was lying?"

"No. You have to understand, Marlowe has always been so certain of herself when it comes to reading dreamprints. But she had never run into anyone like Deene."

"What was he after?"

Zeke's eyes went cold. "We're pretty sure that he had his sights set on nothing less than a Covenant Marriage with Marlowe."

Adam whistled softly. "He wanted to marry into the Jones family? High stakes."

"Deene's father was a ghost hunter who died down in the catacombs shortly before he was born, but his mother was Arcane," Zeke said. "He was registered with the Society at birth, together with his brother and sister.

"If he knew anything about Arcane, he would have known that the Joneses are one of the most powerful families in the Society. Some say the most powerful. Deene wasn't your average fortune hunter, that's for sure. He was going for the amber ring when he tried for a CM with Marlowe.

"Marlowe claims that, in spite of what Deene may have believed, marriage was never in the cards," Zeke continued. "But she let Deene get close. She thought he might be Mr. Right."

"Mr. Right for what? You said she never intended to marry him."

"Just because Marlowe is convinced that she can't

get married doesn't mean she wouldn't like a long-term, stable relationship. She says that managing short-term affairs has become tedious. But after Deene, she told everyone that she was going to take a six-month break from dating."

"She reads dreamprints. How in hell did he manage to deceive her?"

"Deene turned out to be a chameleon talent," Zeke said.

Startled, Adam looked at him. "You mean they actually exist?"

"They're exceedingly rare, but they do show up once in a great while. I ran J&J for over forty years, however, and never encountered one, which should tell you just how scarce they are. Very little information on them in the archives."

"Is it true that they can imitate someone else's dreamprints?"

"Not only that," Zeke said, "they can alter their prints and their energy field to make you sense what you want to sense. In short, they can read you like a book and give you exactly what you want. Perfect con artists."

"No wonder Marlowe got blindsided."

"After it was all over, we realized that Deene had studied Marlowe closely before he made his move. Gave off the vibes of a serious-minded academic who was as passionate about his work as Marlowe is about hers. He shared an amazing number of her interests. And, last but not least, he rode a motorcycle."

"A Raleigh-Stark?"

Zeke's mouth twisted. "Naturally. Found out later that it was rented."

Adam thought about it for a while. "Deene must have generated a hell of a lot of energy to maintain the illusion when he was with Marlowe."

"I'm sure he did."

"Sooner or later he was bound to make a slip. How did he intend to keep up the act long enough to get through a long engagement?

"Who knows? He was good, though. Very strong. Probably assumed that as long as he never spent too much time in Marlowe's company, he could get away with it." Zeke waved the issue aside. "And when you think about it, keeping up the pretense wasn't as hard as you'd expect. Marlowe has never spent a night with a man in her life."

Adam remembered what Marlowe had said during the long walk out of the catacombs. "Always gone by dawn."

"And damn busy at J&J the rest of the time."

"So she never saw him when he was sleeping, the one time when he wouldn't have been able to maintain the pretense."

"No. I think he knew that he was safe on that front, as well."

Adam frowned. "He was aware of the downside of her talent?"

"Evidently. As I said, it's clear that he studied her before he moved in."

"How did she discover that he was a con?"

"Her intuition kicked in, and she did some old-fashioned investigative work. She had already done a routine background check on Deene in the Society's computer records, but after she got suspicious, she went looking elsewhere. Police files and such. It took a while to dig up the truth because Deene covered his tracks well, but eventually the pieces started coming together. Deene and his brother and sister have a long history of shady dealings. A family of con artists."

"In other words, Marlowe saved herself."

"Yes. But as I said, unfortunately, the experience shook her self-confidence. It will take her a while to regain it."

"I wonder how Deene planned to maintain the pretense after marriage?" Adam said.

"The general assumption in the family is that he wasn't worried about keeping up the pretense after the wedding."

"Why not?"

"You know how it is with a CM," Zeke said. "Once you sign the papers and take the vows, you're locked into the marriage for better or for worse for life."

Adam smiled a little. "Something tells me that once the Jones family realized that they had a psi-path con man in the clan who had taken advantage of Marlowe, Deene's life expectancy would have been shortened considerably."

Zeke's smile was equally cold. "Indeed."

"I don't get it. He had to know how powerful the

Joneses are and how they would protect Marlowe. He must have understood the risk he was taking."

"I'm sure that when the truth came out after the wedding, he expected that we would pay him a lot of money to go away and stay away. That's how it's usually done when a CM goes badly wrong."

"Wonder what made Marlowe suspicious?"

"She's a detective to the core. In addition to her talent, she's got a detective's intuition. She followed one of the oldest maxims in the Jones family. If something seems too good to be true, it probably is."

"We say that a lot in my family, too."

Chapter 11

"BEEN A WHILE SINCE WE HAD A DRINK TOGETHER," BEN said. He poured a healthy measure of whiskey into his guest's glass and then filled his own. "When was the last time?"

"Over thirty years ago." Sam Winters held the glass up to the light to study the amber gold whiskey. "Right after you and Fortner and I took down the LeMasters gang."

"Back when we were young and thought we could change the world."

"Or at least change things within the Guilds and Arcane." Sam tasted the whiskey, lowered the glass, and leaned his head against the back of the big leather easy chair. "We didn't make a dent in either of the organizations, did we?"

"No." Ben put the bottle aside, sat down, and picked

up his glass. "The Guilds and Arcane are both as hide-bound as ever. But that's what happens when you've got a lot of secrets to keep."

"What you call hidebound, others call tradition."

"True." Ben looked out the window to the terrace and watched Adam join Marlowe at the stone railing. "But maybe we laid the groundwork that will allow this generation to make a few changes."

Sam came to stand beside him. "They've made one big change already. Adam told me that today a team of Arcane lab techs went below to work with the Bureau people who are already on site at that maze."

"That's a first, all right. Never would have imagined the two organizations sharing that kind of classified information."

They drank their whiskey in silence for a time.

"Do you really think your daughter can save my little girl?" Sam asked after a while.

"I don't know," Ben said. "But when it comes to dealing with dreamlight trauma, Marlowe is the best."

They drank a little more whiskey and contemplated the couple on the terrace.

"Whatever those two have together, it's more than a working partnership," Sam said eventually. "Lot of energy between your daughter and my son. Earlier this evening you could almost hear the snap and crackle in the atmosphere."

"I noticed. So did Elizabeth."

"Working together on a joint project is one thing," Sam said. "But if those two get involved in a serious affair, there could be repercussions throughout both Arcane and the Guild."

"Your family was Arcane once, at least until the Era of Discord. John Cabot Winters made his choice after the conflict. He could have stuck with the Society. Instead, he embedded his family into the heart of the new Guild organization here in Frequency. He had to know that would cut him off from Arcane."

"It's not like they chose different sides during a civil war," Sam said. "They fought together against Vance's rebels. Saved each other's lives more than once, according to the old journals."

Neither of them spoke for a while. They watched the couple on the terrace.

"Well, one thing's certain," Sam said eventually. "It's a good bet that neither of our ancestors foresaw something like this happening. How the hell can it work, Ben?"

Ben looked at the way Adam was positioned beside Marlowe: close but not quite touching, leaning in a little, the way a man did when he was feeling protective, the way a man did when he wanted to make it clear to other men that this woman was his.

"Damned if I know," Ben said. "But if it does work, it could accomplish what you and I used to dream about all those years ago."

"Build some bridges between Arcane and the Guilds?"

"Look what the underworld has done to your daughter, what it might do to the cities. If Adam is right, the destructive power in that maze is enormous. Even if he and Marlowe do manage to resolve this problem, who knows what else is waiting to bite us down below? There are only two organizations that can even begin to deal with the dangers underground."

"Arcane and the Guilds."

"They need to share resources and talents, or the technology the aliens left behind just might get us all in the end. Hell, maybe whatever took out the aliens is still down there, just waiting to pounce."

"What about the liaison that seems to be forming out there on your terrace?"

"I don't know how it will turn out," Ben admitted. "But there's one thing I can tell you for sure."

"What?"

"There's not a damn thing either of us can do to stop it."

Chapter 12

"I AM SO SORRY TO HEAR ABOUT YOUR DAUGHTER'S condition," Elizabeth said gently. "I can only imagine how devastating it must be for you."

"Thank you," Diana Winters said. "It has been so awful. At first the doctors were optimistic that Vickie would recover. But lately they've given up. They won't say it out loud, but I can see it in their eyes. They simply do not know what is going on with Vickie. They admitted that they have never dealt with any parapsych trauma quite like the one that she suffered."

They both looked at the painting on the wall. It was one of Elizabeth's favorites, a scene of the ruins of Old Frequency glowing in the night beneath a lightning-charged thunderstorm.

"You do realize that Marlowe may not be able to help Vickie," she said.

"I know," Diana said. "But at this point we're willing to try anything."

"Of course."

Diana closed her eyes. Tears glistened at the edge of her lashes. "Forgive me. It has all been such a strain on the family. Not only am I worried sick about my daughter, I'm afraid that Adam blames himself for what happened to her. Nothing Sam or I say to him can convince him to accept the truth. It was a terrible accident, but it was not his fault. Vickie was—*is* a professional, and she's a Winters. She wanted to go on that exploratory expedition into the maze, and she was fully qualified."

They walked along the length of the gallery and stopped at the window at the far end. Down below on the terrace Marlowe stood with Adam. The energy of sexual awareness that shivered in the air around the couple was evident, even from this distance, Elizabeth thought. She had been keenly aware of it earlier, during dinner. *Oh, Marlowe, what have you done? You're falling in love with a descendant of Nicholas Winters.*

"I know what you're thinking," Diana said.

Elizabeth smiled wistfully. "Probably the same thing you're thinking."

"Trying to stop whatever is happening between those two would be like trying to stop a hurricane," Diana said.

The tall clock chimed softly at the end of the gallery. Elizabeth glanced at her watch.

"Almost midnight," she said. "Time to go to the clinic."

Diana took a deep breath. "I'm afraid to hope."

There was nothing to say, Elizabeth thought. But she was a mother, too. She understood. She put her arm around Diana. Together they walked back along the gallery to the staircase.

"I see." Nancy said. She came to a halt in front of a partially open door and gave Marlowe a sharp look. "Please be careful. Vickie is more easily agitated late at night."

"Dreamlight is always stronger at night," Marlowe said, keeping her voice equally soft. "If she typically shows more anxiety after dark, that may actually be a good sign."

"Why do you say that?" Nancy asked.

"Because it indicates that her trouble may be a disturbance in the ultradark end of the spectrum."

"And that's your area of expertise?"

"Yes."

Nancy searched her face for a few seconds. Marlowe felt a little shiver in the atmosphere and knew that the nurse was focusing energy through standard resonating amber, most likely her small amber pendant. *Surprise, surprise,* she thought. Nancy Hawkins possessed some degree of talent, and she was using it to take a reading.

Whatever Nancy sensed must have satisfied her, because she beckoned to someone inside the room. A middle-aged woman appeared in the doorway. Her name tag read Tina. A professional sitter, Marlowe thought. Diana Winters had explained that they had hired someone to stay at Vickie's bedside throughout the night.

Tina looked at the small crowd in the hallway and then glanced questioningly at Nancy.

"Is something wrong?" she asked softly.

Chapter 13

❧

"I'M SORRY, BUT I CAN'T ALLOW YOU TO BRING WHA
ever that animal is into the ward," the nurse said. H
name was Nancy Hawkins, and she was not pleased
the late-night visitors to the clinic.

Marlowe reached up to her shoulder to pat Gib
"It's all right. He's a therapy dust bunny."

Nancy did not appear convinced. "I've never
of a therapy dust bunny."

"Trust me," Marlowe said. "I do a lot of
light work. I have discovered that people with
parapsych trauma sometimes respond well
bunnies."

"I've never heard that," Nancy said.

Marlowe felt a little sorry for her. The nurs
prints were those of a dedicated healer v
goal was to protect her patient. But Nanc

"No," Nancy said. "Tina, this is Miss Jones. She's a strong dreamlight talent. The Winters family wants her to examine Vickie."

"I understand," Tina said. She looked at Diana. "But I must warn you that Vickie is somewhat agitated at the moment. In fact, I was just about to call in Miss Hawkins to ask if your daughter should have another dose of medication. I'm not certain this is a good time for a stranger to go into the room."

"I won't stay long," Marlowe said. "I'll just take a quick look. If I see that I can't do anything helpful, I'll leave immediately."

"It's all right, Tina," Sam Winters said.

The sitter said nothing more, but she got out of the way. Adam and the others waited outside in the hall, as promised. Marlowe walked into the shadowed room and stopped next to the crisply made bed. She opened her senses slowly. Gibson muttered. She felt his small paws tighten on her shoulder. Animals had their own psychic natures. They usually responded to subtle changes in the atmosphere before humans picked up the currents.

In this case, however, there was nothing subtle about the dark, chaotic currents of dreamlight that roared and crashed around the sleeping figure on the bed. Vickie Winters was locked in a world of nightmares. Her eyes were closed, but her lashes twitched and her fingers trembled. Small but spasmodic shudders swept through her thin frame. Her hands were clenched.

Marlowe fought her instinctive urge to shut down

her talent in order to protect herself. Instead, she deliberately went hotter, focusing on the seething, churning energy pouring from Vickie's aura. The currents were coming from the darkest end of the spectrum, and they were fluctuating wildly. The underlying pulses appeared strong at the source, but the rogue waves slamming through them destabilized the patterns so that they failed to oscillate properly.

The damage was bad and ongoing, but the fact that Vickie's own powerful energy field was still generating a steady, stable pattern meant that there was hope. Deep down, Vickie was fighting the battle for her own sanity. Thus far she had held the line, but she was weakening. She needed backup.

"It's okay, Vickie," Marlowe said. "I'm here. We'll get through this together."

Gibson hopped down onto the bed. His second set of eyes opened, glowing amber in the shadows, but he did not go into full hunting mode. He hovered next to Vickie's hand.

Marlowe touched him, feeling the sleek little predator beneath the ball-of-lint fur.

"Ready, pal?"

Gibson chattered softly. In these situations he always seemed to understand that they were on a mission.

Marlowe braced for the jolt she knew would come and put her fingertips on Vickie's brow.

The psychic shock waves smashed into her senses. The intuitive elements of her talent interpreted the energy frantically, delivering a senses-disorienting dreamscape.

. . . She was running through endless corridors of mirrors. The brilliant, polished surfaces surrounded her on all sides, forming the walls, ceiling, and floors of the maze. Lightning flashed and burned and ricocheted from one impossibly brilliant surface to another.

Somewhere in the echoing world of reflections she could hear familiar voices calling to her: Adam, her mother, her father. But she could not find them, and they could not find her.

Everywhere she looked she was confronted by infinitely repeating reflections of herself, an infinity of Vickies. They screamed. They laughed. They sobbed. She could no longer tell which image was the real Vickie, so she kept running.

Another, unfamiliar voice was calling her name . . .

"Vickie, you're in a dream, but I know you can hear me. I have suppressed the rogue waves in your dreamlight patterns. You are in control of the dreamscape now. Listen to my voice."

The endless Vickie reflections were receding into the distance, growing fainter. The energy flashing and sparking off the mirrored surfaces was weakening . . .

"Stop running, Vickie. Panic is making you run. You are no longer afraid, because you are in control. Focus on the sound of my voice. You will see the exit from the maze. This is a lucid dream now. You control it."

One entire section of the mirrored corridor dissolved. She could see darkness beyond. Light slanted through the shadows, a familiar kind of light, not the blinding energy that had been bouncing off the mirrors . . .

"Concentrate on the opening in the maze, Vickie. Use your talent to focus on it. Walk through it. Don't try to run. Just walk. You are in control of this dreamscape now."

Vickie opened her eyes. She looked around the shadowed room for a few seconds, confused. Gibson chortled and pushed close to one of her hands. Vickie touched him without seeming to be aware of it. Her fingers tightened in his fur. She grew visibly calmer.

"Welcome back," Marlowe said gently.

Vickie turned her head on the pillow and looked at her.

"Who are you?" she whispered.

"A friend of the family," Marlowe said. Before she could explain, she heard rapid footsteps on the floor behind her.

Diana Winters rushed toward the bed.

"Vickie? Are you really awake?"

Vickie pushed herself up on her elbows.

"Hi, Mom."

Chapter 14

"VICKIE REALLY WILL BE OKAY?" ADAM SAID. "THE FIX is permanent?"

"She'll be fine." Marlowe unfastened the wire lock on the cookie jar, removed the lid, and waited for Gibson to select two perfect High-Rez Energy Bars. "There was no permanent damage done to her underlying field. When she got zapped by the bad energy in that maze, her senses were overloaded. A lot of people, certainly anyone who lacked a very strong parapsych profile, would have been driven insane or died on the spot."

"But she's a Winters," Adam said, not bothering to conceal his pride. "She held the line until reinforcements arrived."

Marlowe smiled. "Yep, she's a Winters."

Chortling gleefully, Gibson hopped down from the

rim of the cookie jar and set about peeling off the wrappers of the two bars.

Marlowe locked the cookie jar and plucked two small glasses and a bottle of Amber Dew out of a cabinet.

She and Adam were alone. Adam's parents had stayed behind at the hospital. Hers had returned home. Adam had driven her back to her condo in the Quarter, and she had invited him in for nightcap. After all, it had been a very long night. And they were partners.

There had been no outbreak of jubilation after Vickie Winters had awakened. The initial reaction was disbelief followed by a lot of tears. Not all of the tears had been spilled by Diana Winters. Marlowe had seen a suspicious glitter in Adam's eyes. Sam Winters had choked up as well.

There had also been questions, mostly from a very confused and disoriented Vickie. She had awakened with no memory of her experience. She had also been utterly exhausted because the trancelike state had not allowed for any healing sleep.

Marlowe set the bottle aside, picked up the two glasses of Amber Dew, and carried them across the room. She put the glasses down on the coffee table and crossed to the wall to rez the flash-rock fireplace. When the flames leaped on the hearth, she went back to the sofa and sat down.

"The inside of that maze is a psi firestorm." Adam lowered himself onto the sofa beside her. He looked at the glass on the table in front of him but made no move to pick it up.

"Vickie reacted to the assault on her senses instinctively." Marlowe picked up her glass. "She shut down and retreated to the darkest end of the spectrum. That's where her talent originates and where she has the most strength. In essence she took cover in a dreamscape. It was a self-imposed trance."

"But she went so deep that she couldn't find her way back out?"

"That pretty much describes what happened, yes."

Gibson finished the energy bars. He carried the empty foil wrappers across the room to a basket that was already half-filled with identical wrappers. He made the additions to his collection and then fluttered across the floor to the dust-bunny-sized door that Marlowe had installed for him. The door was located in the wall next to the glass doors that opened onto the balcony. Gibson chortled once and disappeared outside into the night.

"Probably off to hang with his buddies," Marlowe explained. "I think dust bunnies are quite sociable. Or maybe he's got a girlfriend. I'm not sure what he does when he goes out at night. But he'll be back in a few hours. He hops from balcony to balcony until he gets to the ground."

"Helps to have six paws when you do that kind of mountaineering," Adam said.

Out on the balcony Gibson bounced up onto the

railing. He stood silhouetted against the green light of the ruins for a few seconds and then vanished over the side.

"You and Gibson have done this kind of psychic repair work before?" Adam asked.

She sipped some Amber Dew and lowered the glass. "You know how some people are on a special list of donors for rare blood types?"

"Sure."

"Arcane operates a private clinic for members of the Society similar to the one your sister is in. I'm on a list of rare talents who can be called in to consult on special cases."

He held his glass of Amber Dew up to the firelight and studied the golden liqueur. "The Guild clinics keep lists of parapsych specialists, too. We have some very rare and unusual talents on tap. But none of them could help Vickie."

"Her condition was unique because it was related to dreamlight. Doubt if you have a lot of dream talents in the Guild."

"No," he agreed. "That's more of an Arcane thing."

"I expect you've got some talents on your clinic lists that the Arcane parapsych doctors could use from time to time."

He drank some of the Amber Dew. "Might be useful in the future if the Guilds and the Society shared those lists."

"Yes," she said. "Might be very useful."

She sank deeper into the sofa, letting the gentle heat

of the potent liqueur take the edge off her overstimu-
lated nerves. She had used a lot of energy at the hospital. Now she was in the edgy, high-rez state that always
followed a major burn. Soon she would crash and fall
into a heavy sleep.

But that wouldn't happen for a while. Not that she
was looking forward to sleep. There would be dreams
tonight. Bad ones. But that was just the way the talent
worked. She had a lot of natural resilience. That, too,
was connected to her talent. After a couple of nights,
the images from Vickie's dreams would stop invading
her own dreamscapes.

Meanwhile the Amber Dew was hitting her harder
and faster than it would have otherwise. She knew
from experience that she had a tendency to get chatty
in this condition.

Adam looked at her. "You saved my sister tonight. I
owe you. For the rest of my life, I owe you."

"Stop right there." Marlowe held up one hand. "What
I did for your sister, I would have done for anyone."

"I know that, too. Doesn't change anything."

She swallowed more Amber Dew. "If the situation
had been reversed, you would have done the same
thing."

He watched her with a steady, unreadable expression. "Think so?"

She smiled, feeling a bit smug. "I'm a dreamlight
talent, remember?"

"Oh, yeah."

"And one hell of a profiler. For your information, I

nailed your parapsych profile the first time I met you
in the ruins."

"Is that right?" He raised the glass to his mouth
again, a little amused now. "And just what kind of profile do I have?"

She pondered that, vaguely aware that she was definitely buzzed on the Amber Dew. At times like this it
was usually wise to cease verbal communication, she
reminded herself. Especially when one was engaged in
communication with a man. But for some reason she felt
compelled to tell Adam what she sensed about him.

She held up one finger. "For starters, you are the
kind of man who will always do what you feel is the
right thing, even if doing the right thing requires you
to be utterly ruthless. Which means that you are not,
strictly speaking, always a nice guy."

He winced. "Think that explains my own relationship problems?"

She narrowed her eyes. "Don't tell me a hotshot
Guild boss like you has any trouble getting a date."

"Getting a date isn't the problem. It's the long-term
stuff."

"Gee, you have trouble maintaining a relationship?"
She wrinkled her nose. "Well, don't look to me for ad-
vice. I suck in that department, remember?"

"You did say something about that." He drank a
little more of his Amber Dew.

"But I'm guessing that part of your problem is that
women take a long look at you and decide that you
aren't good Covenant Marriage material," she added.

His mouth twisted. "Thanks."

"Not your fault," she said. "It's the genetic thing. I read those old notes of Nicholas's. Something about a restless spirit being one of the symptoms of the onset of his talent."

"'Each talent comes at a great price,'" Adam quoted softly. "'It is ever thus with power. The first talent fills the mind with a rising tide of restlessness that cannot be assuaged by endless hours in the laboratory or soothed with strong drink or the milk of the poppy.'"

"Well?" she said. "Does that describe you?"

He exhaled slowly. "Probably. Never had a lot of time for relationships, I guess. Always felt like I had to keep searching for something."

"You channeled that energy into your work." She held up a second finger. "As I was saying, you are the kind of man other people will follow into the underworld, even if they don't have amber. Translated, that also means you are not always a nice guy."

"I sense a theme here."

She held up a third finger. "You're an off-the-charts talent, and you have the kind of off-the-charts willpower and self-control required to handle that kind of power. You finish what you start. You are incorruptible. No one could bribe you. Which means that you are—"

"Not always a nice guy." He finished the last of his Amber Dew and contemplated the fire. "Definitely a theme."

"What you are," she said very steadily, "is a natural-born hero."

He frowned. "No. I just do my job."

"And you would do it even if you had to forge a river of ghost energy to get it done."

"That's your definition of a hero?"

"Certainly part of the definition."

He turned back to the fire. "And my relationship problems?"

"Probably similar to my own." She waved one hand. "With the exception of my sleep issues."

"How's that?"

She kicked off her shoes and stacked her ankles on the coffee table. "Look at it from our dates' points of view. We're fun or at least interesting for a while. But soon we become irritating."

"Yeah?"

"We tend to take charge and take over. Before anyone realizes what has happened, we're making all the decisions."

"You make it sound like we're a couple of control freaks."

"Yep." She polished off the Amber Dew and set the empty glass on the table with a small, decisive clink. "That's us. Mega control freaks. Guess that's why they gave us the corner offices with the big windows."

"You've got a corner office?"

"Not exactly. There's actually only one office at J&J, but I've got it."

They both fell silent again, gazing into the fire. Marlowe felt the pull of what she knew would be a deep but troubled sleep. She fought it with a little pulse of psi. That proved to be a dangerous move. When the small burst of energy flashed through her, it became impossible to ignore the electricity in the atmosphere. Adam was close; very close.

"Moving right along," he said softly.

"Right. Now that Vickie is okay, we need to get serious about saving the underworld. I spent today putting out a lot of feelers to my contacts in the antiquities community. Tomorrow I should get some response."

"I've already tried the dealers," he said. "Waste of time. Got zip."

"I doubt very much that you have the kind of connections that J&J does, especially in the underground market. We've been collecting paranormal artifacts for generations. There's an art to it. When Jones & Jones lets it be known that it is looking for a particular relic, seldom-seen dealers who work the very bottom depths of the black market come to the surface."

"Why is that?"

"For one thing, we pay well, no questions asked."

"Always an asset in business," he said.

"But in addition, we're what you might call specialists. We go after the more bizarre items, artifacts that have been infused with a lot of weird psi. Not a lot of collectors in that market."

"Probably because those kinds of relics aren't pleasant to have around."

"People get nervous in the vicinity of powerful relics,"

she agreed, "even people who don't think they have any real talent. They pick up the disturbing vibes. Dealers who work the market that handles those kinds of artifacts are as odd as the relics, trust me. Very low-profile. They tend to be not only secretive but extremely paranoid. It takes years, sometimes generations, to build up business relationships in that world. Arcane has those kinds of connections."

"I'll take your word for it."

There was more silence. The energy level was not going down. If anything, the atmosphere was getting hotter, and the heat had nothing to do with the fireplace. Marlowe tapped her finger against the cushion beside her left thigh and wondered in a dreamy sort of way how Adam would react if she threw herself on top of him and started tearing off his clothes.

Bad idea. They were working a case. Firing up a sexual relationship at this stage would not be wise. In an effort to break the spell, she stirred and made a show of looking at her watch.

"It's getting late," she said.

"I should go," he said.

She turned her head to look at him, intending to say something polite in the way of agreement. But he was right there, so close, watching her. His eyes burned.

The smoldering fire between them flashed into high-rez flames. Adam wrapped one hand around the nape of her neck. His mouth closed over hers. And then she was burning, too.

Chapter 15

HE HAD BEEN WAITING FOR THIS TO HAPPEN SINCE THE moment he had met her, Adam thought. He had known it was only a matter of time. And now the time had come. He was thrilled. There was no other word for it. Thrilled in a way that was unlike anything he had ever experienced.

Marlowe wrapped her arms around his neck and kissed him back, fiercely. The atmosphere in the firelit room got hotter.

She managed to tear her mouth free from his for a few seconds, sucking in a breath.

"Do you think we're going to regret this?" she asked.

"I'm not." He had never said anything with more conviction, he thought.

"Guess we're on the same page here, then," she whispered.

"A joint executive decision."

He eased her down onto her back and sprawled heavily on top of her. She fumbled with the buttons of his shirt. His whole body felt tight and hard. He succeeded in dragging the black silk turtleneck off over her head and went to work removing her bra.

He looked down at her breasts, chills of wonder and excitement sweeping through him. The gentle curves fit perfectly into his hand, as if she had been made for him. When he lowered his mouth to one tight nipple, she twisted beneath him. He felt her nails dig into the muscles of his back.

"Adam."

She got his shirt partway open and pushed her hands inside. He reached down and tugged her skirt up to her waist. Her panties were already damp. The scent of her arousal was more intoxicating than the Amber Dew, a bigger rush than alien psi.

He groaned against her breast. "You're wet."

She found him through the fabric of his trousers. "You're hard."

"Talk about coincidence."

"We at J&J believe there are no coincidences."

"You may be right."

He managed to free himself long enough to sit up on the side of the sofa. He yanked off his low boots. With an effort, he made it to his feet and got rid of his trousers and briefs. He didn't bother to remove his shirt. He just wanted to get back to Marlowe as quickly as possible. The urgency sweeping through him ignited all of his senses.

She opened her arms for him. He settled between her legs and stroked her small furnace. She raised one knee and reached for him with one hand. When her fingers closed around him, it took everything he had not to climax then and there. But he forced himself to pull back from the brink. He needed to be inside her.

"Yes," she whispered, her voice very tight. Her fingers sank into his shoulders, pulling him closer. *"Now."*

The feminine command was more powerful than any siren song. He pushed himself deep into her moist, snug channel. She clenched around him. He'd had some good sex in his life, he thought. But he'd never experienced anything like this.

The energy level in the room climbed even higher. He could have sworn that both of their auras were going to combust. When Marlowe screamed softly and convulsed beneath him, he opened his eyes to watch her face in the moment of release.

She was incredible.

She was his.

He could not wait any longer. His climax stormed through him in racking waves.

SOMETIME LATER, WHEN HIS BREATHING AND PULSE had slowed to normal, he untangled himself from Marlowe's warm body and looked down at her again.

She was sound asleep.

Chapter 16

THE FLASHING, SPARKING, IMPOSSIBLY HOT PSI WAS *everywhere. The lightning strikes bounced from one brilliant mirror to another, enveloping her in a storm that blinded all of her senses. There was nowhere to run, nowhere to hide.*

There was only one hope. She had to find the underlying pattern in the violent currents of energy that were ricocheting off the dazzling quartz surfaces . . .

MARLOWE AWOKE TO THE LIGHT OF A GREEN-TINGED dawn. The glow of the ancient Dead City wall was fading rapidly in the first pale rays of the sun. She was breathing too quickly. Her pulse was racing. Gibson crowded close, mumbling anxiously, both sets of eyes wide-open. She knew it was a sure sign that he was concerned.

"It's okay," she said. She sat up cautiously and cradled his small, furry body close. "Just the usual aftermath crap. Been here before. Thanks for the company."

Reassured, he closed his hunting eyes and chortled a morning greeting, hopped out of her arms, and tumbled off the bed. He headed for the kitchen.

Memories of the passionate encounter on the couch came back in a torrent, followed by hot-and-cold chills. She looked down and noticed that she was wearing her nightgown. She was quite sure that she had not put it on all by herself. In fact, she had no recollection of much of anything after the lovemaking until the dream had awakened her.

"And they say it's men who go to sleep afterward," she announced to the room at large.

Another alarming thought jolted her senses. Where had Adam slept? Where *was* Adam, come to that?

She glanced uneasily at the pillow beside her. There was no way he could have spent the night with her. She wouldn't have slept a wink. But, dear heaven, what if he had? What if she had actually slept with him?"

The pillow was still smooth and pristine.

She did not know whether to be hugely relieved or terribly disappointed. Of course Adam hadn't spent the night in her bed. That was impossible. If he had slept next to her, she would not have been able to sleep at all, even in her exhausted state. But he had put her to bed after she had more or less passed out on him. How embarrassing.

A tiny frisson of energy whispered through her. She

shivered, recognizing her Jones intuition. Something had happened between Adam and herself last night, something more than an episode of passion. She had the eerie, deeply unsettling feeling that some kind of bond had been established. Adam was different from the other men she had known. When the end came, she was not going to be able to walk away as easily as she always had in the past. This was not good, she thought.

Get real. It was great postburn sex. You were both buzzed on adrenaline and psi, and you're attracted to each other. It happens.

But it had never happened quite like that, she thought. Not to her.

She climbed out of bed, found her robe, and wandered into the kitchen to put the water on for tea. The note was on the kitchen counter. She had never seen Adam's handwriting, but she was pretty sure she would have known it anywhere. Besides, his dreamprints were all over the paper.

Hope you slept well. I'll call you in the morning.

Adam

She crumpled the note and looked at Gibson, who was on top of the refrigerator, awaiting breakfast.

"What do you know?" she said. "Looks like Adam Winters is the perfect date for me. Always gone by dawn."

But for some reason that did nothing to lift her spirits. She did not want Adam to be the perfect date, she realized. She wanted something more. She wanted him to be Mr. Right.

Get over yourself. Take what you can get, and enjoy it while you can. Might be a good idea to get to work, too. Trying to save the underworld, remember?

She rezzed up the computer while she waited for the tea water to boil. The message from Tully popped up instantly.

I have what you're looking for. There is interest elsewhere. Arcane is invited to make a preemptive offer. —T

"I was right. Tully found the lamp."

She switched off the tea water, opened the refrigerator long enough to grab a chunk of cheese and some bread for Gibson, and ran for the shower. She didn't need the caffeine now.

A short time later she emerged from the bathroom, hair still wet, and pulled on a pair of jeans, a black turtleneck, and biker boots. She grabbed her leather jacket and headed downstairs to the parking garage with Gibson tucked under one arm.

"Could be just another fake," she told Gibson, who was still munching cheese. "But Tully is the best in the business when it comes to this kind of thing."

Gibson downed the last of the cheese and chortled. She dumped him into the saddlebag, rezzed Dream, and drove out of the garage.

Chapter 17

"IT'S A FAKE," CHARLOTTE DEENE SAID.

An emotion far more intense than disappointment seared her senses. Rage. She looked at the ugly artifact sitting on the coffee table, barely resisting the urge to hurl it against the nearest wall. She had to fight the impulse. She had to remain in control.

"Son of a ghost," Keith whispered. He shivered and wrapped his arms around himself. He was always cold these days.

Tucker stared at the lamp, clearly shaken. "Are you sure?"

Charlotte looked at her brothers. The three of them were triplets, but fraternal, not identical. There was, however, a strong family resemblance. They were all fair-haired with gray eyes. Although they were the same age, Keith looked much older. The warping in his dreamlight currents was taking a physical toll on his body. His face had begun to hollow out, and he was losing weight.

"Believe me, it's not the real Burning Lamp," she said. "I'm a dreamlight talent, remember? I've tried everything. If that vase was infused with even a small amount of raw dream energy, I'd have been able to sense it by now." She touched the rim of the artifact and heightened her senses again, making absolutely certain. "All I'm picking up are some murky dream-prints, most of which were probably left by the museum staff. The artist's prints are on it as well. They indicate that this thing was made sometime around the Era of Discord, not on Earth."

"Shit," Tucker whispered. "I can't believe that after all this time the Arcane experts didn't realize they were storing a fake in the museum vault."

"At the time of the Era of Discord the Winters family must have commissioned a replica of the real lamp, probably to get J&J off their backs," Charlotte said. "A curator stuck it in a vault, and everyone forgot about it. In the intervening decades there has apparently been no reason to dig it out of storage."

"More likely the Joneses just made damn sure it stayed buried," Keith muttered. Another shiver went through him. He pulled his jacket more tightly around himself and wiped the sweat off his forehead with the back of his sleeve.

Charlotte watched him with growing concern. The three of them were alone in the world. They had been since shortly after their birth. Their father had died before they were born. Their mother had been killed in an accident a few months later. Charlotte, Keith, and Tucker had grown up in an orphanage.

For years they had survived on their talents, their looks, and their natural charm, running sophisticated cons, scams, and frauds.

But now Keith was dying, not because of some fatal disease but because he had been unable to resist pursuing the dangerous secrets he'd discovered in the old journal. It was the oldest story in the world, she thought. The ending was always the same. The price for forbidden knowledge was always far too high.

"I can't believe I took all those risks just to steal a fake." Tucker's jaw locked. His eyes burned with hot psi. "I thought the whole gig was going to crash when Marlowe Jones realized I was a chameleon talent. We're damn lucky she concluded I was just a cheap con artist trying to marry into her family."

"You skated on that one," Keith said. He sank wearily down onto a chair. "If she or any of the other Joneses had found out what you were really after, you would have ended up so deep in the tunnels no one would have found your body."

"It didn't happen," Tucker said.

"Trust me, if Marlowe Jones ever does learn the truth, she'll send every J&J agent she's got after you." Keith hugged himself and rocked a little in the chair. "We should never have started this. I knew it wouldn't work. Knew it would end badly. I could feel it in my bones. I want you both to quit now."

"No," Charlotte said fiercely. "Not while there's still a chance."

"She's right," Tucker said. "We have to keep going."

"Don't you get it?" Keith rounded on him. "So far you've lucked out. You haven't attracted the attention of J&J. But that kind of luck won't hold, not when you're up against Arcane."

"We have to find the real lamp," Tucker shot back. "You're dying, in case you haven't noticed."

"Believe me, I've noticed. But do you really think I want to go out knowing I was responsible for the deaths of you and Charlotte?"

"You're my brother," Tucker said. "You know damn well that if the situation was reversed, you'd be doing for Charlotte or me what we're doing for you. We're trying to save your sanity and your life, damn it."

"Stop it, both of you," Charlotte said sharply. "We don't have time for this. What's done is done. Our only hope is to move forward. We've got to find the Burning Lamp."

Keith and Tucker looked at her.

"Speaking of time," Keith said in a flat voice, "how much longer do I have?"

She hesitated as she always did when he asked her to read his dreamprints. She hated looking at the damage. But he was the one who was dying. He deserved the truth. Reluctantly she rezzed her talent and studied

..e seething, warped dreamlight tracks on the floor of .he office. The unwholesome resonance was getting stronger.

"We've got some time," she said. "I promise you." It was the truth, as far as it went.

"How much time, damn it?" Keith whispered.

"I've told you, I can't answer that precisely. According to the old records, Samuel Lodge used the crystals for decades before he died. You just started working with the stones a few months ago. We don't need to panic. Not yet."

But Keith was failing fast, much faster than Samuel Lodge had back in the nineteenth century on Earth. When it came to psychic mutation and evolution, things on Harmony moved much more rapidly and took very different twists than they had back on the Old World. Something in the environment, the experts said.

Keith fixed the fake artifact with a brooding glare. "We just hit a wall. The real lamp was never even in the Arcane vaults. That means we're back to square one."

"Not necessarily," Charlotte said. She went to the window and looked out at the quiet street. "According to the old legend, it takes a dreamlight talent to find the Burning Lamp."

"That was supposed to be you," Tucker said softly.

"I heard that," Keith growled. "It's not her fault."

Tucker slanted him an angry look. "Don't you think I know that?"

"I managed to track the fake lamp to the Arcane vault," Charlotte reminded them quietly.

was the wrong lamp," Keith s

sation in his voice, just a statement

We were looking in the wrong place,"

but stealing the fake may have been the s

thing we could have done under the circumstance

Tucker scowled. "What makes you say that?"

She gestured toward the copy of the *Examiner* o
the table. The photo of Marlowe Jones and Adam Winters occupied most of the front page. "It's no coincidence that Jones and Winters are now an item in the tabloid press. Obviously she consulted him after she realized the lamp had been stolen. I've got a hunch that they are now both looking for it."

Keith and Tucker exchanged uneasy glances.

"Winters is Guild," Tucker said. "The Guild is the only crowd that scares me more than Arcane."

"Think about it," Charlotte said quietly. "According to the legend, it requires the combination of a Winters male and a strong dreamlight reader to find the lamp. That's exactly what we've got working for us now. "

Keith shivered. "You think that part of the legend is for real?"

"It's certainly starting to look that way," she said.

"Just one problem," Tucker added. "If Winters and Marlowe get lucky and find the lamp, we still have to figure out how to grab it so that you can work it for Keith."

"We'll worry about that after they find the lamp," Charlotte said.

Chapter 18

MARLOWE ROUNDED THE CORNER INTO THE NARROW lane that bordered the Old East Wall. She went cold when she saw the flashing lights of the emergency vehicles. An ambulance and two patrol cars were parked directly in front of Tully's small shop. It was only eight o'clock in the morning, but a small crowd had gathered. One of the officers was stringing crime scene tape.

She de-rezzed Dream, kicked down the stand, and swung her leg over the bike. After removing her helmet, she collected Gibson from the saddlebag and walked toward the small group of onlookers. She was just in time to see the medics load a stretcher into the aid car. There was a body bag on the stretcher.

She moved closer to two men who looked like they had been living on the streets for a while. She had learned early on in her work for J&J that in the Quarter it was the locals who had the most information.

"What happened?" she asked.

"Man named Tully who owns that shop got himself killed last night," one of the men said. He looked at Gibson. "Hey, is that a dust bunny?"

"Yes," she said. She did not take her eyes off the shop. "How did Jake die?"

The second man glanced at her, showing some interest. "You knew Jake Tully?"

"My firm has done some business with him."

"I heard one of the cops say that it looks like Tully died of a heart attack. He did have a bad ticker, so that may have been what happened. But the place is all torn up inside. You ask me, I say it was a burglary gone bad."

"Someone stole all his best stuff, I'll bet," the other man said. "Poor Tully. He was always hoping to score one last really big deal so that he could retire from the business."

"Thanks," Marlowe said.

She walked back to the bike, took out her phone, and entered Adam's code. He answered immediately.

"You're up early," he said. "Sleep well?"

The low, rough, sexy, incredibly intimate edge on his words sent a frisson of energy through her. Memories of the passion that had heated up her entire living room last night jangled her senses for a few seconds.

She took a deep breath and reminded herself to focus.

"I got a lead on the lamp," she said.

"Where are you?"

The sexy intimacy in his voice was gone, replaced by the flat, hard tone of masculine authority. The Guild boss taking charge.

"I'm standing in the lane outside the shop of the dealer who may have found the lamp."

"Stay there. I'm on my way."

"Don't bother. Tully is dead. Looks like his place was burglarized last night. His shop is a crime scene now. There's no way the cops will let us inside."

There was a long, thoughtful silence on the other end of the connection.

"Whoever took the lamp from the museum vault must have discovered he stole a fake," Adam said after a while. "He's still looking. Think he found it last night?"

"Only one way to find out," Marlowe said. "We need to get inside Tully's shop."

Chapter 19

"I DIDN'T REALIZE YOU PLANNED TO COOK DINNER," Marlowe said. "I thought when you suggested we eat here at your place that we'd order out."

He snapped the end off an asparagus spear and did his best to look crushed. "Just because I'm a Guild boss doesn't mean I can't cook."

Marlowe absently swirled the wine in her glass and watched him from the opposite side of the kitchen counter.

"I wasn't implying that you didn't have any culinary talent," she said. "It's the time factor. I just assumed a man in your position, given all that you've got going on at the moment, wouldn't have time to plan and prepare a meal for what is essentially a business meeting."

He snapped the last asparagus spear. "I don't order out because I don't like the idea of having to go down four flights of stairs to open the door to a stranger. Call me paranoid, but after avoiding several staged accidents, having my amber warped, and getting shot at, I've concluded that it's a good time in my life to exercise a bit of caution."

She winced. "Point taken."

"Besides, we can't risk going into Tully's shop until later tonight, anyway." He put the washed and dried asparagus spears in a shallow roasting pan. "Might as well eat dinner and talk about the case."

He had sensed her edgy mood first on the phone and again when she had arrived a short time ago. His long history of failed relationships no doubt indicated a lack of perception and understanding of the female of the species. Nevertheless, he was fairly certain that Marlowe's tension this evening was not just the result of what had happened to Tully and their plans for later tonight. It was directly linked to what had happened between them last night. *She feels it now, too,* he thought. *She knows this is not just about sex. There's some kind of connection between us.*

He drizzled olive oil over the spears and sprinkled them with salt, savoring the energy in the atmosphere. There was a cool, touch-at-your-own-risk look in Marlowe's eyes that was probably meant to be a warning flag. He wondered if he should tell her that it was having the opposite effect. He smiled a little.

She was dressed in what he had concluded was her working uniform—jeans, black turtleneck, and boots—ready for the late-night foray into Tully's shop.

Her hair was pulled back into a low ponytail at the nape of her neck. It didn't matter that she was dressed for a bike run, not a date. She looked good here in his home, he thought, like she belonged.

"What did you do with Gibson tonight?" he asked.

"He took off before I left the office this evening. I told you, he does that sometimes." She lounged against the counter, frowning a little. "Although lately he seems to be doing it more often than usual."

"Maybe it's mating season for dust bunnies."

Marlowe stiffened. "Maybe."

He slid the pan into the oven and closed the door. "How did you and Gibson become a team?"

"I found him in an alley outside a crime scene a few months ago. I was working as an agent for J&J at the time. A member of the Society who lived in the Old Quarter had dropped dead of an apparent heart attack. Uncle Zeke called me in to take a look. Turned out to be a homicide."

"Don't tell me the bunny did it?"

Marlowe bristled. "Don't be ridiculous."

"Sorry." He pulled a long loaf of crusty bread out of a paper bag. "Little Guild boss humor."

"It certainly explains why Guild bosses aren't known for their wit." She took another tiny sip of wine and lowered her glass. "Anyhow, I followed the trail of the killer's prints out into the alley. And there was Gibson. A couple of stray dogs had him cornered near a trash container. He was holding them off, but it was two against one."

"So you rescued him?"

"I chased off the dogs. The dust bunny disappeared beneath the trash container. But he showed up at my back door later that night. I gave him a High-Rez Energy Bar. We've been partners ever since."

"If I showed up at your back door, would you give me a High-Rez Energy Bar?"

Marlowe sighed. "You Guild bosses really do have a problem with humor, don't you?"

"Don't worry, you get used to it." He set the bread on a plate, picked up his wineglass, and rounded the edge of the counter. "What do you say we finish our drinks out on the balcony?"

"All right." She glanced back at the preparations for dinner. "You know, you really didn't have to go to all this trouble. I mean, it's not like we're on a real date."

He opened the glass doors at the far end of the room and stood back to watch her walk out onto the balcony. "I like to cook. Gives me a little instant gratification. But cooking for one isn't much fun. It's nice to have someone else around to enjoy it."

She glanced at him, her eyes wary, as she went past. "Yes, it is."

He followed her out onto the balcony, satisfaction roaring through him. No doubt about it. The lady from Jones & Jones was running scared of whatever was going on between them. He doubted if she had ever panicked about a relationship with a man in her entire life. It was a good sign, he decided, a very good sign. She was definitely paying attention now.

"You have a great view," she said.

"One of the reasons I bought the place."

His home was the entire top floor of a two-hundred-year-old Colonial-era building. The structure was five stories high, which made it one of the tallest buildings in the Quarter.

"I couldn't help but notice that three of the four floors below us are empty and dark." Marlowe studied him with a speculative look. "Guild boss paranoia?"

He crossed the balcony and joined her at the railing, careful to keep a little distance between them but close enough to let him savor her intoxicating energy. When he was near her like this, he felt a little buzzed, and not because of the wine or the gentle currents of alien psi that drifted like fog through the Quarter.

"I own the entire building." He rested his elbows on the railing, cradling the wineglass between his hands. "I rent out the ground-floor shops to some people I know very, very well."

She looked knowing. "People you trust."

"Yes."

"A Guild boss version of a neighborhood block watch?"

"Something like that. I like to keep the floors between my flat and the street shops empty."

"And rigged with alarms just in case anyone you don't want to see decides to come calling?"

He contemplated his wineglass. "You know what they say. Even paranoids have enemies."

"How did you sleep last night?" she asked. She glanced down.

He felt the heightening of energy in the atmosphere and knew that she was studying his dreamprints.

"Got in a couple of hours," he said.

"Before the nightmares hit?"

"I told you, I can handle them."

"I did some research in Jeremiah Jones's private case files this afternoon."

Well, it was bound to happen, he thought. He had known from the beginning that sooner or later she'd pull up the old history from the Era of Discord. It dawned on him that he was the one who was wary now.

"Find anything interesting?" he asked, keeping his tone neutral.

"According to Jeremiah's notes, parts of the Winters legend are certainly true. If we find the Burning Lamp, I think we'll be able to use it to stop the nightmares and hallucinations that have been plaguing you these past few weeks."

He did not take his attention off the ruins. "Aren't you worried I might be turning into a real Cerberus?"

"You're not going mad; I've told you that." She rested her forearms on the railing beside him and contemplated the ruins. "But I have a hunch that by now you've discovered the second aspect of your talent."

"My second talent, you mean?"

"No, a new aspect of your original talent," she said

calmly. "You are not a true multitalent. Not a Cerberus. But if we find the lamp and if I can work it properly, I'll be able to turn the key in the lock, as Nicholas Winters wrote in his journal. When that happens, you'll come into the third aspect of your talent. With that level of power, you'll be able to use the lamp as a kind of weapon."

"And if you don't turn the key in the lock properly?"

"The radiation from the lamp will probably kill us both or, at the very least, destroy our parapsych talents."

He looked at her. "Are you sure you want to do this?"

"We don't have any choice. You have to be able to work the lamp in order to try to stop whatever is happening down below in the maze. And according to everything I have been able to uncover concerning the legend, you won't be able to channel the heavy energy in the artifact without a strong dreamlight talent like me."

He watched the glowing towers of the ancient city. "That's the legend, all right."

"I went through all of the old records, Adam. There's no other alternative. It takes two. Just as it did when John Cabot Winters and Sarah Vester worked the lamp to destroy Ignatius Fremont and his lab during the Era of Discord."

He groaned and put his head down for a few seconds.

"You know that story, too?" he asked.

"It's all in Jeremiah's notes. The rebel forces were composed mostly of men who were strong ghost hunters. But a few of them were equipped with a weird crystal weapon of some kind that enhanced their individual firepower. The rebels who carried the crystals were almost impossible to stop. As the war went on, more and more of the weapons made their way into the rebels' hands. Jeremiah identified the scientist who was manufacturing the weapons and located the lab."

"Fremont's facility was located underground in the vicinity of a vortex and very well guarded," he said, taking up the story. "In essence, it was a fortress. There was no way a large contingent of Guild men could get to it. But John Winters worked full-spectrum stone."

"Like you."

"He knew he could get through the vortex, but after that he would be on his own and forced to work rapidly before he dropped into a postburn crash. So he went in with the lamp and Sarah Vester, a dreamlight talent."

"Together they worked the lamp and destroyed Fremont and his lab," Marlowe said. "When the war was over, they got married, abandoned their connections to Arcane, and joined the ranks of the Guild."

"John and Sarah were well aware that the environment on Harmony was accelerating the development of paranormal powers in the population. They had no way of knowing what effect it would have on their own descendants, however, given the twist in John's psychic DNA. They wanted to protect future generations of their family."

"They wanted to protect them from future generations of the Joneses and from Arcane," Marlowe said. She smiled. "Just in case we started to take the Cerberus legend a little too seriously."

"Something like that," he agreed. "No offense."

"None taken. For the record, the Joneses weren't too sure what would happen to their descendants, either, given the twist in our own psychic genetics."

"The formula?"

She shrugged. "While Nicholas Winters was busy frying his DNA with his crystals and the Burning Lamp, Sylvester Jones was adding a few tweaks to his own genes with his alchemical experiments. Both bloodlines were affected."

"Does that make us freaks?"

She turned toward him. "Both bloodlines not only survived, they have thrived."

"And the lesson is?"

She smiled. "Some mutations work out nicely. Are you going to tell me how the second aspect of your talent manifests?"

"Maybe," he said. "Someday. Not tonight."

Chapter 20

"I CHECKED THE GUILD SECTOR CHARTS FOR THE CAT-acombs in the vicinity of Tully's shop," Adam said. He opened what had appeared to be a hall closet door, revealing a small elevator. "There's a hole-in-the-wall located in the adjacent building. We'll go in that way."

Marlowe followed him into the elevator. "How do we get into Tully's shop from there?"

"The same way any self-respecting pair of burglars would. Through the back door."

The elevator sank silently downward. When the door opened, Adam rezzed a flashlight and led the way across the vast, dark space. It took Marlowe a moment to realize that they were walking through an abandoned underground parking garage.

When Adam reached the far wall, he unlocked a

mag-steel door. A familiar green glow shimmered through the opening.

The green quartz that formed the catacombs was impervious to human tools and weapons, but at some time in the distant past, cracks, fissures, and jagged holes had been created in the tunnel walls. Some experts theorized that the same alien machines that had been used to build the underworld had also been used to punch holes in the stone. Others were convinced that earthquakes had created the fractures.

Whatever the case, the jagged openings in the tunnels were common underground in the Old Quarters of the cities. They were frequently discovered and used by drug dealers and other criminals on the run. Treasure hunters, indie prospectors, thrill seekers, and Guild bosses who liked the idea of having an emergency escape route were also fond of them.

Adam de-rezzed the flashlight and went through the opening in the quartz. Marlowe followed him into the glowing catacombs.

"I keep a sled down here," Adam said. He checked his locator and backup amber. Then he moved toward a nearby chamber. "It's in there."

Marlowe went after him and saw a small, two-seater sled. She stepped up into the little vehicle and sat down on the bench seat.

Adam got behind the wheel and drove out of the chamber. Traveling by sled was certainly faster than walking underground, but there was not a lot of power

in the simple, low-tech amber-rez motors. More tech-
nologically sophisticated engines would not function
at all amid the heavy currents of psi. Like guns, they
were inclined to explode.

Adam piloted the sled through the maze of tunnels
for about fifteen minutes before gliding to a halt near
another hole-in-the-wall. They got out and stepped
through the opening into yet another darkened space.
Marlowe recognized the damp, dank smell characteristic of old basements.

The beam of Adam's flashlight gleamed on a door.
He opened it, and they went up three flights of stairs.
The door at the top was unlocked. They went through it
and into an unlit room. The floor was coated with dust,
and the windows were obscured by layers of grime.

The door opened onto the alley. The back door of
Tully's shop was immediately adjacent. Ignoring the
crime scene tape, Adam took out a small device and
used it on the lock.

"I think those lockpicks are illegal," Marlowe said.

"Is that right? I hadn't heard that."

"I'm aware of that particular little factoid because
I've got a drawer full of them," she said. "I hand them
out to my agents like candy."

"If I lose mine, I'll know where to go to get another
one."

He got the door open. They moved into the shop and
closed the door.

As was her custom at crime scenes, Marlowe did a
quick survey before heightening her talent. Sometimes

those with a lot of paranormal ability tended to forget that they could detect a great deal of information with their normal senses.

The light from the old wall filtering through the window illuminated the chaotic scene. A variety of alien artifacts—tomb mirrors, vases, and urns of various shapes and sizes—were scattered around the floor. There were also a number of Early Colonial items including old boots and clothing and some high-tech tools that had become useless two hundred years ago after the closing of the Curtain.

A dozen or more leather-bound, handwritten books and journals had been swept from the shelves. They were similar to other First Generation volumes that Marlowe had seen. She knew they contained whatever scientific, technical, and historical data the desperate colonists had been able to salvage from the Old World computers before the machines went dark forever.

"Doesn't take any talent to see that whoever killed Jake Tully was looking for something," she said.

"The lamp," Adam said. He sounded very certain.

"In his note, Tully said there was interest elsewhere."

"Looks like the other collector decided to bypass the auction," Adam said. "I don't want to use the flashlight if we can avoid it. The streets around here are empty at this hour of the night, but some insomniac in one of the nearby apartments might notice the light and call the cops."

"I don't need the light," she said.

She opened her other sight cautiously and concentrated on the murky pool of dreamprints that covered the floor. It was not the first time that she had investigated a death in the Old Quarter, and it was always like this. People had been coming and going from the Colonial-era buildings for two centuries. Most of the tracks were faint and murky, the accumulated residue of psi light left by former proprietors, customers, and all of the others who had come to the shop over the years. Some of the tracks still seethed and simmered with strong emotions, even though they were decades old. But most merged into a fog of energy that glowed faintly in the shadows.

Some of the freshest prints, however, burned with an ominous, oily luminescence that sent another frisson of energy through her. She wrapped her arms around herself.

"Are you all right?" Adam asked.

"Yes. Just give me a moment." She steadied her nerves and her senses and walked toward the hottest, darkest pool of dreamlight. "Tully died here. The authorities called it a heart attack. Tully was an old man. Not in good health. But there was a struggle."

"He was attacked, then?"

"Yes, but death was sudden. It's entirely possible that the authorities were right. He probably did die of a heart attack or stroke, but I think it was brought on by the shock of the assault."

"That makes sense."

She glanced at him. "I think the assault was paranormal in nature, not physical."

In the eerie green light, Adam's face was a hard mask carved in shadows. "Are you saying that someone used psi energy to kill Tully?"

"That's what the prints tell me. Talent that strong is extremely uncommon." She examined the seething pool of dreamlight more closely. "But there's something else going on here. "The killer's pattern is warped."

"What does that mean?"

"The basic pattern is that of a cold-blooded para-sociopath. This is a true predator, a powerful talent who lacks any vestige of a conscience. And he's intelligent. Smart enough to blend in with normal society. A real wolf in sheep's clothing."

"That doesn't exactly narrow our list of suspects."

"No, but there is one other fact that might," she said. "Whoever he is, he's dying."

Adam stilled. "You can detect that?"

"Yes. The early signs are all there, although they might not be obvious yet. The origin of the illness is psychical in nature. It will take a while to affect him physically, but it will kill him. Sooner, rather than later, I think. He'll go crazy first, though."

"You're sure the killer was male?"

"Yes," she said. "That, too, is in the dreamlight."

"So we're looking for a smart psi-path who is mortally ill. Why would he want the lamp?"

"I can think of only one reason," she said. "He thinks he can somehow use it to save himself. Which tells us he is very familiar with some of Arcane's most ancient secrets and legends."

"A member of the Society."

"That is certainly a strong possibility."

"The question is, did he find the lamp?"

"Maybe not." She walked forward slowly, following a trail of prints. "Most of the older dreamlight residue that Tully left is faint, but over the years I can see traces of excitement here and there. The most recent hot prints are only a day old at most."

"You're thinking that they are indications that he was anticipating a lucrative auction?"

"I can't think of anything else that would have caused him to get so excited." She rounded the corner and stopped short when she found herself facing a wall. "Hmm."

Adam came to stand beside her. "What?"

"The trail leads right up to that wall and disappears," she said.

Adam regarded the paneling for a moment. "Looks like Tully may have had himself a secret vault."

"If he did, I don't think the killer found it. There's no sign of his tracks on the floor in this part of the room."

Chapter 21

IT TOOK HIM LESS THAN FIVE MINUTES TO FIND THE concealed lock, another sixty seconds to pick it. A section of the wall swung open with a soft hiss of levers and gears. Marlowe came to stand beside him. Together they looked at a narrow flight of stairs that led down into the basement. Alien psi wafted up from the darkness.

"Tully had his own hole-in-the-wall," Adam said. "What do you want to bet he used it as a safe for his most valuable antiques?"

"His hot footsteps go down the stairs," Marlowe added. "And come back up."

Adam rezzed the flashlight. They went down into the darkness. Green light emanated from a narrow opening at the bottom.

"The problem," Adam said, "is that if Tully hid the

lamp somewhere underground, we don't have a prayer of finding it. Not unless he left a record of the coordinates. The catacombs are the perfect vault for a hoard of valuable antiquities or anything else, for that matter. The only person who can locate the cache is the one who hid it."

"Or someone who can read dreamprints," Marlowe said quietly.

The cool confidence in her voice riveted him.

"Can you really track dreamlight inside the tunnels?" he asked.

"Not always," she said. "But when it was laid down with this much energy and adrenaline, yes."

"Damn. No wonder they made you the head of J&J." He watched her step through the crack in the tunnel wall. "You know, the Guild could use someone like you."

"I work for Arcane, not the Guild."

"A good Guild boss doesn't let petty details bog him down."

He checked his locator coordinates and followed her into the tunnel. She walked a short distance, turned a corner, and stopped at the entrance to one of the multitude of chambers that opened off the long passage.

"Oh, yes," she said very softly.

He came to a halt behind her and looked over her shoulder. Crates and boxes were stacked high against the green quartz walls.

"This was Tully's vault, all right," he said.

She looked at him. "Can you feel it?"

He knew what she meant. Familiar alien psi stirred his senses, but there were other currents as well. Waves of ultradark dreamlight energy freighted with power roiled the atmosphere. He recognized them in a way he could not explain. An icy anticipation surged through him.

"Yes," he said.

She watched him, her eyes intent. "I would think that it would be a lot like looking into a psychic mirror. Whatever it is in this room that is giving off those vibes could only have been created by someone in your bloodline."

"A psychic mirror." He thought about that. "Yeah, that comes very close to describing what I'm sensing now."

The dark dreamlight emanated from a plain wooden crate stashed in the corner. Nearby was a rusted metal toolbox that looked like it dated from the Era of Discord. He opened the lid and selected one of the old tools inside

"Your basic crowbar hasn't evolved much over the centuries," he noted. "A classic example of form following function."

Marlowe watched him pry open the lid of the crate. He was aware that she was jacked, too. Her eyes were hot, and her face was alight with fascination and curiosity. Energy and power sizzled in the air around her. He realized that as badly as he wanted to open the crate, he wanted even more to have sex with her again. And somehow it was all connected.

The last nail popped free. He tossed the old crow-bar aside and opened the crate. The bulky object inside was shrouded in black silk.

"The fabric looks old," Marlowe said. "But certainly not two hundred years old. It didn't come from Earth. But whatever is inside surely did."

He started to unwrap the silk. "You can sense the age of this thing?"

"Dreamlight carries a psychic date stamp. That thing is old."

"Seventeenth century?"

"That is certainly within reason."

He untwisted the last length of the black silk. He and Marlowe studied the artifact in silence for a long moment.

"It looks like a cross between a rather ugly flower vase and a chalice cup," Marlowe said at last.

The Burning Lamp was about eighteen inches high. Marlowe was right, he thought, it did look a lot like a vase or a chalice. It was made of a strange, gold-colored metal. The lower, narrower portion was set in a heavy base inscribed with alchemical designs. The lamp flared up and out toward a rim set with a ring of murky, gray crystals.

"I can sense the energy in the thing," Marlowe said. "So much raw power and all coming from the dark-est end of the spectrum. I never would have guessed that it was possible to infuse an object with such a vast amount of energy and keep it trapped in stasis like this. How did Nicholas Winters forge such a thing?"

"No one knows for sure. According to the records, he created it using the secrets of some ancient science called alchemy."

She examined the lamp more closely. "The next question is, how can the energy be safely accessed and channeled?"

"According to those same old records, that's your job."

"I was afraid you were going to say that. One thing is certain; I'll need some time to get a feel for the artifact and to do some more research."

"I'm not sure how much time we have." He got to his feet. "The energy in the maze is growing more unstable every day. There's no way to know when it will dissolve into chaos."

And no way to know how much longer I'll be able to stay in control long enough to try to stop the process, he thought.

She watched him very steadily. "Now that you've found the lamp, do you still think you can use it to correct the instability in the mirrors?"

"Maybe." He wrapped the length of black silk around the lamp. "There's a lot of power in this thing, and it is definitely coming from the same end of the spectrum as the energy in the mirrors."

The sense of urgency that had been gnawing at him for weeks was at flashpoint now. It took everything he had to keep it under control. He started toward the stairs that led up to the shop. "Looks like another part of the legend is true."

"Which part would that be?"

"The part that says it takes a dreamlight reader to find the lamp."

"There is some logic to the premise, I suppose," she said. "My kind of talent does give me an affinity for that type of energy. But you can sense it, too."

"Not down here in the tunnels. I would never have been able to find it without the coordinates. This isn't the first time the lamp has gone missing. Family legend claims it has a habit of getting lost. Whenever some-one in the Winters clan decides to go looking for it, he discovers he needs a dreamlight reader to help him find it."

He went through the doorway into the darkened shop, his senses fully aroused by the combination of the dark psi leaking out of the lamp and Marlowe's dis-turbingly feminine energy. Nothing like the hot mix of sex and power to distract a man.

Which was, he concluded, an instant later, why it took him a couple of seconds too long to realize that something was very wrong.

Energy crashed through the atmosphere. He recog-nized it at once—ghost fire, a lot of it. He turned, in-tending to get Marlowe back down the basement stairs to safety.

But it was too late. Paranormal flames erupted in the darkness, encircling them, cutting off the possibil-ity of retreating into the safety of the tunnels.

Chapter 22

TWO SHADOWY FIGURES APPEARED ON THE OTHER side of the circle of green fire. *Ghost hunters,* Marlowe thought. Only men with a talent for manipulating the alien psi that infused the underworld could channel the stuff into weapons outside the catacombs. But in theory no hunter, regardless of how powerful he was, could generate this much psi aboveground.

Through the flaring ring of green psi flames she could see that each man gripped an object in his hand. At first she thought they were holding flashlights. But the devices were emitting a hot green light that was the same eerie hue as ghost energy.

"Stay close," Adam said quietly.

She did not argue. She stood next to him, touching him. His fierce features were etched in acid green light and the darkest of shadows. His eyes burned with a

cold green fire that somehow appeared more dangerous than the energy flaring around them.

Adam looked through the encroaching flames at the
two men generating the fire.

"You do realize that this much ghost light is going
to attract attention out there on the street, sooner or
later," Adam said.

"You don't have to worry about it," one of the men
said. "You're going to be a dead man soon."

"So will you," Adam said. "Drake and O'Conner
sure as hell won't let you live after you take care of me.
You know too much."

"Shut up," one of the men snarled.

"Finish it," the first man ordered. "Hurry. We can't
risk hanging around here long."

The circle of flames tightened. Marlowe felt the
crackling energy snapping and hissing at her senses.
Psi fire was more like lightning than flames. Sometimes
you could survive a burn, but too much was lethal.

"This is a waste of time," Adam said. "I'd really
like some answers, but I don't think this pair is going
to be helpful."

The flood tide of nightmare energy caught her by
surprise, roaring across her senses. Shocked, she realized in a dazed way that Adam was generating the violent energy. The fact that she was in physical contact
with him meant that she was catching the full brunt of
the storm.

She sucked in a breath and took a step back so that
her shoulder was no longer touching his arm.

The screaming started. She turned to look at the two ghost hunters. They were keening in terror. Their bodies jerked and twitched. The flashlights fell from their hands and winked out.

The circle of fire evaporated, but the awful screaming continued for another few seconds before it ceased. Both hunters collapsed, unconscious, on the floor.

The cascading nightmares stopped as suddenly as they had begun.

Adam went to the first man, crouching to check for a pulse.

"This one's still alive," he said. He rose and checked the second hunter. "So is this one." He looked at her, his eyes still demon-hot. "Are you all right?"

She took a deep breath and concentrated on lowering her frazzled senses.

"Yes," she said. She took another breath. "That was a demonstration of the second aspect of your talent, I take it?"

His expression tightened. "You caught some of the backwash, didn't you?"

"Hard to avoid it under the circumstances. The physical contact acted like a channel of sorts. But I'm okay, really."

Adam took out his phone and punched in a code. Whoever he called must have answered on the first ring, because he started issuing orders immediately, crisp, sharp commands that rang with authority.

Marlowe leaned against the counter to steady herself. By the time she had her breathing back to a level that more or less resembled normal, Adam had closed his phone. He looked at her from the other side of the room.

"There's a Bureau team on the way to collect these two," he said. "We can leave as soon as they get here. But I don't want them to see you or the artifact, so you're going to wait down below."

"I don't understand. You don't want the Bureau people to know that we found the lamp?"

"Not yet. Given what just happened, I'm going to assume that there is at least a possibility that Fortner has a leak somewhere in his organization."

"But you're going to let the Bureau take these two into custody?"

"I don't have much choice. Not like I can call the cops. I can't explain my own presence here in a dead man's shop, let alone why a couple of ghost hunters tried to take me out."

She walked to one of the unconscious men, crouched, braced herself, and touched his forehead gingerly. The dreamlight pattern was steady but at very low tide.

She stood and crossed to the second man and put her fingertips on his forehead.

"I've seen this kind of pattern before," she said, straightening. "It's typical of a deep state of unconsciousness. It could be a couple of days or longer before either of them wakes up. When they do, I doubt that they'll remember much of anything about what happened here tonight."

"All I want from them is information, but that's the one thing I probably won't get."

She circled the fallen hunters, studying their dreamlight. "There's something wrong with these currents."

"As you just pointed out, both men are unconscious."

"No, something else." She leaned down for a closer look. "I see the same kind of disturbance in these prints that I saw in the killer's tracks."

He scooped up the odd flashlights and walked across the room to join her. "Any idea what's going on?"

"No." She glanced at the flashlights. "But until we know otherwise, I think we should assume that the warping in the currents is linked to whatever those things are."

He unscrewed the top of the flashlight and held it up to the light from the window. Marlowe peered over his shoulder.

"It's a crystal of some kind," she said. "That settles it, whatever you do, don't try to activate it. You'd better warn your lab people not to run any human tests on it, either. Tell them to stick to instrument analysis."

Adam frowned. "Are you sure the crystals caused the damage in the prints of those two men?"

"No, but there's enough old history regarding crystal weapons to make me very cautious. I think it would be best not to take any chances."

"All right." He screwed the top of the flashlight onto the handle. "But I think these things may explain how this pair managed to rez so much psi outside the tunnels. Supposed to be damn near impossible to pull that much ghost light aboveground."

"I think you're right. They were using the crystals to enhance their natural talent for manipulating ghost light."

"I'll send these devices to the Bureau lab," Adam said. "See what the techs can tell me."

"Just to clarify something here," she said coolly. "You can send one of those flashlights to the Bureau lab. I get one for the Arcane lab."

"This is a Bureau operation, Marlowe."

"Not any longer. It became a joint Bureau–J&J operation when I agreed to help you look for the lamp." She tapped the artifact she held in the crook of her arm. "Let it be noted that I'm holding up my end of the bargain."

"The fewer people who know what's going on, the better."

"I agree. But as you just said, there's a possibility that you may have a leak in the Bureau. Might be a mistake to trust all of the evidence to that lab. There's something else to consider, as well."

He eyed her with obvious skepticism. "What's that?"

"As I keep reminding you, Arcane has been conducting research into the paranormal since the seventeenth century, Earth time. We've got a lot more expertise in the field than anyone else around, including the Bureau. Admit it."

He thought about that for a beat or two. "You can have one of these gadgets. But I want a guarantee that you'll keep it under the strictest security."

"Give me a break. The one thing Arcane knows how to do is keep secrets."

"I seem to recall that over the years the Society has had a few problems keeping the founder's formula under wraps," he said.

"Well, it isn't like the Winters family hasn't had a few security issues of its own. You can't even hang on to the lamp."

The sound of a vehicle in the alley distracted them. They both looked toward the rear door of the shop.

"That'll be the Bureau team," Adam said.

Marlowe held out one hand. "We have a deal."

His jaw tightened but he put one of the crystal flashlights in her palm.

"I want your word that I'll get the full report and lab analysis," he said. "Not a scrubbed version."

"I want the same promise from you."

He nodded. "Deal."

Chapter 23

"ARE YOU SURE YOU'RE OKAY?" HE ASKED.

"I'm fine," Marlowe said. "You're the one who just went through a major burn."

He was amazed by the cool, steady tone of her voice. In spite of all she'd been through tonight, in spite of what she had just watched him do to the two men who had attacked them, she was still in control. Definitely the sexiest woman he had ever met. It was all he could do not to stop the sled and pull her into his arms.

They were on their way back through the tunnels. It had taken less than ten minutes to brief the Bureau team and send the two unconscious hunters together with one of the strange flashlights off to the lab at Bureau headquarters.

He whipped the sled around another corner. Marlowe grabbed the dashboard to steady herself.

"Out of sheer curiosity, when did you discover the second aspect of your talent?" she asked.

She was bound and determined not to refer to it as his second talent, he thought.

"The usual way," he said. "By accident. Remember the jungle drug lab case I told you about? The one I was working when I sensed the mirror maze?"

"Yes."

"In the course of the raid, things went wrong. One of my people was taken hostage by the drug lord who was running the lab. The guy had a knife at Harry's throat. They were both about fifteen feet away. Suddenly I just knew how to stop the man with the knife."

"You hit him with a wave of nightmare energy?"

"He didn't even scream, the way those two did tonight. He just collapsed and died on the spot."

"Did the members of your team know what you did?" she asked.

"No. They figured the man suffered a stroke or a heart attack." He frowned, thinking about the incident. "But Harry didn't get the blowback the way you did tonight. He didn't feel anything, even though the guy with the knife was standing right beside him."

"Maybe the only reason I got singed was because of my talent. I was running hot when you hit that hunter with the nightmare energy. My senses were wide-open."

He tightened his hands on the wheel. "You're sure you're okay?"

"I'm very sensitive to dreamlight, but I've also got a

very strong ability to manipulate it. I was able to protect myself. Don't worry about me. We need to stay
focused."

She was right, he thought. The problem was that he
could not stay focused, not when she was so close to
him and the artifact was summoning him in ways he
could not explain. He thought about the old legend as
he brought the sled to a halt near his private hole-in-
the-wall.

Marlowe slipped off the bench seat and stood looking at him. "Speaking of the Burning Lamp myth,
there are a couple of details of the traditional version
of the legend that we should talk about."

His insides tightened, but he managed not to show
any reaction. He climbed out of the vehicle and picked
up the lamp.

"Talk about a psychic intercept," he said. "I was just
thinking about the legend, myself."

She walked around the rear of the sled to join him.
"According to the records, a physical connection is required between the man who wants to access the lamp's
power and the Dreamlight reader who assists him."

He started toward the opening in the quartz. "You
know how it is with old legends. There's always a sexual element in the story." He stepped through the hole-
in-the-wall into the darkened parking garage. "But in
this case, it's just a myth. According to the family records, physical contact is necessary. Just touching each
other is sufficient."

"So, all we have to do is hold hands?" she asked without inflection.

"As you have just pointed out, contact enhances focus and power."

"Yes."

He watched her angle herself through the rip in the quartz. Silhouetted against the alien psi light spilling through the opening, she looked exotic and mysterious and so hot he was starting to sweat.

"Were you really worried that we might have to go to bed together again to make the damned thing work?" he asked.

"Of course not. I never thought that anything more than a handshake was required." She halted just inside the garage. "Just wanted to clarify your understanding of the legend, that's all."

"In other words, you wanted to make sure that I wasn't hoping to get laid again."

"Stop putting words in my mouth." She cleared her throat. "Some people are inclined to take old tales very literally."

He walked forward and stopped directly in front of her, very close but not touching. Marlowe did not retreat, but he felt the rising tide of energy in the atmosphere and knew that she had heightened her senses instinctively, the way people of talent did when they felt threatened. *Or when they were aroused,* he reminded himself.

He should not be thinking about sex, but he couldn't

seem to stop thinking about it. Not just sex, but sex with Marlowe. The situation was fraught with danger and possibilities and a hell of a lot of energy.

"You make it sound like sleeping with me again would be a deeply traumatic event," he said.

"Oh, for pity's sake. That's not what I meant, and you know it."

"Do I?"

He set the silk-wrapped artifact on the concrete floor and moved a little closer to her. The atmosphere around them shivered with heat.

"It's been a busy evening," she said, her voice husky and low. "Lots of adrenaline and psi going on here."

"Like last night?"

She took a deep breath. "We probably shouldn't discuss last night."

"Why?"

She stared at him. "Because I'm not sure what's happening between us."

"And it makes you nervous?"

"Yes." She drew another breath. "What's going on here is probably nothing more than simple sexual attraction enhanced by proximity and the natural bonds forged between two people who have just come through a dangerous experience. In addition, you are in the middle of a major postburn buzz."

"Like you were last night. Is that why we had sex? So you could work off the burn?"

"No."

"Got a problem with this natural bond, mutual attraction, postburn rush we've got going?"

"I probably should have a problem with it," she said. "I'm sure I'll think of one tomorrow."

"What about tonight?"

"No problem tonight," she whispered.

He leaned in very close and brushed his mouth across hers. She did not try to avoid the kiss.

He kissed her again, taking it deeper, letting the heat build between them. This time she responded. Her mouth softened under his. He heard a faint cry. Not a sigh of surrender or a moan of passion. More like a half-stifled murmur of frustration, he decided. She clutched him close, demanding more.

He pulled her hard against him and kissed her until she opened her mouth for him, until her arms tightened around his neck, until her breathing was fast and shallow and she sounded desperate.

He came up for air, crouched in front of her, and pulled off first one boot and then the other, leaving her in her socks. When he rose, she gripped the lapels of his khaki shirt and started kissing his throat. Her leg hooked around his calf.

They were locked in sensual combat. He pushed up the hem of the black turtleneck and put his hands on her bare waist. Her skin was warm and supple.

He unfastened her jeans and shoved them, along with the dainty panties, down to her ankles. She kicked free of the denim.

When he felt her hands on his belt buckle, he held himself very still while she unfastened his trousers. She was exquisitely careful. She took him into her hand.

He slid his fingers through the soft triangle of curls and found her swollen core. She cried out softly when he stroked her and clenched her fingers around his shoulders.

"Nothing has ever felt this good," he said against her throat.

"No," she whispered. "Nothing."

He gripped her by the waist, lifted her, and braced her against the concrete wall. She wrapped her legs around him and used her hand to guide him into her.

"Okay," he managed, his voice hoarse with the effort it took to hang onto his control. "I was wrong. Nothing has ever felt *this* good."

He drove into her, going as far as possible. Her legs tightened around him. So did her passage.

"Oh, Adam."

The stunning intimacy ripped the oxygen from his lungs and dazzled his senses. He rode the crashing waves with Marlowe, each thrust taking both of them higher. He was determined that she would come first. He wanted to make sure she understood that her pleasure was his highest priority. More than that, he wanted her to realize that he could satisfy her fully. He wanted to make sure that she did not forget him, not ever. He was going to be the man she could not leave before dawn.

Her fingers sank into his shirt and the skin beneath

it. He sensed the tension that tightened her entire body now. She was wound to the breaking point.

With a soft, low cry, she came undone. The small spasms of her orgasm pulled him over the edge. He went willingly, glorying in the release. His surging climax sent another wave of hot energy through both of them.

He was distantly aware of his own long roar of satisfaction echoing off the walls, floor, and ceiling of the old garage for what seemed an eternity

Chapter 24

MARLOWE REALIZED THAT HER BACK WAS STILL PLAS-
tered against the cold wall and her legs were still
wrapped around Adam's waist. He was leaning over
her, supporting both of them, his hands flattened
against the concrete behind her.

In the glow of the tunnel radiation she could see that
his forehead was damp with perspiration. His eyes were
closed, and his dark hair was mussed from her fingers.
She listened as his ragged breathing quickly returned to
normal.

She let her legs slide bonelessly back down to the
floor. When her bare feet touched the concrete, she
discovered that the muscles of her inner thighs were
trembling. She had to keep her back against the wall in
order to stay vertical.

nd looked at her. His

even better if we'd

could have been im-

le mattress and a couple of
rete wall. It's the little things
romance to a relationship."

at."

push-up against the wall that brought
gh to kiss her again. It was a lazy, sen-
ure masculine satisfaction this time, not
heavy kiss that had started the encounter.
be we should consider a do-over upstairs,"
suggested, nuzzling her throat. "For compari-
purposes."

he would fall asleep and start dreaming,
An pleasant little fantasy would be destroyed, she
thought. Better to end it now.

"Sounds tempting," she said brightly. She made a show of checking her watch. "But look at the time. It's nearly two in the morning. I don't know what kind of hours you keep at the Guild, but J&J opens at eight."

He nibbled on her earlobe. "You're the boss. You get to set your own hours."

"Uncle Zeke always told me that the boss has to set the example."

He watched her very steadily, eyes faintly narrowed.

Ultraviolets, ultragreens, ultra... with those of
blazed across cold concrete.
Adam's body went rigid, his ... work with a great
twisted in a mask of mortal ago... a key in a lock
He dropped the lamp. The a... mpleted and that
thud, barely missing Marlowe's ... he potential of the
immediately. Adam collapsed, un...
lamp.

...ters had written in
the third and final
who can work dream-
survive must find
key in the lock that

plate the enormity of
taken. A blaze of en-
e psi rainbow became
g the darkened garage
t end of the spectrum.

---

lamp. We don't
h energy."

out of sync. I'll

certainty, easing
inside the lamp.
am's patterns so

Jayne Ca

"This isn't about the r
able to sleep with

"It's better

"Not s

Sh

she
Fortun

She s
into her je
she noticed t

"Adam," she

"What?"

"The lamp," she

He turned to follo
stared at the black bund
rage. A pale, paranormal l
folds of black silk.

"What the hell?" He started

"I think you lit it," she said.
now when we . . . Oh, damn. Mayb
to that part of the legend. Sex produ
energy."

He stood over the black bundle. "So
he said softly.

"We've got to shut it down."

"Why?" He picked up the bundle. At his tou
bundle glowed brighter. "The whole point of this

Jayne Castle

before we run any experiments on the
want to take any chances with this mu

"What are you going to do?"

"Some of your currents are a little
just make a few minor adjustments."

Sh
her o
Obey
that
the a
Sh
deal
and o
tell A
they
lamp.
Lik
Th
his jo
"G
power
the Bu
light e
opens
Wh
The
the ste
ergy e
blindin
in all t

Jayne Castle

HIS PHONE RANG AS HE FOLLOWED MARLOWE OUT
of the elevator into his living room. He glanced at the
code. Adrenaline spiked.

"It's Fortner." He opened the phone. "Winters. Did
that pair I sent to you last night wake up?"

"The two hunters are still unconscious." Elliot said.
He sounded grim and weary, as if he, too, had spent
the night keeping watch. "The parapsych doc says that
even if they do wake up, they won't have much in the
way of coherent memory. But we ID'd them. Couple of
hunters who moonlight as hired muscle."

"Working for O'Conner and Drake?"

Elliott snorted. "You must be psychic. They're free-
lancers but, yes, as it happens they have done some odd
jobs for O'Conner and Drake."

Marlowe stopped in the middle of the room, listening. Gibson wriggled out of the crook of her arm and
tumbled to the floor. With what appeared to be unerring instinct, he headed toward the kitchen.

"What about that flashlight weapon?" Adam said
into the phone. "Anything on it yet?"

"Not much. There is a crystal of some kind inside,
but the lab techs tell me they've never seen anything
like it. Their instruments say that it's dead, though. No
energy left in it at all."

"Alien technology?"

"Certainly a possibility. Wouldn't be the first artifacts of power to come out of the jungle." Elliott
paused. "You said there was only one of these devices
at the scene?"

Adam met Marlowe's eyes. "Right. You're thinking there may be more?"

"Who the hell knows?" Elliott exhaled heavily. "Like I told you, watch your back."

"Any word from Galendez and Treiger?"

"Last report was that O'Conner and Drake come and go from their office, but there are no signs of any unusual activity. Are you sure you don't want to move on them? This is your call, but after what happened last night—"

"Not yet," Adam said. "I need to know what they're up to before we take them down. That goes double now that we know about the crystal weapon. Talk to you later."

He closed the phone, aware that Marlowe was watching him with an interested expression.

"Nothing on the flashlight?" she asked.

"Lab techs think it might be alien technology. But whatever it is, it's gone dark. They don't think it's capable of generating any energy now."

She unzipped her small leather backpack and took out the flashlight she had commandeered. She contemplated it for a moment.

"I'll bet this one is dead, too. I think we can attribute that to your second talent."

He cocked a brow.

"I mean the second aspect of your talent," she corrected hurriedly. She dropped the flashlight into the backpack. "When you hit those men with that crushing wave of nightmare energy, they were both fully rezzed. You scrambled their senses while they were both running hot and focusing through the flashlights. Got a hunch the power surge probably blew out the crystals."

"Like melting amber?"

"Yes. The crystals most likely need to be tuned to function, just like amber. Finely tuned instruments or machines of any kind are always delicate. Doesn't take a lot to throw them out of whack or destroy them."

He headed for the kitchen. "Which means your lab techs probably won't find anything helpful when they examine that one."

"Maybe not. Adam?"

He picked up the coffeepot and turned on the faucet. "Yeah?"

"You lied to your boss about last night," she said.

"Elliott's not my boss. Not any longer."

"You lied to him from start to finish. He doesn't know that I have the second flashlight. He doesn't even know that you have the lamp, does he?"

"It's better this way. I told you, I think he's got a leak in the Bureau. Best bet is that O'Conner and Drake have someone inside, close to Fortner. Someone he trusts."

"Wow. And I thought I was paranoid. You really don't trust anyone, do you?"

"That's not true." He finished filling the pot and turned off the faucet. "I trust the members of my family."

"That's it? Just your own family?"

HIS PHONE RANG AS HE FOLLOWED MARLOWE OUT of the elevator into his living room. He glanced at the code. Adrenaline spiked.

"It's Fortner." He opened the phone. "Winters. Did that pair I sent to you last night wake up?"

"The two hunters are still unconscious." Elliot said. He sounded grim and weary, as if he, too, had spent the night keeping watch. "The parapsych doc says that even if they do wake up, they won't have much in the way of coherent memory. But we ID'd them. Couple of hunters who moonlight as hired muscle."

"Working for O'Conner and Drake?"

Elliott snorted. "You must be psychic. They're free-lancers but, yes, as it happens they have done some odd jobs for O'Conner and Drake."

Marlowe stopped in the middle of the room, listening. Gibson wriggled out of the crook of her arm and tumbled to the floor. With what appeared to be unerring instinct, he headed toward the kitchen.

"What about that flashlight weapon?" Adam said into the phone. "Anything on it yet?"

"Not much. There is a crystal of some kind inside, but the lab techs tell me they've never seen anything like it. Their instruments say that it's dead, though. No energy left in it at all."

"Alien technology?"

"Certainly a possibility. Wouldn't be the first artifacts of power to come out of the jungle." Elliott paused. "You said there was only one of these devices at the scene?"

He looked back down at the lamp. "You're certain?"

"Absolutely. Trust me; I would know."

She sounded very sure. He exhaled slowly.

"Did you notice that one of the crystals remained dark?" she asked.

"Can't say that I was paying close attention," he admitted. "But according to the old records, every time the lamp has been lit, one crystal has always stayed dark."

"The Midnight Crystal."

"That's what Nicholas Winters called it. The family concluded centuries ago that it was dead. The theory is that Nicholas was already going insane and losing his talents when he forged it. All he cared about was vengeance. He deceived himself into believing that he had infused the last crystal with some kind of psychic command."

"Which is, technically speaking, impossible," Marlowe said.

"Yes. But it leaves us with the next question." He looked at her. "Will I be able to work this thing to stop the dissonance in the maze?"

"I can't answer that. But I can tell you that you don't have a chance of channeling the energy in the artifact without me."

He smiled faintly. "Still partners?"

"Someone's got to save the underworld."

"That would be us," he said. "Let's go upstairs and get some breakfast, partner."

* * *

after five. You were only out for three hours. I did go upstairs to make some coffee at one point."

He swallowed some of the coffee and couldn't remember the last time anything had tasted that good. Because she had made it for him, he realized.

"Thanks," he said. He sounded surly, even to his own ears. He couldn't help it. He'd passed out last night. He didn't like knowing that she had seen him in such a weak, helpless state.

She smiled. "It's okay. I went to sleep on you the night before last."

"Right." It wasn't the same thing at all, but he decided there wasn't much room to argue. "Where's the lamp?"

"Over there."

He followed her gesture and saw a dark lump in the shadows.

"Why did you put it way over there?" he asked.

"It gives off a lot of disturbing energy, even when it isn't lit. I thought it might interrupt your sleep."

He crossed the garage and picked up the lamp. For a moment or two he contemplated it. Marlowe waited quietly. After a while he looked at her.

"Think I came into my third talent last night?" he asked.

She glanced at the garage floor beneath his feet. He knew she was reading his prints.

"You came into the third *level* of your talent," she said deliberately. "You are no Cerberus."

The elevator doors hissed open. Marlowe walked out, a mug in her hand.

"I'm the one with the coffee," she said. She came toward him through the shadows. "When I checked your dreamlight a few minutes ago, it looked like you were about to wake up. How do you feel?"

He thought about the question. "Good. Very good." He pushed aside the blanket, got to his feet, and took the coffee from her. "Okay, maybe a little stiff from sleeping on the garage floor, but all in all, I feel a hell of a lot better than I have in a month."

"Sorry about leaving you down here in the garage all night. After you crashed I couldn't wake you. There was no way I could get you upstairs, so I brought the blankets and pillows down here."

"Thanks. I appreciate it."

She moved through the angled light from the catacombs. He saw that she was wearing the jeans, turtleneck, and boots she had worn last night. Her hair was scraped back into a knot. The shadows under her eyes told the story.

"You didn't sleep, did you?" he asked.

"I wasn't sure how the lamp had affected you. I thought it best to keep an eye on you until you woke up."

The realization that she'd felt obliged to stand guard annoyed him.

"You spent the night watching me sleep?" he said.

"I wanted to be sure you were okay. It's just a little

Chapter 25

HE CAME AWAKE TO A REALM OF DARKNESS LIT ONLY by a long shaft of underworld light. It took him a few seconds to realize that he was lying on the floor of the garage. There was a blanket underneath him and one over him. A pillow cushioned his head.

"What the hell?"

A cheery chortling sound made him look to the side. He saw Gibson sitting nearby. The dust bunny was munching on a cracker. The cracker looked familiar, Adam decided. It looked like it had come from the stash upstairs in his kitchen.

"Good morning to you, too." He pushed himself to a sitting position and checked his watch. Five o'clock. "I don't suppose you've got any coffee to go with that cracker?"

Ultraviolets, ultragreens, ultrareds, and ultrayellows blazed across cold concrete.

Adam's body went rigid, his head flung back, face twisted in a mask of mortal agony.

He dropped the lamp. The artifact landed with a thud, barely missing Marlowe's bare toes. It went dark immediately. Adam collapsed, unconscious, beside the lamp.

Adam raised his dark lashes and looked at her. His eyes still burned.

"This probably would have been even better if we'd made it upstairs to bed," he said.

"Hard to imagine how it could have been improved."

"Maybe with a comfortable mattress and a couple of pillows instead of a concrete wall. It's the little things that add an element of romance to a relationship."

"I'll remember that."

He did a small push-up against the wall that brought him close enough to kiss her again. It was a lazy, sensual kiss of pure masculine satisfaction this time, not the hot and heavy kiss that had started the encounter.

"Maybe we should consider a do-over upstairs," Adam suggested, nuzzling her throat. "For comparison purposes."

And then he would fall asleep and start dreaming, and her pleasant little fantasy would be destroyed, she thought. Better to end it now.

"Sounds tempting," she said brightly. She made a show of checking her watch. "But look at the time. It's nearly two in the morning. I don't know what kind of hours you keep at the Guild, but J&J opens at eight."

He nibbled on her earlobe. "You're the boss. You get to set your own hours."

"Uncle Zeke always told me that the boss has to set the example."

He watched her very steadily, eyes faintly narrowed.

"This isn't about the rules at J&J. It's about not being able to sleep with me. About being gone by dawn."

"It's better this way, trust me."

"Not so sure about that." He fastened his trousers.

She realized that her panties were still draped around one ankle. A wave of heat rose in her cheeks. Ridiculous, really, after the wild parking garage sex, she thought. But she felt frazzled and unsure of herself. Fortunately, the deep shadows hid the blush.

She stepped hastily into the panties and shimmied into her jeans. She was fastening the waistband when she noticed the lamp. She stilled.

"Adam," she whispered.

"What?"

"The lamp," she said. "Look at it."

He turned to follow her riveted gaze. They both stared at the black bundle lying on the floor of the garage. A pale, paranormal light was seeping through the folds of black silk.

"What the hell?" He started toward the artifact.

"I think you lit it," she said. "Or maybe we did just now when we . . . Oh, damn. Maybe there is some truth to that part of the legend. Sex produces a lot of strong energy."

He stood over the black bundle. "Son of a ghost," he said softly.

"We've got to shut it down."

"Why?" He picked up the bundle. At his touch, the bundle glowed brighter. "The whole point of this exercise is to figure out how this thing works. Looks like we've made a good start."

"We don't know what we're doing here," she reminded him. "I need time to study the artifact. Time to do some research."

He began to unwrap the silk cloth. "Time is one commodity we don't have."

"I really don't think it would be a good idea to mess around with that thing tonight. We should come up with some sort of strategy before we tackle this project."

"According to the records, we have to rely on our intuition, not research and strategy."

He pulled away the last of the cloth. She saw the shudder that jolted through him when his hands came in direct contact with the artifact.

"Are you all right?" she asked.

"You should feel the power in this thing. It's incredible."

The lamp no longer appeared solid. The strange, gold-toned metal was becoming translucent. Currents of psi shifted in the relic.

"I can feel the forces in it," she said quietly. "I think it's getting stronger. It's responding to your own currents."

"Yes." His eyes were heating again.

"There's too much power in that thing for one person to control," she warned. "We know that much. You can't do this alone."

He held the lamp in his hands and looked at her.

In the rising glow of the artifact he looked like some ancient alchemist gazing into its fires, like Nicholas Winters.

"I know I can't handle the energy in this thing alone," he said. "That's why I need you. Now. Tonight."

His voice was once again shaded with lust, but she realized that it was not sexual desire that drove him this time, rather a bone-deep hunger to control the power of the lamp. The need to manipulate the energy of the artifact was, quite literally, in his genes.

She knew then that nothing she said would convince him to try to de-rez the lamp tonight. Perhaps there was no way to stop what had been started. There was only one thing she could do now, and that was to help Adam control the device.

She crossed the short space that separated them. He used both hands to hold the lamp by its base.

"It would probably be best to have physical contact," she said.

He said nothing, waiting for her to make the next move.

She covered one of his hands with her left palm and gripped the rim of the artifact with her right hand.

Energy slammed through her. Psychic flames flashed across her senses. The shock stole her breath for a few heartbeats, but she did not pull away.

The initial flash diminished quickly. In the next instant she was in the currents, soaring on the waves of raw power. There was no more pain, just an exhilarating sense of certainty. She knew how to do this.

Adam watched her with hot, knowing eyes.

"Feels good, doesn't it?" he asked. "Like the sex we just had."

The sensation was, indeed, unnervingly akin to what she had experienced during their heated sexual encounter.

The base and body of the lamp were still undergoing some kind of alchemical change. As they watched, the gold metal became translucent. Energy built higher in the atmosphere and inside the artifact.

In another moment the lamp was abruptly transparent, as though it were made of the purest crystal. A seething storm of ultradark light flared and roiled inside the artifact.

All but one of the murky crystals set into the rim heated with paranormal fire. Each displayed a different color of the dreamlight spectrum. Without warning, a rainbow of psi lanced out from the circle of stones and splashed against the walls of the garage.

"So much power," Adam whispered. "I understand now. I can channel it, but only if you hold the center."

"Yes," she said.

Probing gently, she found the rhythm of the heavy, shifting waves of raw dreamlight. The pulses and oscillations of the storm infused into the lamp were almost but not quite identical to Adam's. His own wavelengths were astonishingly strong, but here and there she sensed a slight lack of harmony in the currents.

"I think I've found the source of your nightmares and hallucinations," she said. "I should fix the problem

before we run any experiments on the lamp. We don't
want to take any chances with this much energy."

"What are you going to do?"

"Some of your currents are a little out of sync. I'll
just make a few minor adjustments."

She went to work with a sense of certainty, easing
her own energy into the storm brewing inside the lamp.
Obeying her intuition, she tuned Adam's patterns so
that his dreamlight currents resonated with those of
the artifact.

She finished the last bit of repair work with a great
deal of satisfaction. *Just like turning a key in a lock
and opening the right door,* she thought. She started to
tell Adam that the small task was completed and that
they could now proceed to explore the potential of the
lamp.

Like turning a key in a lock.

The old words that Nicholas Winters had written in
his journal slammed through her.

*"Grave risk attends the onset of the third and final
power. Those of my line who would survive must find
the Burning Lamp and a woman who can work dreamlight energy. Only she can turn the key in the lock that
opens the door to the last talent."*

What had she done?

There was no time to contemplate the enormity of
the step she and Adam had just taken. A blaze of energy erupted from the lamp. The psi rainbow became
blindingly brilliant, illuminating the darkened garage
in all the colors of the darkest end of the spectrum.

He glanced at her. "And you, Marlowe. I trust you."

She smiled. "Well, naturally. Partners have to trust each other."

"No," he said. "They don't. But it certainly helps if they do."

Chapter 26

"YOU'RE LATE, BOSS." RICK PUT DOWN THE COPY OF *Harmonic Weddings* magazine that he had been reading and surveyed Marlowe. "I was about to call you."

"I'm the boss," Marlowe said. "Rank has its privileges. But as it happens, I have a good excuse. I had to drop something off at the lab, and then I stopped by Uncle Zeke's place to get a few of the old private case files out of the J&J vault."

"I'm telling you, those old files should be computerized."

"Probably. But to date every Jones who ever had my job has been too paranoid to put the data online. As Uncle Zeke says, once it's in that format, it's accessible to anyone who has a thirteen-year-old available."

"That's not true. J&J computer security is extremely sophisticated."

"There's still the paranoia factor. Hard to overcome it after several centuries of tradition."

Gibson bailed out of her backpack and fluttered across the floor. He bounded up onto the desk to greet Rick.

"Hey, there, biker dude, how's it hangin'?" Rick patted Gibson affectionately and then went to work removing the wire lock from the cookie jar.

When he got the lid off, Gibson jumped up onto the rim and studied the array of High-Rez Energy Bars with an expression that could only be described as lust.

Rick squinted at Marlowe through his gold-rimmed spectacles. "No offense, but you don't look like you got a lot of sleep last night, boss."

"Comments like that will not get you a raise." She shrugged out of her backpack. "How's the wedding planning going?"

"Dan and I have an appointment with the wedding planner this afternoon. We're going to choose the invitations." He held up the copy of *Harmonic Weddings* and assumed an ominous air. "Did you know that blush pink and cerulean blue are the fashionable colors for CMs this year?"

"Hadn't heard that." She never liked to talk about the subject, because it only made her aware that she would never have a Covenant Wedding of her own. But she tried to show some enthusiasm. She was fond of Rick, and he had found the love of his life. That was something to be celebrated.

"Dan refuses to wear pink or blue," Rick said.

"Can't blame him. I'm not a fan of pink and blue, myself. What are you going to do?"

"Something untraditional. The wedding planner suggests copper and bronze."

"That sounds—" She broke off, searching for the right word. "Interesting. Are you sure that you and Dan won't look like a couple of statues standing at the altar?"

"Hadn't thought about it that way, but now that you mention it, we may want to reconsider."

Gibson made his selection and abandoned the cookie jar. Rick replaced the lid and secured the wire.

Marlowe walked around the desk, heading toward the inner office. "Did Tony Chula report in on the Parker case?"

"About ten minutes ago. He said he had no trouble picking up the killer's trail. The wife, just like you thought."

"I was afraid of that." She set the pack on her desk and removed the two old volumes inside. "When a Covenant Marriage goes bad, it goes really, really bad."

Rick came to stand in the doorway. "Divorce might be next to impossible, but you'd think two civilized people who got trapped in a bad CM could just agree to live apart with their respective lovers."

"That only works when both of the parties involved have lovers. In this case, Mr. Parker had his young, attractive yoga instructor. Mrs. Parker had her bridge club. Evidently, the two did not equate in her mind."

"Guess not. Tony says the case isn't ready to hand over to the cops, yet. He's still working on evidence, but he doesn't think it will be hard to find."

Marlowe sat down and opened one of the old books. "I'm expecting a call from Dr. Raymond at the lab. Put him through immediately."

"You got it, boss."

Marlowe started to read.

TWO HOURS LATER, SHE FOUND WHAT SHE WAS LOOK-ing for. She picked up the phone and entered Adam's private code.

"Hello, Marlowe."

She tried to ignore the sexy, intimate tone in his voice, but the truth was, she was getting addicted to it.

"I've been going through some old J&J records. The private case files of Caleb and Lucinda Jones."

"The founders of Jones & Jones?"

"You know the history?"

"My family has always kept close tabs on yours. Besides, one of my ancestors, Griffin Winters, had some dealings with J&J back in the days when Caleb and Lucinda Jones ran the agency." Adam paused a beat. "Something to do with an old lamp, as I recall."

"It's all here in the files. But there's some other in-formation, as well. In the course of that case, some odd red crystal weapons showed up. According to Caleb Jones's notes, they could be tuned in a way that allowed a person with talent to enhance and focus his natural psychic energy."

"You're thinking there's a connection to the crystals in those flashlights?"

"Well, the color of the crystals is different, but, yes, I think there is a link." She pulled the second volume closer and peered at the page. "What's more, weapons of a similar nature showed up again in the early twenty-first century, according to the case files of Fallon Jones. Again, the crystals weren't red, but I think we're talking about the same kind of technology."

"Old Earth technology?"

"Old Earth alchemy, to be precise."

"Alchemy was a dead science by the nineteenth century," Adam said.

"Got news for you. Alchemy has never been dead within Arcane. The Society was founded on alchemical science."

"Do you think the crystal guns we took off that pair last night date from the nineteenth or twenty-first century?"

"No. Those flashlight devices are definitely of modern manufacture. I can sense the age of artifacts, remember?"

"That leaves us with two possibilities," Adam said. "The first is that someone rediscovered the same alchemical technology that others discovered at various points in the past."

"Coincidence and serendipity happen," Marlowe

said. "The wheel was probably invented several times by a number of different people before it caught on."

"The second possibility is that someone got hold of some of those old Arcane files that you're looking at and found the method for creating the crystals."

"Here's the interesting part. Caleb and Fallon Jones deliberately did not include the instructions in their records. They both believed that the crystals were too dangerous."

"So we're going with the coincidence and serendipity theory."

She cleared her throat. "Actually, there's another explanation."

"Yeah?"

"Turns out that the original set of instructions for manufacturing talent-enhancing crystals came from the early works of Nicholas Winters."

There was a long silence on the other end of the line.

"That old alchemical recipe," Adam said neutrally.

"Listen, I understand the need to keep family secrets, believe me. But in this case—" She stopped mid-sentence because the phone was ringing. "That's my other line. Hold on."

She heard Rick answer.

"She's with a client, Dr. Raymond. Let me see if she's available."

"I'm available," she called into the other room. She turned back to the phone. "That's the Arcane lab,

Adam. Dr. Raymond must have an initial report on the crystal I gave him this morning. I'll call you right back."

"Do that," Adam said. "Oh, and Marlowe?"

"Yes?"

"We need to go down into the rain forest as soon as possible. I just got a report from the on-site team. After your people arrived, they took their own measurements and observations. They indicate that the rate of deterioration in the dissonance currents is accelerating even faster than we thought."

"We really should do some more experiments on the lamp before we try to use it underground in that heavy psi atmosphere."

"We don't have time. Can you be ready to go below this afternoon?"

She took a deep breath. "Yes."

Adam ended the call. She picked up the other line.

"This is Marlowe, Dr. Raymond. What have you got?"

"A preliminary report only, Miss Jones. But you did say that you wanted to be notified of our findings on that crystal flashlight as soon as we learned anything."

"Yes. Thank you for the fast analysis."

"Don't thank me yet. At this point I can't tell you a lot. But I can confirm that the crystal is certainly not alien technology. Definitely human engineering. In addition, our instruments tell us that the device might have been capable of channeling and focusing human psi, but it appears to be quite dead now. It would require a special kind of talent to retune it."

"Crystal talent?"

"Yes, a very powerful crystal talent." Dr. Raymond hesitated. "One other thing: I believe your initial suspicions are correct. Things such as amber that allow a person to focus his or her natural talent are, generally speaking, harmless. But devices like that crystal that can actually enhance talent are different. They are inherently dangerous to the user because over time they warp the individual's underlying patterns."

Like the founder's formula, she thought. But she did not say it out loud. There was no need. Everyone in Arcane knew about the dangers of the ancient alchemical recipe that Sylvester Jones had concocted.

"Thank you, Dr. Raymond."

"One more thing, Miss Jones. Whoever created this crystal device knows a great deal about crystal science, certainly more than I or anyone on my staff knows. We're talking very cutting-edge technology, Miss Jones."

"Or very ancient technology," Marlowe said quietly. "As in Old Earth alchemy. Call me if you come up with anything else."

"Of course."

She reconnected with Adam.

"Anything new from your lab?" he asked.

"No. But Dr. Raymond did confirm that the crystal weapons are potentially very hazardous."

"Yeah. I noticed that last night."

"Not just to the victim," she said patiently, "but, long-term, to the user."

"Which explains the warping that you saw in the dreamprints of those two men. I agree, the crystals are a problem. But they're linked to O'Conner and Drake. That means that, for now, they're at the bottom of my priority list. Ready to save the underworld?"

"Sure. Not like Gibson and I had anything more exciting to do today."

Chapter 27

HER INTUITION HAD BEEN REZZED FOR DAYS. NOW IT was screaming at her. *Time to disappear,* Gloria Ray thought. A chill shivered through her. *Past time.* She had left the decision until too late. That was not like her. She should have been on her way out of town by now, not standing here, alone, in dear Hubert's extremely private office.

She had been Hubert O'Conner's mistress for several months now and had hoped to continue for a while longer. Dear Hubert had been very generous with jewelry, furs, cars, and exclusive spa memberships. But when the Chamber had put its heavy, booted foot on the necks of the local Guild Council and installed Adam Winters as the new CEO of the Frequency organization, she had seen the writing on the wall.

There was only one reason the Chamber would have

overridden the Frequency Council. It had finally concluded that the Frequency organization needed to be
cleaned up and that the housekeeping would not take
place without a new boss from outside. She knew that
meant that Hubert would not be on the Council much
longer. He wielded a lot of power, but he was also as
dirty as they came.

When you opted for a career path like the one she
had chosen, Gloria thought, you learned to depend on
your intuition. As it happened, hers was very highly
toned. It had kept her out of trouble this long, and it
was shrieking at her now.

Get out.

But there was one more thing she had to do before she left town with her suitcase full of expensive
jewelry.

Hubert O'Conner's official office was at Guild headquarters. But he and his old buddy, Douglas Drake,
had always maintained a private office deep in the
heart of the Quarter here near the South Wall. They
had grown up together in the neighborhood, joined the
Guild together, and started out working as a team in
the catacombs.

Over time they had clawed their way up through the
ranks of the corrupt Frequency organization, watching each other's backs at every step. But neither of
them had ever lost touch with the old neighborhood.
The mean streets near the South Wall constituted their
power base.

In this tough part of the Quarter, O'Conner and

Drake were the go-to men for anyone looking to do business in the vicinity, including drug dealers, pimps, and entrepreneurs who worked the illegal antiquities trade underground. If you didn't cut O'Conner and Drake in for a slice of the action, you didn't last long.

She did not need to turn on the lights. She had been here before, and she knew her way around. There was enough green psi coming through the grime-covered windows to enable her to see what she was doing.

Unlike the offices at Guild headquarters, this was a sparsely furnished space containing only a battered desk and a couple of chairs. She knew that as far as O'Conner and Drake were concerned, the most important amenity was a closet that concealed a staircase that led to a bolt-hole into the underworld. O'Conner often used it to come and go from his secret office on occasions when he did not want anyone in the neighborhood to see him. He had brought her with him a number of times. He liked to have sex down in the catacombs. A lot of hunters liked it that way. Something about the alien psi. She had secretly made a note of the coordinates.

An unnerving frisson shivered through her. She should leave. *Now.* She had packed her gym bag earlier, filling it with only the essentials: the collection of expensive amber and gold jewelry that Hubert had given her, the new ID that she had bought secretly online, the brown wig that she would use to cover her blonde hair, and the amber contacts that would darken her blue eyes. She'd hated leaving the gorgeous clothes and the lovely new crimson Siren behind, but, really, there was no other option. You couldn't carry out a decent disappearing act when you were traveling with a half-dozen large, overstuffed suitcases and a flashy sports car.

Hurry, she thought. *Do what you have to do and get out of here.*

She went to the wall and felt for the concealed seam in the paneling. She found it quickly. A small section slid aside, revealing the safe.

She rezzed the code that O'Conner did not know that she had found, thanks to her intuitive talent. Her fingers trembled a little.

This was not the first time she had been obliged to end a relationship with a potentially dangerous lover. She was a pro. She had been planning for this day since the moment she had managed to engage Hubert O'Conner's attention a year ago. Men like O'Conner—high-ranking Guild Councilmen—were excellent financial investments. They lavished their mistresses with the best of everything.

But such powerful men were also high-risk. At best they simply lost interest when a younger, more beautiful woman came along. Generally speaking, she accepted that possibility with a degree of equanimity, even good grace, if she did say so herself. Losing out to the competition occasionally came with the territory and now that she was getting older, it was bound to happen more frequently.

But there was a worst-case scenario when it came to

terminating such relationships, and her talent told her that was what she was facing now. She had learned too many of O'Conner's secrets, and recently she had discovered the most dangerous one of all. Powerful men got nervous when they realized that a mistress knew too much. Guild men like Hubert tended to be somewhat old-fashioned when it came to protecting themselves. O'Conner was quite capable of making certain that she really did disappear—straight into the tunnels or the rain forest.

Leaving town and changing her identity would not give her sufficient protection. She needed an insurance policy, leverage. The journal stored in the hidden safe would give her at least a fighting chance if O'Conner decided to send his goons after her.

She rezzed the lock, opened the safe, and took out the journal. She carried the volume back to the desk and opened it.

Reaching into her low-cut blouse, she took the tiny camera out of the pocket inside her bra. The pocket was designed to hold special pads to enhance cleavage. She did not need that kind of enhancement. Her very fine breasts had been expertly constructed by one of the best surgeons in the city. But the pockets in the bra were useful for concealing other items such as the camera and a little emergency backup amber. When you hung around Guild men, you learned to carry tuned amber.

She took several shots of the most recent pages in the journal, tucked the camera back into her bra, and replaced the volume inside the safe.

When she withdrew her hand, her fingers brushed against a hard, round object about half the size of her fist. *A crystal or stone of some kind,* she thought. The surface was faceted, but the object was much too large to be an item of jewelry. She groped around inside the safe and discovered two more crystals.

She did not need her intuitive talent to tell her that if O'Conner kept them in the safe, they were not only extremely valuable but very likely dangerous.

She knew she should leave, but she was unable to resist a closer look at the crystals. She picked up one of the stones and brought it out into the light.

In the green glow filtering through the window she could not make out the color of the crystal, but she sensed some kind of energy in it.

Briefly she contemplated the notion of taking one of the crystals with her. But again her talent stepped in, voting strongly against the idea. O'Conner would be certain to notice that it was missing. He would put that fact together with the fact that she had also disappeared and leap to the worst possible conclusion.

Decision made, she put the crystal back into the safe, secured the lock, and slid the concealing panel into place.

She crossed the room to the closet, intending to leave the same way she had arrived. But when she put her hand on the handle of the closet door, her intuition surged.

Don't open the door.

She released the handle as if it had seared her palm,

took a quick step back, whirled, and started toward the only other exit from the room, the front door.

It opened before she was halfway across the office. One of Hubert's men, a thug named Kirby, walked into the room. He had a mag-rez in his hand.

"Looks like Mr. O'Conner was right about you, Miss Ray," he said. "He told me to keep an eye on you. Said you'd been acting a little different lately."

"What are you talking about, Kirby?" she snapped.

"Mr. O'Conner figured you might be planning something, but personally, I never thought you'd be stupid enough to search his private office. Always figured the dumb blonde act was just that, an act."

"You idiot," she said, putting as much disdain as possible into her voice. "I'm here because Hubert asked me to meet him here tonight. If he finds out you pulled a gun on me, he'll be furious."

"I don't think so," Kirby said. He sounded oddly wistful. "Too bad things turned out this way. I sort of liked you. Of all the women Mr. O'Conner has had, you were the nicest to me and the other guys. You had class, y'know?"

"Listen, Kirby. This is all a misunderstanding. Just give me a minute, and I can explain everything."

The closet door opened behind her. Hubert O'Conner walked out of the tunnel entrance.

"Kirby's right, Gloria," he said. "You had class. I'm going to miss you."

"Hubert, this is ridiculous. What's going on? I got your message telling me to meet you here."

"We both know I never sent you a message," he said.

She worked up some convincing outrage. "Well, someone sure as hell did. Whoever made that phone call to me an hour ago must have been trying to set me up."

"Why would anyone go to the trouble?" O'Conner asked. "You're just a whore."

"The idea was to distract you, of course. Make you look in another direction. Hubert, listen to me. We both know you've got enemies. Someone is plotting against you. Whoever it is wants you to think that you can't trust me."

O'Conner ignored her. He went to the wall, opened the panel, and unlocked the safe. He took out a small flashlight and examined the interior.

"Nothing's missing," he said to Kirby. "Get her amber. I don't think any of it is tuned, but no point taking chances."

"Yes, sir." Kirby holstered his weapon and moved forward. "Sorry about this, Miss Ray. You going to hand over your amber, or do you want me to take it the hard way?"

"You're making a mistake, Hubert," Gloria said quietly. She stripped off her amber ring and removed her amber earrings. "A very big mistake. Whoever set me up will laugh when he finds out how easily he made a fool out of you."

"Shut up," O'Conner growled. "Are you finished, Kirby?"

"Yes, Mr. O'Conner. Got her amber."

"Take her down into the tunnels."

Gloria's heart was pounding now. She could scarcely breathe. Kirby had not found the small piece of tuned amber that she kept in her bra pocket. As soon as Kirby released her down in the catacombs, she would use the tuned stone to find a way out. But meanwhile, she had to make this look good.

"Please, Hubert," she whispered. "After all we've meant to each other, surely you aren't going to send me underground to die."

He jerked a thumb toward the closet. "Get rid of her."

"Yes, Mr. O'Conner." Kirby started to wrap thick fingers around Gloria's arm.

"Wait," Hubert ordered. "You're right, Kirby, Gloria, here, isn't as dumb as she looks. I think I'd better take one more precaution." He reached under his overcoat and unclipped a small case from his belt.

Gloria watched, her senses screaming. Hubert opened the case. He took a chunk of what looked like pale pink quartz out of the pocket of his coat.

"Hubert?" she said. "What's going on here?"

"Just a little insurance in case you've got some amber tucked under all that blonde hair. Stand out of the way, Kirby."

Kirby quickly moved aside.

O'Conner held the quartz in the palm of his hand and concentrated. The quartz brightened. Gloria sensed energy heightening in the atmosphere, but nothing happened as far as she could tell. A few seconds later, the quartz lost its pale glow.

"That will take care of your backup amber," Hubert said.

"What do you mean?" she asked. "Kirby just took my amber."

"Maybe he got it all, maybe he didn't. It doesn't matter now." O'Conner held up the pink quartz. "This stuff destroys tuned amber. If you've got any left, it just went dead."

Her mouth went dry. "That's not possible."

He was genuinely amused now. "You'll see when you start running. That's the thing about the cata-combs, you know. Put people down there without good amber, and sooner or later they always start running. Makes people crazy, they say. Get rid of her, Kirby."

Chapter 28

THE HEART OF THE UNDERWORLD WAS A VAST FROZEN lake of searing, seething, quicksilver psi.

"It's incredible," Marlowe whispered.

She stood with Adam on the rim of the canyon and looked down at the solid sheet of flashing, sparking mirror quartz that filled the valley below. It was hard to look directly at the impossibly brilliant energy for more than a few seconds at a time.

She took out her sunglasses and put them on. The heavily tinted lenses reduced but did not eliminate all of the glare as far as her normal vision was concerned. The glasses did nothing at all to dampen the dazzling effect on her other senses.

"That's just the surface of the maze," Adam said. "The real action is inside."

Perched on Marlowe's shoulder, Gibson grumbled

uneasily. He had become increasingly alert for the past two hours as they made their way through the jungle toward the maze. She reached up to touch him. He huddled closer as though he needed to be reassured.

The three of them were not alone. There was a lot of scurrying in the underbrush and rustling in the leafy canopy. Dust bunnies.

Almost immediately after they had entered the jungle, Marlowe and Adam had become aware of the small creatures trailing them through the underworld. There had been only a handful at first, but the number had increased steadily during the hours it had taken to reach the canyon. Marlowe estimated that there had to be dozens of dust bunnies concealed in the undergrowth now, possibly hundreds. Occasionally she heard them calling to each other. Sometimes Gibson chattered with their unseen companions. But for the most part the bunnies remained eerily quiet, as though sensing that something of great import was happening, something that would affect them.

The sounds of other denizens of the rain forest had grown less frequent as they had neared their destination. Marlowe hadn't heard a birdcall or seen one of the ubiquitous iridescent lizards for the past hour.

It had taken longer than anticipated to arrive at their destination because they'd been forced to detour around two deadly ghost rivers and one psi storm.

"They weren't here the last time I came this way," Adam had said. "Got a feeling that the deteriorating resonance pattern in the maze is generating a lot of unstable energy throughout the jungle. The situation is getting worse."

Marlowe looked down at the shimmering quicksilver surface of the maze. Bracing herself, she opened her senses cautiously. The shock was both thrilling and energizing. There was an enormous amount of power coming at her in invisible, pulsing currents. It was as if she had taken a hit of an astonishingly potent drug. Everything inside her stirred wildly. She had to fight for control.

She felt Adam's talent quicken and knew that he was also responding to the energy rolling off the quicksilver lake in a steady tide.

"It's definitely some kind of dreamlight energy," she said. "And definitely from the ultradark end of the spectrum. But it's unlike anything I've ever encountered. There's no emotion, no dreamscape images. Just raw power."

"Probably because the energy is being generated mechanically, not by a living creature. The maze is a machine, a generator."

"Theoretically it's supposed to be impossible to generate artificial dreamlight," she reminded him.

He glanced down at the leather bag that contained the Burning Lamp.

"What about this thing?" he asked. "It's a device that is capable of producing a hell of a lot of dreamlight."

"Well, yes, but only if you ignite it and have someone to help you control the forces inside. And you're the only one who can direct the energy infused in it.

When you get right down to it, the power of the lamp can only be accessed and activated by human psi, specifically your genetic version."

He studied the lake. "The aliens are long gone. There's no one around now to focus bio-paranormal energy through that quartz, but that big generator is still sending out a huge amount of psi."

"All indications are that it has been humming along, doing its thing, whatever that is, for centuries," she said quietly.

He glanced at her. "You can sense the age of that mirror quartz?"

"Only in a very rough way. It's always difficult to come up with a precise date when you're dealing with antiquities that are so ancient, especially alien antiquities. But, yes, we're talking centuries here, probably a couple thousand years."

"Which is the approximate age that the para-archaeologists have come up with for the age of the ruins, the catacombs, and the jungle."

"Yes," she said.

Gibson mumbled in her ear. She heard some answering dust bunny chittering in the nearby brush.

"Wonder what's up with the dust bunnies," Adam said. "It's like they know something serious is going on."

"Animals have their own kind of sensitivity. Maybe they're picking up the faint distortion underneath the dominant currents pulsing from that quartz. The other wildlife has fled the area."

"So why are the bunnies here?"

"I'm guessing it's because of Gibson," she said. "They sense that he's with us and that we're all here to try to fix whatever has gone wrong."

"Our own private cheering section." Adam glanced at her, his eyes unreadable behind the dark lenses of his sunglasses. "You can feel it, can't you?"

She knew what he meant.

"Yes," she said. "You're right. There's something just faintly off about the resonating patterns."

"It gets worse once you're inside. You'll see what I mean."

She studied the quicksilver surface of the maze. "Do you really think that weird generator is what keeps the whole underworld running?"

"Yes, and I think it's what keeps the lights on in the ruins aboveground as well. The mirror maze was the aliens' artificial sun, the source of the psi that powered the bioengineered world they had to create in order to survive here on Harmony. At least, that's what my intuition tells me."

A chill slipped down her spine. "I think you're right. But it's huge. How can we possibly hope to affect the currents of a massive machine like that with something as small as the Burning Lamp?"

"When I took the team in two weeks ago, I was able to determine that the destabilizing energy is emanating from only one small section of the maze. The distortion is starting to affect some of the other quartz, but

I think that if we adjust the currents in that one chamber, everything else will revert to normal." He paused. "Whatever the hell normal is for that generator."

She adjusted her backpack. "In other words, we're just going in to change a couple of lightbulbs?"

"Might be a little more complicated."

"You know, I could make a joke here. Try to lighten the atmosphere."

"How many J&J agents and Guild bosses does it take to change a lightbulb?"

"Something along those lines." She contemplated the shimmering lake of quartz fire. "Trouble is, I don't know the punch line."

"What do you say we go find the answer."

THEY MADE THEIR WAY AROUND THE RIM OF THE CANyon to the research lab that the Bureau had established. Gibson stayed put on Marlowe's shoulder when she and Adam walked out of the jungle into the clearing, but the rest of the herd of dust bunnies that had followed them through the rain forest remained in hiding.

"This is impressive," Marlowe said. She surveyed the array of tents and jungle gear that had been erected. "But you should have called in Arcane earlier."

Adam looked at her. "You may be right."

Marlowe counted at least a dozen men and women moving purposefully around the compound. Most of the staff was dressed in standard-issue Guild jungle gear, which meant there was a lot of khaki and leather.

But she saw two men and two women wearing lab uniforms emblazoned with the emblem of the Arcane Society. One of them noticed Marlowe.

"Hey, Marlowe," he called. "Good to see you. We can use you down here. We're short on dreamlight talents."

"Hi, Ralph," she said. "How are things going?"

"Not good." Ralph Tripp walked toward her. He was a portly, middle-aged man who enjoyed his work. But today he looked uncharacteristically serious. "This is not just a dreamlight problem, it's an alien technology problem. To be honest, none of us knows what the hell we're doing." He eyed Adam. "You're Winters, aren't you? The new Guild boss."

Marlowe stepped in quickly. "Adam, this is Dr. Tripp. He's a crystal talent."

Adam inclined his head politely. "Dr. Tripp. I take it there has been no improvement in the situation?"

"I'm afraid the readings are deteriorating. All we can do is watch and observe. I agree with Dr. Nyland, however, that we'll have some sense of when things turn critical. At that point it would be prudent to issue the evacuation orders."

The atmosphere around the encampment had the feel of a hospital trauma ward minus the blood. People appeared calm, cool, and competent but very, very focused. Marlowe did not need her talent to sense the tension and adrenaline.

Adam looked at one of the Bureau technicians. "Where's Dr. Nyland, Liz?"

"Lab A, sir." Liz indicated the nearest of the two large tents. "He's charting the latest set of readings taken by the spectrum talents."

"Thanks." Adam indicated Marlowe. "This is Marlowe Jones, Liz. She's a very strong dreamlight talent."

Liz looked relieved. She smiled at Marlowe. "That's very good news. As Dr. Tripp just told you, everyone is convinced this is a dreamlight problem, but your type of talent is hard to find, especially in the higher ranges."

"As I keep telling Adam, the Bureau should have come to Arcane at the start," Marlowe said.

Liz flicked an uneasy glance at Adam and then turned back to Marlowe. "This was a highly classified Bureau project."

Marlowe smiled. "Well, now it's a highly classified Arcane project, as well."

Ralph Tripp looked pained. "To be precise, it is a para-physics problem."

"You're right, Dr. Tripp," Adam said. He turned to Marlowe. "Let's talk to Nyland. He'll have the latest reports. Then we need to go into the maze."

"Right." Marlowe said. She made to follow him.

"Cute dust bunny," Liz called after her. "Didn't know they made good pets."

"His name is Gibson," Marlowe said over her shoulder. "He's not a pet, he's a pal. Works part-time as a therapy dust bunny."

"We've spotted several of the little critters around

here," Liz said. "Sometimes we feed them. They seem to like energy bars. But they won't get too close."

Marlowe smiled. "They're suckers for the High-Rez brand of energy bar."

Liz chuckled. "That's what we stock in the chow tent. Standard issue for Guild teams."

Marlowe turned back and saw that Adam had already disappeared through the flap of the tent. She hurried after him.

Inside the lab tent she found herself looking at an array of instruments, meters, and gauges. The equipment was all of the simplest, most basic amber-rez design. The average third grader used more sophisticated technology to carry out a science project. There was no point hauling high-end computers and calculators underground, because they would not function in that environment.

Doing science in the underworld was a laborious process that consisted of gathering data with basic equipment and making observations and then taking the information back to the surface to process through computers.

Adam was at the far end of a long workbench. He stood with another, older man. They were studying a wide strip of graph paper spread out on top of the bench. When Marlowe got closer, she saw that all of the notations on the chart had been entered by hand.

Adam glanced up briefly when she approached. "Marlowe, this is Fred Nyland. Fred, Marlowe Jones. She's with the Arcane team."

"How do you do, Miss Jones?" Fred nodded at her. "Adam tells me that you're going into the maze with him. You're a dreamlight talent?"

"Doctor." She returned his polite nod. "In answer to your question, yes. Although, as I warned Adam, I've never encountered any dreamlight like the kind coming out of that maze."

"We weren't even sure if it was dreamlight for the first few weeks, although Adam, here, insisted that it was," Fred said. "Looks like he was right. Think you can work it?"

She glanced at the gym bag in Adam's hand. "Maybe."

Adam tapped a finger on the last entry on the graph. "The distortion is getting stronger."

"You know how it is once psi starts oscillating out of rhythm," Fred said. "The disturbance worsens more quickly as the distorted wavelengths create their own new patterns. I have to tell you both, I don't think we've got a lot of time left here. At the rate this is going, the Bureau is going to have to give the order to evacuate the major cities along with the catacombs at the end of the week." He looked at Marlowe. "Your Arcane people concur."

Adam looked at Marlowe. "Let's go change some lightbulbs."

Chapter 29

MARLOWE CONTEMPLATED THE ENTRANCE TO THE mirror maze. It was about fifteen feet wide and perhaps twenty feet high, a little narrower at the top than it was at the threshold. As with everything else the aliens had built, the proportions seemed slightly off to her human eyes, but there was an odd, ethereal grace in the architectural lines and a strange beauty in the runes etched around the edges of the entrance.

"Is this the only way in?" she asked.

"Who knows?" Adam said. "It's just the only one we've found so far. Haven't had time to look for more, but this place is huge, so I wouldn't be surprised if there are some other entrances and exits."

Gibson muttered and shifted a little on Marlowe's shoulder. He was not reacting to the promise of a major thrill ride with his customary enthusiasm, she noticed.

Instead, he seemed to be taking the entire business in a serious, intent manner, the same way he dealt with therapy sessions.

Worried that he might not be able to handle the heavy alien psi, she had made one attempt to leave him behind with Liz. Gibson had protested vigorously, leaped out of Liz's arms, and dashed after Marlowe. It was clear he had made his own decision. She had accepted it because there was no alternative. She knew that he would follow her into the maze.

She studied the strange engraving that marked the entrance.

"Wonder what it says," she mused.

Adam glanced briefly at the elegant alien inscriptions. "Probably, 'Danger, Keep Out. Trespassers Will Be Really, Really Sorry.'"

"Probably something like that," she agreed.

Unlike the quicksilver-bright surface of the huge construct, the interior of the maze was not illuminated with eye-dazzling light. Instead, to her wide-open senses, it glowed with the eerie hues of the ultradark end of the spectrum, the colors of dreams and midnight. Dreamlight.

She was aware of the small crowd of technicians, researchers, and security guards watching from the rim of the canyon, but she could not take her attention off the fantastic rainbow of night light that illuminated the entrance to the maze.

The power flowing out of the opening riveted all her senses. Adrenaline was fizzing through her. The energy emanating from the realm of glittering midnight was intoxicating, energizing, euphoric. Tendrils of her hair had come free of the clip that she had used to secure it and now danced around her head. A little more of this white-hot psi, and she might actually be able to fly, she thought.

Gibson chortled, catching the wave of excitement.

"This," she announced, "is really something else, Adam. What a rush. Just like taking the bike out on Old River Road at night under a full moon. Except more so."

"You know, the thought of you going out all alone on a motorcycle at midnight scares the hell out of me," he said.

"Does it scare you more than this maze?" she asked.

He thought about it. "Maybe about the same."

She knew then that he was experiencing the same rush that was heating her blood.

She smiled at him. He leaned forward a little and brushed his mouth against hers. When he pulled back, she saw that his eyes were very green; psi green.

And then, in a heartbeat, he was all business, all Guild boss. He wrapped a long length of leather around her waist.

"Listen up, Jones," he said, his voice hard and flat, the voice of the man in command. "Going into the maze is like going into an alien house of mirrors. Two steps inside the door, and you'll start feeling disoriented. Ten feet inside, you won't be able to find the entrance."

"Just like the catacombs and the jungle."

"No. Most people can navigate the tunnels and the rain forest, provided they have good amber and a little training. This place is different. Standard rez amber isn't enough. The only thing we know for certain that works is full-spectrum and tuned mirror quartz. Whatever you do, hang on to the chunk that Nyland gave you."

She touched the quartz pendant that she wore on a chain around her neck. "Don't worry, I will."

"Even with tuned quartz, most people can't handle the interior of this maze."

"I see what you mean." She studied the endless waves of seething energy flooding her senses. "I think that only someone whose talent comes from the dark end of the spectrum could get through this stuff."

He finished securing the strap to her and then wrapped the other end around his own waist and tied an elaborate knot. There was no more than six feet of slack in the strip of leather that bound them together.

"I feel like I'm on a leash," she said.

"Good." He hoisted the gym bag and started toward the entrance. "I want to make damn sure you don't get out of my sight."

She thought about what had happened to his sister. "Understood."

Neither of them turned to wave good-bye to their audience. Side by side they walked through the glittering entrance into a world of midnight mirrors.

Marlowe felt the rapid increase in the intensity of

the dreamlight psi as they moved into the maze, but it was the dark infinity of reflections that truly disturbed her senses. Everywhere she looked, up and down and on every side, she was confronted with endlessly repeating images of Adam, Gibson, and herself.

The not-quite-right proportions of the interior architecture compounded the disorienting sensations. It was incredibly difficult just to make out various twists and corners in the maze. More than once she blundered into a mirrored surface. After the first encounter with solid quartz, she walked with one hand extended in front of herself.

"You were right," she said. "This is freaky."

"The trick is to try to ignore what you see in the mirrors and concentrate on the underlying energy patterns," Adam said. "We're following the currents that are slightly distorted."

"Got it." She narrowed her eyes in an attempt to cut down some of the visual special effects and reached up to touch Gibson. He chattered in response and hunkered down on her shoulder. She wondered if he, too, was disturbed by the infinity of scenes that surrounded them, or if he was able to tune them out.

She quickly realized that Adam was right. The faint disturbance in the currents acted like a subtle beacon. Once she started to concentrate on the unstable oscillations and ignore some of the other feedback that her normal senses were receiving, her stomach settled down and her head stopped spinning.

They moved still deeper into the twisting maze.

Marlowe decided that the structure was not unlike the catacombs in that there appeared to be endless corridors, chambers, and rooms. But it was, as Adam had warned, vastly more bewildering to the senses.

"The out-of-sync currents are definitely getting stronger now," she said.

A hundred thousand Adams turned their heads to look back at her. "The warp in the patterns has increased significantly just since the last time I was in here."

"Any idea how much farther we have to go?"

"Distances are hard to measure in this place, but in terms of time, we should arrive at the chamber in about twenty minutes if we keep walking at this pace and if we don't take any wrong turns," he said.

They kept moving. The thin currents of distorted energy got sharper and more distinct with every step.

Adam went around one last corner and stopped.

"This is it," he said. "If I'm right, the disturbance is emanating from this chamber."

They walked through a high, narrow opening and stopped in the middle of the room. Marlowe looked around. The mirrored chamber was identical to many of the others they had passed along the way, but the energy in it was wildly distorted.

She closed her eyes and concentrated only on her para-senses. The source of the disturbed energy was suddenly clear. She opened her eyes and looked at the troubled mirror. The infinity of Marlowes and Gibsons gazing back at her were as visually out of sync as the currents were psychically.

"There is definitely something wrong here," she said. "I think you're right, the problem is confined to that one chunk of mirror quartz. There just might be enough energy in the Burning Lamp to handle one or two bad lightbulbs."

"Good to hear," Adam said.

He set the gym bag on the floor, leaned down, and started to unzip it. He stopped halfway, staring at the bag. Marlowe followed his gaze.

"Oh, geez," she whispered.

A familiar pale light spilled out of the bag.

"Looks like just walking through all this dreamlight energy with our senses on high was more than enough to light the damn thing," Adam said.

He finished unzipping the bag and reached into it for the lamp. Marlowe saw him tense. His jaw clenched. She knew that a jolt of energy had just snapped across his senses.

He straightened and held up the lamp. Untold thousands of repeating images of the illuminated artifact appeared in the mirrored surfaces of the chamber.

In Adam's hands, the lamp grew brighter. As Marlowe watched, the relic became translucent

"This is not good," she said. "We need to get control of that thing, and fast."

"Yes," Adam said.

In the eerie radiation produced by the room and the

artifact, his hard face was etched in the paranormal light of a nightmarish dreamscape. Gibson muttered, the way he did in a therapy session.

Marlowe moved closer to Adam, took a deep breath, and put her fingertips on the rim of the lamp.

Energy flashed through her, shocking her senses. She gasped and struggled to regain control. She knew that Adam was fighting the same battle. Gibson rumbled and went into full hunting mode. He sleeked out, and all four eyes appeared.

"It feels even stronger than it did the first time," Adam said. He sounded like he was speaking through clenched teeth.

"I think that's because the energy in this room is resonating with it," Marlowe managed. "Augmenting and enhancing the currents. But in a way, that proves your theory. We need to work quickly, though. If the energy in the lamp gets out of control—"

She did not finish the sentence. There was no need. Adam could surely sense the danger, just as she had.

Gibson hissed softly. His hind paws tightened on Marlowe's shoulder.

The lamp shifted from opaque to translucent and then became transparent. Marlowe could see the dark storm swirling inside it now. All but one of the crystals in the rim began to heat.

An instant later, a blazing, senses-dazzling, paranormal rainbow lit up the chamber of mirrors. The energy of the stones sparked and flashed on the glittering surfaces.

She clenched her fingers around the rim of the lamp. She must not lose control. When she looked at Adam, she saw that he was working equally hard to handle the forces they had unleashed.

She found the core pattern of the lamp's currents and eased into it. She did not try to fight for control. That would have been impossible. Instead, she set about weaving tendrils of her own power into the surging waves.

"Like riding Dream," she whispered.

Adam said nothing. He watched her steadily with his fierce green eyes.

"Okay, I've got it," she said after a few seconds of concentration. "But I don't know how long I can hold the center. Do what you have to do, Adam."

He focused the energy of the lamp with a sudden rush of power. She held on for dear life. Gibson's hind paws gripped her shoulder more securely. The psychic winds buffeted them in all directions. The rainbow of psi grew hotter.

No human was ever meant to channel this much energy, she thought. But she and Adam had no choice. They either rode the storm to the end, or they died there in the chamber. She knew that beyond a shadow of a doubt.

She also knew that she needed more power to control the lamp. She willed it from the depths of her being.

Then, in some way she would never be able to explain, she sensed that Gibson was adding his own psi to hers. He was just a small dust bunny, but all living things gave off energy across the spectrum. She and Gibson shared an animal-human bond that was intensely strong in its own way. They had worked together in the parapsych ward at the Arcane clinic, and they were working together now.

She felt the precise instant when Adam seized the vast forces roiling in the lamp and sent them hurtling into the distorted currents of the chamber. Again and again he sent strong, stable waves soaring into the glittering quartz. She realized that he was relying on the mirrored surfaces of the room to enhance and intensify the lamp's power.

Within seconds the dark mirrors began to reflect the stable currents of dreamlight, forcing the erratic pulses back into a steady rhythm. Gradually the chamber began to settle. There was no way to know what normal was for this place, Marlowe thought, but it was simple enough for a dreamlight talent like her to recognize stable energy when she saw it.

She looked at Adam, triumph sweeping through her. *"We did it."*

On her shoulder, Gibson returned to full-fluff mode and bounced a little, chortling.

Adam did not speak. He was staring at the lamp.

"Adam?" She realized that the artifact was still fully illuminated, still running hot. "We need to shut it down now."

"The Midnight Crystal," Adam said. "Look at it. The damn thing is supposed to be dead."

Gibson muttered, uneasy again.

Marlowe glanced down at the ring of crystals set in the rim of the lamp. The stone that had remained dark the first time they had activated the lamp was on now, on fire with all the colors of midnight.

"Shut it down," she whispered.

"I can't."

"We have to stop this," she cried.

The nightmare roared out of the mirrors, engulfing them all.

Chapter 30

THE SHOCK OF THE PSYCHIC IMAGES THAT HAD BEEN locked in the Midnight Crystal slammed through Adam. The dark dreamscape took on form and substance in the mirrored room.

It was like any other nightmare, he thought, borne on the waves of dreamlight energy that came from the darkest end of the spectrum. But he retained enough awareness to know that this was not his dream. Not Marlowe's either.

"Nicholas Winters," Marlowe said. She looked around at the rapidly coalescing dreamscape. "This is his work. Somehow he managed to infuse the Midnight Crystal with these images. When we rezzed it just now, we released the dream."

"And maybe the psychic hypnotic command that he embedded in that stone."

"According to the files, that's just a myth."

"Like the lamp and founder's formula? We've got to get out of here. Now."

"Good grief, surely you don't think Nicholas was able to actually infuse that stone with some kind of hypnotic command? He died centuries ago."

Gibson growled.

Marlowe broke off, staring at the figure that was materializing in the mirrors.

Adam watched as an all-too-familiar face looked out at them with demon-green eyes. It was the face he saw in the mirror every morning. The only difference was that the man in the mirror was dressed in an archaic fashion characteristic of the late seventeenth century on Earth.

"Let's go." Adam gripped Marlowe's upper arm, intending to propel her toward the doorway of the chamber. "Move."

She did not argue. But even with the aid of their para-senses, they dared not run. They had to move cautiously or risk crashing into one of the mirrored walls.

Two feet from the door, the surge of rage and madness and raw power hit Adam like a closed fist. He lost his hold on Marlowe and staggered back into the center of the room.

"Hear me now, heir of my blood. I bequeathed to you the gift of the Burning Lamp. You have proven your worthiness by controlling the three powers and by unleashing the Midnight Crystal. You are fit to be the agent of my vengeance."

The old English was so heavily accented and so archaic Adam doubted that he would have been able to
comprehend a word of it if he had not studied Nicholas's
journals. But even if his ancestor had been speaking an
ancient, long-dead language instead of a six-hundred-
year-old version of English, there could have been no
misunderstanding the meaning and intent of what the
old alchemist was saying. Dreams did not depend on
language. They conveyed messages, warnings, and
knowledge in a far more elemental way: through the
psychic energy of dreamlight.

Marlowe reached out and grabbed his hand.

"Hurry," she said, urging him toward the door.

Adam pulled hard on his talent and managed to take
a single step forward.

Another blast of energy seared his senses. In the
mirror quartz, the alchemist's eyes blazed with the
force of the hypnotic command he was delivering, but
his voice was glacial.

*"You will use the great powers of the lamp to de-
stroy all who carry the blood of my enemy, Sylvester
Jones . . ."*

The words were accompanied by another shock of
energy. Adam felt a terrible fury well up inside him.
*Marlowe carries the blood of Sylvester Jones in her
veins.*

"Can you hear him?" he asked. Even to his own
ears, his voice sounded strange, thick and raspy.

She concentrated. "Yes, at least my intuition can
translate the dream message. He's wielding hypnotic

energy, trying to force you into a trance. I can't feel the power of it, though. I think only someone of his bloodline can do that."

"I'm fighting it, but I don't know how much longer I can hold out."

He tried for the door again, but it was as if he had hit a wall. He knew then that he would never escape the chamber. Time to prioritize.

Marlowe. She was the most important thing in the world. He could not hurt her. He would die before he allowed himself to harm her in any way. That made it easy. He had a plan now. To save Marlowe, he had to end things here.

He suppressed the rage with an act of will. The fury and the glittering shards of madness that accompanied the emotion belonged to Nicholas Winters, not to him. He was experiencing what Nicholas had felt countless generations earlier.

Bastard. This is your dream, not mine.

But it was rapidly becoming his nightmare. The dreamscape around him seemed increasingly real. The chamber was filling with the foggy, undefined atmosphere of dreams, a paranormal realm with no beginning or end, no top or bottom.

It would not be long before he was no longer aware that he was dreaming. Once that happened, he would not be able to control his actions. The psychic command would overwhelm him. He would destroy Marlowe. That must not happen.

The infinity of alchemists spoke again.

"The psychical command I have locked in the Midnight Crystal can be accessed only once. You, who have unleashed the forces of the stone, are charged with carrying out my vengeance. You must not fail."

Adam had to concentrate fiercely to unknot the leather bond that linked him to Marlowe. When she was free, he methodically started to strip off every piece of tuned standard rez and full-spectrum amber that he carried: his watch, the ring, the stone in his bolo tie, the concealed chunks in the heels of his boots, his locator, and his belt buckle.

He dropped all of the amber and the spare chunk of tuned mirror quartz that he had brought with him into the heart of the Burning Lamp.

"Adam." Marlowe stared at the stones. "What have you done? The forces inside that thing will probably destroy your amber."

"Take Gibson and the lamp and go," he said through his teeth.

"Are you crazy? You'll never find your way out of here without your spectrum amber or the quartz."

That's the point, he thought, but he did not say it aloud.

"Make sure J&J takes good care of the artifact this time," he said. "It may be needed again in the future to fix another lightbulb in this place."

"Once the hypnotic command is complete, you're going to walk off into the maze, aren't you?" Marlowe made no move to take hold of the lamp. "You'll walk forever. It will be just as if you went into the tunnels without good amber. I won't let you do that. We're in this thing together, Adam Winters. We're partners, remember?"

The trance energy was bounding and rebounding off the mirrored walls, intensifying in force with every oscillation. It was a thousand times stronger than Nicholas Winters could ever have dreamed, thanks to the multiplying effect of the mirrors. Adam knew that the hurricane of psi would soon overwhelm him with rage.

"I can't take the risk of allowing you to stay with me," he said to Marlowe. "I think the lamp will be reasonably safe for someone else in my bloodline to use again, if that ever becomes necessary. You heard what Nicholas said: the energy of the Midnight Crystal can be unleashed only once. What's done is done. No putting that genie back into the bottle."

"Damn it, Adam . . ."

He let go of the lamp, forcing her to grab it. She did so reflexively, catching it by the base. When it was secure in her hands, he gripped her shoulders, pulled her close, and kissed her. She returned the kiss with searing force.

He felt her strong, positive, healing energy sweeping over him, temporarily pushing back the storm of the command. For a few seconds he could think clearly again. He wanted to hold her forever, but doing so would be the equivalent of signing her death warrant. All he could allow himself was one last taste of her.

"All who descend from Sylvester must die. All that

*he created must be extinguished. This is the only fit-
ting penalty for the crime that he committed against
me. For he has surely destroyed me. It is only a matter
of time now before I shall lose all my great powers. I
am doomed because of the treachery of a man I once
called friend and the rage of a jealous woman."*

It took every scrap of willpower that Adam possessed to break off the kiss. He released Marlowe and
stepped back. She watched him with psi-hot eyes. So
did Gibson.

"I'm staying here," Marlowe announced.

"When this nightmare ends, I'm going to be a true
Cerberus. I will be a danger to you and everyone else
in your family."

"It's just a dream, Adam."

"I know that now. But it won't be long before I don't
know it."

"You're stronger than Nicholas ever was," she said.

"There's no way you could possibly know that."

She put her fingertips on the rim of the lamp. He
saw the shiver that went through her, but she did not
release the artifact. Instead, she tightened her grip.

"Nicholas Winters left his prints all over this
thing." She waved one hand to indicate the myriad images that surrounded them. "What's more, the energy
emanating from the Midnight Crystal and bouncing
all over this chamber is his. I can read it as surely as
I can read yours. Trust me, while you are descended
from him, the two of you are not the same person.

You are the stronger talent. It makes sense when you think about it."

"What the hell are you talking about?"

"It's true you carry his psychic genetics, but the blood of the powerful dreamlight reader who bore Nicholas's son also runs in your veins along with that of generations of other strong talents. You are Nicholas's direct descendant, but you are also the descendant of Griffin Winters and Jack Winters and Adelaide Pyne and Chloe Harper. You are not a clone of Nicholas Winters."

Adam looked at her, wanting to believe what she was saying. But the storm was growing hotter around him.

"Sylvester knew that he could not destroy me with his own powers. We are too evenly matched. But he crafted a plan whereby the dreamlight reader would use the lamp to strip me of my talents. He played to her jealous nature, promised that he would take care of her and the babe after I was gone. The truth is, he desired her for himself. He wished to mate with her, as he had with other women of power, in order to discover if his own talents would combine with hers to produce offspring possessed of surpassing psychical abilities . . ."

"Chatty, isn't he?" Marlowe asked. "Trying to justify himself, I suppose."

Adam looked at her. "Marlowe, if I'm stronger than he was, why can't I escape this room?"

"You can. But first you must break out of the trance."

"How do I do that?"

"You said it, yourself; you're trapped in a dreamscape. But this is still a lucid dream. That means you can control it. You can end it by shutting down the lamp and the Midnight Crystal."

"I tried to do that."

"You tried to do it alone. The energy of the lamp can only be controlled when we work it together, remember? Touch the lamp, Adam, and take my hand."

He stared at the lamp, half afraid that physical contact would draw her into the dreamscape with him. Then he looked at the hand she held out to him. When he met her eyes, he saw absolute certainty and power. She smiled.

"You're the boss of the Frequency Guild, and I'm the head of J&J," she said. "We just saved the underworld. We can do this."

And suddenly he believed her. He could accomplish anything with Marlowe at his side.

"No wonder they put you in charge of Jones & Jones," he said.

He gripped the rim of the lamp and wrapped his other hand around hers.

Psi fire seared his senses.

"Hear me, you who carry my talent in your veins. The heirs of Sylvester must all die. My bloodline must triumph."

"Ignore him," Marlowe said. "He's been dead for a

few hundred years. Okay, I've got the center. Remember, this lamp is basically a force multiplier designed to enhance your own talent. The mirrored quartz around us is having a similar enhancing effect. All you have to do is destabilize a few of the trance currents. Once the process starts, I'm betting the energy pattern of the Midnight Crystal will fall apart very quickly."

"You're betting?"

"Just do it, Winters."

He did not try to swamp the fierce energy pounding at him the way he had earlier when he rebooted the unstable energy emanating from the quartz. Intuitively, he edged in carefully, found a single, oscillating current in the trance pattern, and sent out a counterpoint wave. Almost at once, the current fell apart, fracturing and weakening.

The process felt oddly familiar.

"Just like old times in the tunnels," he said. It wasn't easy to get the words out because his jaw was rigid with the effort he was making to focus so much energy. "Like de-rezzing hot ghosts."

"That makes sense. Energy ghosts are inherently unstable at the core. I'm told the trick is to disrupt a few of the currents that hold one together."

"When you get it right, the whole thing disintegrates and vanishes."

"Like a ghost," Marlowe said.

He went to work on another current and got a similar effect. The process accelerated as he methodically isolated individual pulses and dampened them.

Gibson chortled, excited now.

Nicholas Winters was still speaking, but the energy that laced the command was weakening rapidly.

"I shall not live to see my vengeance, but I know that it will come to pass, for my powers are vastly greater than those of Sylvester, and I have locked them into my blood. My son carries the seeds of my great talents. He will bequeath them to his sons down through the generations . . ."

Adam zapped a few more currents. The mirrored quartz was working for him now. The dreamscape became murky, dissolving like morning mist in the sunlight. The myriad ghostly images of Nicholas grew fainter.

With one last sparking pulse of energy, the Midnight Crystal winked out, taking the fragments of the nightmare trance with it. He was free.

He shut down the Burning Lamp. All of the crystals went dark. The transparent artifact grew translucent, then opaque, and finally became solid once more.

He reached into the lamp and grabbed his amber. He still had a grip on Marlowe's hand. He urged her toward the chamber entrance.

"Now we leave," he said.

"Good idea."

They went deliberately but with some speed through the doorway. Adam checked his watch.

"I can't believe it," he said. "Still good."

"Probably because it's full-spectrum. Standard rez amber would never have survived the forces in that lamp. One thing I don't understand, though."

"Only one thing? Consider yourself lucky."

"I realize that Nicholas somehow found a way to trap the energy of a hypnotic command in the Midnight Crystal, but how did he capture an image of himself?"

"Why does that strike you as strange? You're the dreamlight talent. You've told me that when you touch someone, your intuition translates some of the energy into images."

"Yes, but that's the whole point. Back in that chamber we were viewing images from Nicholas's own dreamscape that he somehow managed to trap in that crystal. Yet we saw Nicholas, himself, in that dream world."

"So?"

"Think about it. You never see yourself in a dream."

"He put himself into a kind of trance, a lucid dream, in order to generate the images that we perceived, right?"

"Yes, I think so."

"He saw himself in the trance, so we saw him, too."

"But how did he see himself in his own dream?" she asked.

"I'm no dreamlight expert, but I can think of one way he could have done it."

"What way is that?"

"He stared into a mirror when he went into the dream state," Adam said. "He saw his own reflection while he was in that trance, so we saw it, too."

Chapter 31

SHE AWOKE TO THE SOFT DRUMMING OF RAIN FALL-
ing in the jungle. There was no other sound like it, she
thought. Even here in the lush, bioengineered underworld, it conveyed its own kind of psychical meaning:
nature's gift of life and renewal.

There was no other scent like that of rain in the rain
forest, either. She lay quietly for a moment, breathing
in the elemental fragrance.

She stirred a little and realized that she was still
dressed except for her boots, but she was securely enveloped in the silk sleeping sack she had brought with
her in her pack. Someone had spread the sack out on
the cot and stuffed her into it, someone who understood about her little eccentricity. Adam, she thought.
She smiled.

The rush of adrenaline and psi that had gotten them

through the ordeal in the mirrored chamber had carried them to the exit of the maze. It had even gotten them partway up the long quartz staircase that led to the rim of the canyon. At that point, however, several people had come rushing down the steep flight of steps to assist them.

By the time they had arrived at the top of the staircase, she had been on the verge of exhaustion. She had fallen into a heavy post-burn sleep while listening to Adam explain to the others what had transpired inside the maze.

She stretched, opened her eyes, and looked out the plastic window of the tent into near-impenetrable darkness. Midnight in the jungle.

She heightened her senses, testing the faint currents of maze energy that echoed up the canyon walls to the rim. The resonating patterns felt strong and stable. There was no longer even a hint of underlying disharmony.

There was, however, another kind of dreamlight energy in the tent, a very familiar pattern. Startled, she turned her head.

"Adam?" Conscious of the fact that there were half a dozen other tents filled with sleeping people in the vicinity, she kept her voice to a whisper.

"Better not wake up expecting to find some other man sleeping next to you in this tent," he said. He kept his voice pitched very low, as well.

The darkness inside the tent was utter and complete. She could not see him, but when she put out her hand, she felt the edge of a second cot positioned alongside hers.

"I don't understand." She levered herself up onto one elbow. She still could not see a thing with her normal vision, but when she heightened her talent, Adam's prints became visible. "What are you doing in here?"

"Let's review and see if we can figure out the answer to that question."

There was a rustling sound. She saw energy shift in the depths of the night and concluded that Adam had rolled onto his side, facing her. His eyes glowed green in the dense shadows.

"We both went through a really bad burn down there in the maze," he said. "Depleted all our reserves. By the time we got back to the top of the canyon, we had almost exhausted our physical energy, as well. You conked out right in the middle of what was, I felt, a brilliantly coherent debriefing, considering the shape that I was in and how many details I had to leave out."

"Yes, well, I can see where you wouldn't want to go into the whole Winters Family Curse thing with a lot of Bureau and Arcane staff."

"Not good for the Guild boss image. Anyhow, you went sound asleep on my shoulder in front of the entire lab crew just as I was getting to the good part."

"What was the good part?" she asked.

"The punch line in the how many Guild bosses and J&J agents does it take to change a lightbulb joke."

She winced. "Oh, right."

"Figuring that under the circumstances, you might

not want to have a dozen people staring at you while you slept—"

"Lord, no."

". . . I thought you might appreciate some gentlemanly consideration. I picked you up and carried you to this tent. I managed to get your boots off and get you into your security blanket."

"Thanks," she whispered.

"You're welcome. However, that last bit of noble, manly exertion did me in. I told everyone to wake us in the morning, sealed the tent flap, and more or less collapsed on this cot. I remember nothing after that until Gibson woke me a few minutes ago."

"Gibson." She searched the darkness for a pair of glowing baby blues and saw nothing. "Where is he?"

"I heard him scratching at the tent flap, so I got up and let him out. I think he went hunting. I saw his second pair of eyes pop open just before he disappeared into the undergrowth. Got a hunch he joined his buddies for a little night sport."

The energy of Adam's dreamlight was getting hotter. So were his eyes. She knew he was aroused. In response, an urgent warmth began to pulse through her veins.

She cleared her throat. "I see. You, uh, couldn't get back to sleep after you let him out?"

"No."

"Thinking about what happened in the maze?"

"Mostly I was thinking about you," he said.

"Oh."

"I'm sorry, Marlowe." He exhaled heavily. "I didn't mean to fall asleep in here. I couldn't go another step. Literally. I know you have this thing about not being able to sleep in the same space with someone else who is sleeping. But I was out of it at that point."

"It's okay, you didn't disturb me. That was a very heavy burn we went through, and the sleep state that followed was bound to be much heavier and deeper than normal. We both more or less passed out for a few hours."

"Yeah, felt like that. I'm sorry."

"I was so zonked that I probably could have slept through a tornado."

"How do you feel now?"

She thought about it. She had awakened feeling amazingly normal, as if she had just surfaced from a deep, replenishing sleep. But now she was intensely aware of Adam.

"I feel fine," she assured him. "Really."

"Want me to leave?"

"It's raining, and it's pitch-black out there."

"The crew put up some amber lanterns. Don't worry, I can make it to one of the other tents."

She eased aside the top sheet of the silk bag. "I don't want you to leave, Adam. I may not be able to go back to sleep, but I don't mind. I'd rather spend what's left of the night with you."

"That's good to know, because I want to spend the night with you, too."

She heard more rustling in the darkness and watched

his energy patterns with her other senses. In the glow of dreamlight, she saw him sit up on the edge of the cot. The camp beds were only inches apart.

He lowered himself down on top of her with exquisite care. The cot squeaked in protest, but it did not collapse.

Marlowe wrapped her arms around him and discovered that he had taken off his shirt but not his trousers. His skin was enticingly warm to the touch.

"Adam."

"Hush." He smothered a choked laugh that was half groan against her mouth. "Sound carries in the jungle, especially at night. There are other people sleeping out there."

"Right, sorry." She kissed his mouth, his jaw, his throat, inhaling his scent. "I'll try to remember."

He stifled another groan and gently nipped her ear. "You might have to remind me from time to time, too."

They fumbled with each other's clothes. Adam got her shirt open. The next thing she knew, his mouth was on her breasts. When he tugged gently on one nipple, she felt the currents of fire all the way to the center of her being. In a matter of a few heartbeats, she was tightly clenched and wet with need.

She managed to unfasten his belt and then his trousers. When she got her hand inside his briefs, she found him thick and rigid.

He unzipped her pants and shoved them down over her thighs to her ankles. She struggled impatiently to wriggle free of the garment. With each twist and turn of her body beneath his own, she sensed Adam getting hotter. His sleekly muscled back grew damp beneath her fingers.

He managed to get himself out of his own trousers and briefs. She heard a soft, muffled plop when the clothes dropped to the floor of the tent. He came back to her. She opened herself for him, wrapping him close.

"I can't get enough of you," he whispered hoarsely.

He slipped his fingers into her, pressing deliberately upward. She tightened around him. He used his thumb to work the taut bundle of nerve endings.

She gasped, bit back a cry, and sank her nails into his shoulders. As if that was the signal he had been waiting for, he shifted position and thrust heavily into her.

The force of their union pulsed and crashed invisibly in the atmosphere. It seemed to her that their auras fused briefly in a moment of shattering intimacy.

She got tighter and hotter, and then her climax was sweeping through her in small convulsive waves. In the midst of the dazzling release, she realized she could not catch her breath. It took her another second to comprehend that the reason she was having trouble breathing was because Adam had covered her mouth with his own to silence her. Only then did she realize that she must have cried out.

The muscles of his back were quartz-hard. He tore his mouth away from hers. She heard the beginnings of a long, low, howl of triumph and satisfaction deep in his throat. Hastily she clapped a hand over his lips.

His climax seemed to go on forever; he surged into her, emptying himself. When it was over, he collapsed, sprawling on top of her. She laughed a little, tears in her eyes, and held him close and snug against her.

THE RAIN HAD STOPPED. HE DECIDED THAT WAS WHAT had awakened him. His internal clock told him that dawn was arriving in the jungle. He shifted a little and realized that he was tangled up in a silk sheet and Marlowe's silken body. For a moment he kept very still, not wanting to shatter the magic by tumbling off the side of the very narrow cot that he and Marlowe shared. It felt so good to be locked close to her like this.

He opened his eyes and saw that she was sound asleep. With him.

Satisfaction swept through him, as intense as the sexual release during the night.

A scratching sound and a soft chortle on the other side of the tent flap distracted him. He tried to gently disengage from Marlowe's warm body, but in spite of his care she stirred, yawned, and opened her eyes.

She looked straight at him with a dazed, faintly bewildered expression, as if finding him this close, his face only inches from her own, was the very last thing she had expected. It probably was. He watched with a sense of triumph as understanding lit her eyes.

"Adam?"

He smiled. "That would be me."

"I don't understand."

"Try. Try real hard."

She frowned. "I went back to sleep after we had sex."

"You went back to sleep after we made love," he corrected very deliberately. "We both went back to sleep, as a matter of fact. I just woke up, myself."

"Hmm. Well, this is certainly very weird."

"You slept with me," he said. "We slept together. Get over it."

"Maybe it's the heavy psi levels here in the jungle," she said, frowning a little. "Perhaps they affect the way I pick up dreamlight when I'm sleeping."

"And maybe you were actually able to sleep with me."

Her eyes widened. "I've never been able to sleep with a man. There must be some explanation. The energy in that maze, maybe."

He brushed his mouth lightly against hers. "I think we're going to need to conduct a few tests when we get back to the surface."

She blinked again. "But if it's true, what does it mean?"

"It means you can sleep with me. I suggest you don't try to complicate things here, Marlowe. You know what trained detectives always say."

"No, what do they say?"

"The simplest explanation is usually the right explanation."

"But this isn't simple."

The scratching noise sounded again. This time it was accompanied by another muffled chortle.

Marlowe glanced toward the sealed opening of the tent. "That's Gibson."

"Our little hunter is home," Adam said. "I'd better let him in before he decides to chew through the tent flap."

He pushed aside the silk sheeting, sat up, and reached for his briefs and trousers. He pulled on the clothes and got cautiously to his feet, careful to keep his head down so as not to hit the top of the tent.

He unsealed the flap. Gibson chattered cheerfully. He had half an energy bar in one paw. He tumbled into the tent and fluttered up onto the cot to greet Marlowe. She smiled and patted him affectionately.

"Something tells me it's better if I don't know exactly what you were doing out there in the jungle all night," she said. "By the way, where did you get that energy bar?"

Through the tent opening Adam watched Liz and one of the female Arcane technicians emerge from a nearby tent. They were dressed for the day, chatting in low tones with each other. They both turned to look toward the tent that he and Marlowe shared, smiling a little, speculation sparkling in their amused expressions. When they saw him, they blushed, embarrassed at having been caught checking out the boss's sleeping arrangements.

He lifted a hand in a casual salute. "Good morning, ladies."

"Morning, sir," Liz stammered. "Jill and I are in charge of breakfast this morning. Coffee and scrambled eggs will be ready in a few."

"Sounds good," he said.

The women hurried off toward the kitchen tent. He let the flap fall back into place and turned to look at Marlowe, who was pulling a fresh shirt out of her pack.

Her brows rose. "What? Something wrong down at the maze?"

"Nope, no problem in the maze that I know of." He cleared his throat. "Remember what I said about sound carrying in the jungle at night? I think that might have happened last night."

"Sound carried?"

"From this tent."

"Ack." She made a face but looked resigned. "Well, I suppose it was inevitable. Even if there hadn't been any, uh, sound transmission, everyone knows we spent the night together in this very small space."

"They do know that, yes."

"Relax, we've got the world's best cover story."

"That would be the cover story that implies that you and I are involved in an affair?" he asked neutrally.

"That one." She grimaced. "Still, it is sort of embarrassing, though."

"What is embarrassing? Everyone thinking that a respectable member of the Jones family is having an affair with a Guild boss?"

"No." She shot him a quelling glare. "That was not

what I meant. I was referring to the sound transmission in the jungle issue."

He grabbed his pack, opened it, and yanked out a T-shirt. "Look, I'm sorry about this, Marlowe, but given all that's been going on lately, you have to admit that in the grand scheme of things, it really isn't important."

"Not important? You're saying our relationship isn't important?"

"Damn it, you know I didn't mean it that way," he said. "Are you saying we have a relationship?"

"What would you call it?"

"Don't look at me like that," he said. "You're the one who keeps saying we're *partners*."

"We *are* partners." She paused. "Sort of."

"In case you haven't noticed, the basis for our partnership disappeared yesterday when we reestablished the rhythms in that maze."

She got to her feet. "Why are we arguing like this?"

"Beats the hell out of me, partner."

She stepped around the corner of the cot and went into his arms.

"Adam, this is ridiculous," she said against his chest.

"I agree." He smiled into her hair. "So, does this mean that you'll be my date for the reception on Friday night?"

"What reception?"

"The official welcome reception for the new boss of the Frequency Guild."

"Oh, that reception," she said, her voice muffled against his shirt.

"Just think. Our first real date."

He caught her chin on the edge of his hand and started to raise her mouth for a kiss.

An outraged screech from somewhere outside the tent stopped him cold.

Marlowe stepped back quickly. "What in the world?"

"I think it came from the direction of the kitchen tent," Adam said.

He released her to raise the flap. He saw Liz and Jill standing in the center of the small compound, hands planted on their hips, grim expressions on their faces.

Heads popped out of the neighboring tents.

"What's wrong?" a tech asked.

"We've been raided," Jill announced. "The food is gone."

"All of it?" Dr. Nyland asked, perplexed.

"Eggs, fruit juice, biscuit mix, sausages, jam," Jill said. "And that's just the breakfast stuff. You can forget lunch and dinner, as well. They ripped off almost three days' worth of supplies. There isn't even a single energy bar left. We're all going to be foraging in the rain forest this morning."

"The only thing they didn't take was the coffee," Jill said. "Probably because the cans were too heavy for the little suckers to cart off into the jungle."

"What little suckers?" Nyland asked.

"Dust bunnies," Jill said. "Saw the last one scurrying out through the hole in the tent just as we got there."

"Uh-oh," Marlowe said.

Adam noticed that she was looking at Gibson, who was sitting on the cot, polishing off the energy bar.

"I think I know what you were doing last night," Marlowe said to Gibson. "And here I thought you were boldly hunting wild game and having torrid sex in the rain forest, doing the nature in the raw thing."

Gibson chortled and ate the last of the energy bar.

"Why hunt when you can round up a bunch of your buddies and raid the humans' kitchen tent?" Adam asked.

"What about the torrid sex in the jungle part?" Marlowe said.

"As I recall, we were the ones doing that."

Chapter 32

SHE GOT BACK INTO HER OFFICE THE FOLLOWING DAY shortly before noon. Rick grabbed the two newspapers on his desk and held them up so that she could see the headlines.

"You're famous again, boss," he said. "Nice work. This is going to be so good for business."

Gibson chortled a greeting, leaped nimbly out of Marlowe's leather pack, and hopped up onto the desk.

"You're famous, too, biker dude," Rick said. He showed Gibson the copy of the *Examiner*. "See? That's you sitting on the big Guild man's shoulder."

Gibson displayed no interest in the picture. He sidled across the desk to the locked cookie jar and assumed a hopeful air. Rick put down the papers and went to work opening the jar.

"Help yourself, dude," Rick said. He raised the lid

with a flourish. "You deserve it. You're one of the heroes of the hour."

Marlowe peeled off her leather jacket and hung it on a hook. She went to the desk and glanced down at the headlines. The picture on the front of the *Examiner* had been taken just as she and Adam emerged from the rain forest through the main gate.

They had walked out to find a large crowd of reporters, bloggers, curiosity seekers, and city officials waiting for them. Marlowe knew that was no accident. Adam had cold-bloodedly plotted the entire media frenzy before they had left the camp. He had sent a small group of lab techs up to the surface first to contact the Chamber and tell them what had happened. The Chamber's press office had taken over from there. The Frequency Guild desperately needed a public image makeover, and the story of what had happened in the rain forest was perfect.

The headline in the sober, sedate, ever-so-serious *Amber Intelligencer* was a publicist's dream.

DISASTER AVERTED BY NEW GUILD CEO
AND LOCAL PI

Authorities Say Explosion in Alien Ruins Would Have Been Devastating Aboveground as Well as Below

The headline in the *Examiner* took a slightly different slant on the news.

GUILD BOSS AND MISTRESS
SAVE THE UNDERWORLD

"Oh, geez," Marlowe said. She tossed the *Examiner* down onto the desk. "Somehow I don't really think that being labeled the new boss's mistress is going to bring J&J a lot of business."

"Wait and see." Rick looked knowing. "I'm telling you, J&J is going to be the hottest psychic private investigation agency in town."

"Meanwhile, I should get back to work on the few cases we've actually got. Where's the museum theft file?"

"On your desk," Rick said. "Let's talk about the important stuff first, though. What are you wearing to the big Guild affair tonight?"

"Gee, I dunno. I'm thinking maybe my leather jacket, chaps, and boots."

"The dominatrix look is classic, of course," Rick said. "But in this particular instance, you'll be representing Jones & Jones. I feel that you should go with something a bit more elegant."

"I'll have to see what I've got in the back of the closet."

SHORTLY AFTER THREE O'CLOCK THAT AFTERNOON, the phone rang again for what had to have been the hundredth time. Marlowe ignored it to concentrate on the file she was reading. The door to the reception area was open, however, so she heard Rick repeat the message he had delivered dozens of times that day.

"I'm sorry, sir, but Miss Jones is not giving interviews to the media. I have been instructed to refer all calls of this nature to the public relations office of the Frequency Guild. Yes, Miss Jones will be attending the reception for the new CEO of the Guild this evening."

Rick ended the call. The phone rang again almost immediately.

"I'm sorry, ma'am, but Miss Jones is not available to appear on your program."

Marlowe tuned out the conversation and finished the file. When she was done, she closed the folder and sat quietly for a while, thinking. It was at times like this, she decided, that Uncle Zeke would have opened the bottom drawer of the desk and taken out the bottle of Alien Ruin whiskey that he had always kept there. He claimed it helped him focus his talent.

She looked at Gibson, who was dozing on the cushion of the client chair. He was stretched out flat on his back, all six paws in the air.

"What do you say we go for a ride, pal?"

Gibson's blue eyes popped open. In one neat little twist, he was on his feet, chortling enthusiastically. Marlowe rose, went around the desk, and scooped him up.

She went out into the small reception area. Rick was just ending another call.

"I'm going to be gone for an hour or so," she told him. "If I'm not back by five, go ahead and close up."

He looked up, squinting a little through the stylish glasses. "Something wrong, boss?"

"I want to take another look at a crime scene."

"Which one?"

"The museum theft. I went back over the file. There's something that bothers me."

"Still worried because everyone except Dr. Lewis has a mag-steel alibi?"

"It's Dr. Lewis's dreamprints at the scene that bother me. I'm going to take another look at them."

"Fine, but it's after four. You need to allow plenty of time to get dressed. All eyes will be on the new Guild boss and the lady who helped him save the underworld tonight."

"Oddly enough, the reception is not the kind of appointment a person tends to forget. Right up there with going to the dentist."

"Hah. It's one of the most glamorous events of the season, and you and Adam Winters will be the center of attention. You should be thrilled."

"I'll do my best." She took her leather jacket and helmet off the wall hooks and headed toward the door with Gibson tucked under her arm.

"Remember, you're going for elegant, boss."

"I'll try to keep that in mind."

She opened the door and went out into the late-afternoon light. She plopped Gibson into the saddlebag, settled the helmet on her head, pulled on her gloves, and got on board Dream.

She rezzed the powerful flash-rock engine and

cruised away from the curb, working her way deeper into the Quarter. The building that housed the Society's collection of paranormal artifacts and the research facilities associated with them was a hulking, nondescript Colonial-era structure located near the wall.

From the outside, the building resembled its neighbors on the street: just one more aging, down-at-the-heels Old Quarter warehouse. In keeping with Arcane's six-hundred-year-old tradition of maintaining a low profile, there was no sign out front.

She drove around the corner and cruised down the alley behind the museum. At the back door, she stopped, kicked down the stand, and plucked Gibson out of the saddlebag.

She went up the three steps and rang the doorbell. Eleanor Gilling, one of the curators, responded.

"Oh, it's you, Marlowe," Eleanor said. "We're just getting ready to close for the day."

Marlowe moved through the entrance into a cluttered office area. "I won't be long. I want to take one more look at the entrance to the vault where the old lamp was stored."

"Certainly." Eleanor's eyes lit with excitement. "We all saw the news in the papers today. The reason we're closing early is so that the entire staff can watch the opening ceremonies of the reception for the new Guild boss. You're going to be there with Adam Winters."

"So I'm told," Marlow said.

"This is so exciting. To think that you'll be on the rez-screen tonight."

"I'm sure the attention will be on Adam Winters, not J&J or Arcane."

"True, but still, for those of us in the Society, this is quite thrilling. After all, you and Mr. Winters saved the underworld and very likely the Old Quarters and the Dead Cities, as well. Those of us in the field of para-archaeology will be forever grateful."

"We all had a vested interest."

"Quite true," Eleanor agreed. "Now, then, you're here about the theft of that old artifact, aren't you? Have you made some progress with the investigation?"

"Things are coming along rapidly," Marlowe said. "We should be able to identify a suspect very shortly."

Uncle Zeke had made it clear to her the first day on the job that the number one priority in any investigation was to make it appear that progress was being made. *It not only reassures the client, it often works to shake loose a few leads. Bad guys get rattled when they think you're actually getting somewhere.*

"It will be such a relief to have the mystery solved," Eleanor said. "There have been rumors that it was an inside job, but none of us believes that. Come with me; I'll escort you down to the storage vaults."

"Thank you."

While the outside of the museum building showed its age, the interior was state-of-the-art. The labs and workrooms were filled with gleaming equipment and sophisticated instruments. Computers sat on every desktop, all of them heavily encrypted. Marlowe wondered if Arcane would ever leave behind the old habit of keeping secrets.

She noticed that most of the staff had already departed for the day. There were only a handful of people still at their desks. They greeted her enthusiastically. A couple offered Gibson cookies, which he graciously accepted. Marlowe saw copies of the *Herald* and the *Examiner* at several workstations.

"Who knew that academics read the tabloid press?" she murmured to Gibson.

They followed Eleanor down into a belowground chamber lined with mag-steel walls. Rows of display cases filled the room. An array of artifacts were arranged inside the cases. Many of the relics were from the Old World. But Arcane had begun acquiring rare and unusual objects with paranormal provenances immediately after arriving on Harmony.

Given the nature of the New World and the long-vanished civilization that had once colonized it, there were a lot of psi-infused artifacts around. Many had been literally lying on the ground. The result was that there was a wide variety of alien antiquities and oddities in the collection.

Eleanor led the way deeper underground to another steel-lined chamber. But this room was fitted with a bank-vault-style door embedded in one wall. The curator opened the lock and pulled the heavy door open.

The familiar green light of the catacombs spilled out of the jagged tear in the quartz. Before going into the tunnels, Marlowe opened her senses and looked at the layers of dreamprints on the floor. Nothing had changed since her first visit to the scene.

Inside the catacombs, Eleanor powered up a locater, clicked in the coded coordinates, and led the way to the series of chambers that had been converted into storage rooms for the museum's vast collection.

They stopped in front of the vaulted room in which the fake lamp had been stored. With her talent tuned to the max, Marlowe took another look around.

There was nothing fresh in the way of clues. Not that she had expected to uncover any startling new evidence that would change her conclusions, she thought. She had told herself that she needed to check one more time to be absolutely certain, however.

"Thanks, Eleanor," she said. "That will do for now."

"That's it?" Eleanor's brows rose. "You're finished?"

"That's all I need to see today," Marlowe said.

"I know you're a dreamlight profiler, not a chaos-theory talent," Eleanor said. "Did you find a new clue?"

"Not a new one. Just one I should have spotted the first time. I know who is responsible for the theft of the lamp."

Me, she thought. *I gave him the opening, let him get close. So what does the new head of J&J do when the person who is responsible for the crime turns out to be the new head of J&J?*

*   *   *

GIBSON CHATTERED A LITTLE, UNCHARACTERISTI-
cally agitated when Marlowe put him back into the
saddlebag. She knew that he had sensed her despon-
dent mood.

"I sure don't feel like playing Guild boss mistress
at that reception tonight," she told him. "I think I need
to go for a ride, see if I can clear my thoughts. I've got
some decisions to make."

She glanced at her watch. It was not yet five. She
had time for a run along the Old River Road.

Gibson watched her from the leather bag, grum-
bling.

She pulled on her gloves, fastened her helmet,
climbed aboard the bike, and drove out of the alley. A
deep twilight was settling on the Quarter. The amber
lights of the old-fashioned streetlamps glowed in the
mist. The ruins were starting to brighten.

She drove through the Colonial section of the city
and turned onto the narrow, two-lane road that par-
alleled the winding course of the mighty Frequency
River. To her left the tree-studded hillside rose gently
away from the edge of the pavement.

At one time the old road had been a main thorough-
fare, but the new highway on the far side of the river
had lured away the commercial and commuter traffic.
Old River Road was rarely used now.

She opened the throttle and gave herself over to the
exhilaration that flooded her senses whenever she was
on the bike. It had been like this since her childhood.
She had started out riding dirt bikes as a kid with her

father and brothers. When they had realized that her interest was not a passing fancy, that she was truly hooked on the thrill of riding, they had made sure she learned how to manage a bike in all kinds of weather conditions and on all types of terrain.

Out here on the open road, running free, she did not have to think about her responsibilities and obligations or the consequences of screwing up. Out here, for a time, she could forget how her talent complicated her life.

There was, she reflected, only one other activity that provided a sensation that equaled and even surpassed this intoxicating experience: making love with Adam.

Hastily she corrected herself. Having sex with Adam was the other experience that matched being out here on the bike. There was most certainly a bond of sorts between them, she thought, and plenty of sizzling physical attraction. But the connection she felt could be explained by the high drama they had experienced together in the past few days.

She had known him for such a short time. It was impossible that she could have fallen in love. Now that the underworld had been saved, she and Adam would return to their normal lives. Things would change. Things always changed in relationships, especially her relationships. And they never changed for the better.

Meanwhile, she had a case to close.

She leaned into another curve. When she checked the rearview mirror she saw Gibson. He had his head poking out of the bag. The wind plastered his fur back against his body, providing a rare glimpse of his nose and tufted ears. He was enjoying himself enormously, as usual, and his delight was contagious. Dust bunnies had it right, she thought. They were always in the moment.

In spite of everything, she laughed.

And in that instant she saw the truth in all its shattering clarity, as though it had been written in hot dreamlight. She was in love with Adam.

For a few seconds her spirits took wing and flew on the thrilling currents of that acknowledgment. *She was in love with Adam.*

She went into another turn. When she came out of it, reality struck hard. She was in love with Adam. Fine. Now what?

She glanced into the rearview mirror again, looking for Gibson's reflection. He was right where he was supposed to be, his nose in the wind. But there was something else in the mirror, as well: a big black Oscillator 600. The huge SUV was accelerating rapidly out of the curve—too rapidly.

She didn't need her Jones intuition to tell her that something very dangerous was going on. But on the off chance that she was overreacting, she drove a little faster. The Oscillator responded by picking up speed, closing the distance.

The next curve was coming up fast. Marlowe leaned into it and juiced the throttle on the far side. Behind her, tires shrieked. The Oscillator was all muscle, a vehicle hyped on steroids. It was designed to send a message of power. It certainly suited the image and ego of the stereotypical high-ranking Guild man.

But, while the 600 could attain high speeds on the straightaway, it was not made for the kind of nimble maneuvering the curves on Old River Road demanded. At its heart, the Oscillator was still, in all, a truck.

When she checked the mirror again, she saw that she had gained some distance.

The reprieve did not last long. The Oscillator came out of the curve at full throttle, engine roaring. She thought about the road ahead. She had driven this way countless times over the years. She knew every inch of it. There was only one more bend coming up. After that, the pavement ran straight for nearly a mile along the river. Dream was not built for racing on the flat. There was a very good chance she would not be able to outrun the Oscillator. One swipe from the big car's fender, and she and the bike would be in the river. The treacherous currents would do the rest.

That left only one option.

"Hang on," Marlowe shouted to Gibson. She doubted that he could hear her above the howling wind, let alone comprehend the words. But he was very good at sensing her moods.

She went into the next turn a little too fast, wondering if the Oscillator would be tempted to do the same. But the SUV was more cautious this time, slowing a little. The driver must have realized he could catch up with her on the far side of the curve. He saw no reason to risk his neck.

Just the executive decision she had hoped he would make, she thought. She had bought herself a few seconds of breathing room. She braked, did a quick slowdown, and turned the bike toward the bank that sloped up into the woods. She downshifted, goosed the throttle, crossed the oncoming lane, and jammed Dream up the hillside.

The bike responded eagerly, bucking and growling. Dirt, small rocks, and dried leaves churned beneath the tires. Marlowe thought she heard Gibson chortling.

She frequently went off-road with the Raleigh-Stark. It was the reason Dream was endowed with a stiffer suspension than was customary for a bike that was used only on the highway, why the tires had an aggressive tread designed for a variety of conditions.

She wrestled the handlebars for control, drove the bike a short distance into the trees, and brought it to a shuddering halt.

Down below on the road she heard the Oscillator emerge from the turn, engine screaming. She looked back over her shoulder and watched the SUV charge down the straightaway at full throttle. The driver had not yet realized he'd lost his quarry.

She raised the faceplate of her helmet and anxiously checked the saddlebag.

"Gibson? Are you okay?"

Gibson chortled wildly and bounced up and down, intoxicated on dust bunny adrenaline.

There was a lot of adrenaline going through her, as well, she thought. Her heart was pounding, and her senses were on full alert but not in a good way.

"Okay, I'm glad you had fun, but don't get the idea that we're going to do this a lot," she said. "I think I scared myself just now."

She reached into the pocket of her leather jacket and took out her cell phone. Her hands were shaking. She had to concentrate hard to punch in Adam's code.

He answered halfway through the first ring.

"Where the hell are you?" he said, his tone fierce. "Are you all right? I've been trying to get hold of you for nearly ten minutes."

The savage, barely controlled urgency in his words caught her by surprise. "I'm out on the bike. The phone was in my jacket. Couldn't hear it. What's wrong?"

"You tell me." But he sounded as if he was breathing a little easier now. "Sorry to jump at you through the phone. I've been a little edgy for the past half hour. A few minutes ago I got a feeling that you were in serious trouble, and I couldn't shake it. Called your phone. When you didn't answer, let's just say I got a whole lot edgier."

"Talk about your psychic intercept," she said.

"There is no such thing," he said automatically. "Hold on, are you telling me that something did happen? Where are you, anyway?"

"Old River Road. And, yes, something did happen. I think a big Oscillator 600 just tried to run me down."

"Talk to me," Adam said.

She gave him a brief version of events.

"I suppose it could have been a bad case of road rage," she concluded. "Or maybe some idiot's idea of a game. But given the official J&J policy regarding coincidences, I tend to think that someone was either trying to scare the daylights out of me or—"

"Or kill you."

"What are you thinking, Adam?"

"That an Oscillator 600 is a classic Guild car. Got a whole fleet of them in the garage here at headquarters."

"That did occur to me. But why would anyone in the organization come after me? Killing a Jones would be awfully stupid. It would guarantee a full-scale police investigation, to say nothing of what my family would do. The Joneses would tear Frequency apart to find the killer."

"I don't suppose you got a license plate?"

She thought back to the image of the vehicle in her mirror. "I admit I wasn't paying a lot of attention, but I don't think there was one."

"Figures. How far out of town are you?"

"Not far. Maybe twenty minutes away from my condo. I was about to turn around and head home when the 600 started chasing me."

"I'll meet you at your place," he said.

"You said you'd pick me up at eight. I haven't forgotten."

"No, I mean, I'll meet you at your place as soon as you get back into town."

She glanced at her watch. "But it's only going on six."

"I'll be waiting."

"You're that worried?"

"I'm that worried."

"But why would anyone in the Guild go after me?"

"Think about it, Marlowe. What connects us?"

Understanding slammed through her. "We've both got people working on the crystal flashlights."

"See you in twenty."

"Wait, before you hang up, I'm pretty sure I know who stole the fake lamp."

"Inside job like you thought?"

She exhaled slowly. "You could say that."

"Tell me about it when you get home. And Marlowe?"

"Yes."

"Drive really, really carefully."

Chapter 33

THE RUINS IN THE HEART OF THE QUARTER WERE FULLY illuminated by the time Marlowe pulled into the garage beneath her condo building. She eased Dream into the parking space next to her little Float, cut the engine, and kicked down the stand.

She dismounted, removed her helmet, and tucked it under one arm. Gibson bustled out of the saddlebag and up onto her shoulder.

She started toward the elevator. "One would think that I'd had enough excitement for one day," she said to Gibson. "But, no. Now I get to go to a Guild reception and make nice with a bunch of people, one of whom may have tried to turn me into roadkill today. You know, by the time I get to bed tonight I'm going to be exhausted."

Gibson growled. In a flash, he went from fluffy to full-rez predator mode, all four eyes wide.

Marlowe stilled, her senses instinctively heightening along with another surge of adrenaline. She looked at the floor of the garage. Dark waves of dreamlight seethed and burned there, indications of both a strong talent and desperation.

She tracked the hot dreamlight to the stairwell. The door was partially open.

"I know you're there inside the stairwell, Tucker," she said. Her voice echoed against the concrete walls. "You've been waiting for me, haven't you? Why don't you come out? We'll talk."

A few seconds of tense silence passed. The door to the stairwell squeaked as it was pulled inward. Tucker Deene moved out into the garage. He held a mag-rez in a two-handed grip.

"I'm sorry about this," Tucker said.

There was a quaver in his voice and his hands trembled. It was the latter observation that worried Marlowe. Tucker was a professional con artist, not a professional shooter. She suspected that he knew very little about guns. In addition, he was clearly at the edge of his control.

Gibson growled again.

"It's okay, Gibson," Marlowe said. "You know Tucker. He won't hurt me."

"You have to come with me," Tucker said. "We'll use your car. You'll drive."

"Someone you know is in trouble, right?"

"My brother."

"You stole the lamp because you thought you could

use it to help him, but you discovered that the artifact was a fake. Now you're hoping I can fix your brother."

"You're a dreamlight reader. You once told me that you can help people whose parapsych profiles are all messed up."

"Only sometimes, Tucker. It depends on the nature of the underlying trauma."

"You have to help my brother."

"What's wrong with your him?"

"Keith is dying," Tucker's voice rose. "Those damned crystals he forged are killing him."

Adam emerged from the stairwell behind Tucker. It was obvious that he had come straight from the office. He had removed his black jacket, but otherwise he was in full Guild exec black. His polished leather boots made no sound on the floor of the garage as he moved up behind Tucker.

"You can put the gun down now, Tucker," Marlowe said. "I'm here. I'm listening."

Tucker ignored her, his eyes feverish. "My sister is a dreamlight talent. We all knew about the lamp because of Keith's work with crystals, you see."

"I understand," Marlowe said.

"When Keith's psi patterns started to go bad, Charlotte thought she might be able to work the energy of the lamp to reestablish the normal resonance patterns, but the damn artifact was a fake, and now you're the only option we've got left. You have to help Keith."

Adam reached around Tucker and snapped the magrez out of his hand.

"She's not going anywhere with you, Deene," Adam said.

Tucker's handsome face crumpled. He started to cry, making no sound.

Marlowe glanced at her watch. "Three hours until the Guild reception starts. We'd better hurry."

"I was afraid you were going to say that," Adam said.

Chapter 34

THEY TOOK HER FLOAT. ADAM DROVE. UNDER HIS guidance the normally sedate, unobtrusive little compact cut through the early evening traffic like a shark through a school of small quartzfish. Marlowe rode on the passenger side, Gibson perched behind her on the back of the seat. Tucker huddled forlornly in the back.

"Tell me about the crystals," Adam ordered.

"What do you want to know?" Tucker asked.

"You said your brother forged them."

"Yeah."

"How?"

"How?" Tucker shrugged. "He's a crystal talent. He used a furnace. Some raw crystals. A lot of his own psi."

"Creating crystals that can enhance a person's talent isn't the kind of thing you learn how to do in chemistry class or on the Internet," Adam said. "It's alchemy, an Old Earth science. Your brother must have found the instructions somewhere."

"Yeah. He got hold of a copy of some old journal."

"What old journal?" Adam asked evenly.

There was a long silence from the backseat.

"Keith told us that he found some notes supposedly copied from one of the early journals of Nicholas Winters," Tucker said finally.

Marlowe felt energy heat the atmosphere. Adam was not a happy Guild boss.

"How many of those crystals did your brother make?" Adam asked, slicing through a narrow alley.

"A dozen," Tucker replied.

"How many did you sell?"

"All of them."

"I want the names of the buyers."

"There was only one," Tucker said tightly. "He took every one that Keith made. Said he'd buy all that we could produce. And before you ask, yes, he was a Guild Councilman. At least we think so."

Adam glanced at him in the rearview mirror. "What makes you think he was a Councilman?"

"The deal was done through a go-between, a broker who handles those kinds of arrangements. Guy named Joey. He made it pretty obvious that the client was not only a strong talent but very well connected at the top of the Guild. No offense, but we thought you might have been the buyer. If it wasn't you, must have been a Councilman."

Marlowe turned in her seat to study Tucker. "How do you know the buyer wasn't from the criminal world?"

He gave her a wry smile, the smile that had first attracted her weeks ago.

"Not much of a difference between the criminal world and the Guild here in Frequency, is there?" he asked.

Out of nowhere, anger flashed through her. No one could seriously defend the badly tarnished reputation of the Frequency Guild. But for some obscure reason, she reacted to the slur on the organization as if it had been aimed directly at Adam.

"Things will change now that Adam Winters is in charge," she said coldly. "He's going to clean up the Frequency Guild."

Adam's mouth kicked up a little, but he said nothing.

"Good luck with that," Tucker said, monumentally unconvinced.

"It's not like you're exactly a shining beacon of integrity, now is it, Tucker?" Marlowe snapped.

Adam whipped the Float down a narrow, tree-lined street. "You two might want to save the sparkling repartee for some other time. We've got other issues on the agenda at the moment."

Marlowe winced. "Good point." She turned back to Tucker. "But I am a PI, if you will recall. I like answers. I want to know exactly why you are so sure that the person who bought the crystals wasn't a politician or a businessman or a serial killer or some lunatic trying to fire up a cult?"

Tucker slumped deeper into his seat and stared glumly out the window. "We've worked with Joey before. We know him, and we trust him."

"You're talking about a guy who brokers deals on the black market," Adam pointed out.

"Joey is a professional in his own way," Tucker said. "He's been in business for a long time. The good brokers survive for the simple reason that everyone involved, buyers and sellers alike, know they can be trusted."

"Does this Joey the broker have a last name?" Adam asked.

Tucker hesitated. "Why?"

"Because I want to talk to him," Adam said. "Give me a name, Deene."

Marlowe narrowed her eyes. "We need a name, Tucker."

Tucker crumpled again. "I can't give you one. He's just Joey the broker."

"How do you find him when you need him?" Adam asked.

"Hangs out at a bar called the Green Hole," Tucker replied.

Adam took a phone out of his pocket. He spoke briefly to whoever answered.

"Guy named Joey," he said. "Works the black market as a go-between. His office is at the Green Hole. Pick him up."

He closed the phone and glanced at Marlowe. Her surprise must have been plain on her face, because his brows rose a little.

"What?" he asked.

"I'm just wondering how you got the authority to send someone after a known criminal, let alone have him picked up for questioning. You're not a police detective."

"You know the code, the Guild polices its own."

"Yes, but Joey the broker isn't Guild."

"If he's selling illegal weapons to someone in the Guild, he has to deal with Guild law."

A SHORT TIME LATER, ADAM BROUGHT THE FLOAT TO a halt in front of a modest house. He de-rezzed the engine and surveyed the quiet neighborhood.

"For the record," he said, "I'd just like to mention one last time that this is probably not a good idea."

"What do you mean?" Marlowe unfastened her seat belt. "According to Tucker, this involves the crystals. We've been trying to get a handle on them. This is the perfect opportunity."

"There are other ways to do that." Adam glanced at Tucker, who already had the rear door open. "I don't trust this guy."

"Well, he is a chameleon and a professional con artist," Marlowe allowed. "Of course, you can't trust him completely."

Tucker looked crushed. "I never meant to hurt you, Marlowe."

"Skip it," Marlowe said. She scooped up Gibson. "Adam's right; you can't be trusted far. But there is one exception."

"What's that?" Adam asked.

She looked at him over the roof of the Float. "Tucker cares about his brother. It's in his dreamprints. This is about family, not about pulling off another score."

Tucker drew a deep breath. "Thank you, Marlowe."

Adam glanced at Tucker, shrugged, and closed the car door.

Marlowe considered Tucker. "It's too bad, you know."

"Too bad that we got off on the wrong foot?" Tucker said quietly. "I agree. It was my fault."

"True."

"You and I, we had something special going for us, Marlowe."

"Ghost shit," Adam said, coming up behind Marlowe.

"I wasn't talking about us," Marlowe said to Tucker. "I meant it's too bad you can't be trusted, because J&J could use someone with your kind of talent."

Tucker was dumbfounded. "Me? An agent for J&J?"

"Boggles the mind, doesn't it?"

"Marlowe—" He extended a hand toward her, as though to take her arm in the familiar, intimate way that he once had.

Gibson growled. Marlowe took a quick step back out of reach and came up hard against Adam. His hands closed around her shoulders, intimate and possessive.

"Let's get on with this project," Adam said. "Time's running out."

Tucker dropped his hand. He led the way up the walk.

"How did you know I was the one who took the lamp?" he asked Marlowe.

"You imitated Dr. Lewis's dreamprints when you went into the vault to steal the relic," she said.

"Yes." Tucker exhaled heavily. "But how did you figure it out?"

"Good question," Adam said. He looked at Marlowe. "How did you discover that Deene was the thief?"

"Something about the prints I tracked in and out of the chamber where the lamp was stored bothered me from the start," she said.

"Because they had been left by a trusted employee?" Adam asked. "You couldn't believe that Lewis would steal from the museum?"

"Not just that," Marlowe said. "It was the fact that the prints weren't hot. Dr. Lewis is a quiet academic who has dedicated his entire professional life to preserving artifacts in the museum. He suddenly decides to do something totally out of character and steal one of the artifacts, but there's no strong emotion in his prints at the scene? It didn't make sense."

"Right." Adam nodded, comprehending immediately. "At the very least, he should have been nervous as hell. Scared."

"I know Dr. Lewis," Marlowe said. "He would have been terrified. There would have been plenty of energy burning in his prints."

Tucker's jaw tightened. "I can imitate the basic resonance patterns of someone else's prints, but I can't generate the individual's emotions when I do it."

"What about your own emotions?" she asked, her professional interest aroused. "Why aren't they visible in the prints that you imitate? You must have been hyped on adrenaline at the very least, when you went into the vault."

"Are you kidding? I was freaked. Hell, I was stealing from Arcane. The energy is probably there in the prints, according to my sister. But it's masked by the chameleon effect. Even a strong dreamlight reader can't see it."

Marlowe nodded. "Which is how you got close to me."

"Damn it, Marlowe—"

"Like I said, a very useful talent."

Adam's jaw was set at an unforgiving angle. "Don't even think about hiring him as an agent. You can't trust him, remember?"

"Yes, but now that I know that, I might be able to work around that issue," she said, thinking about the possibilities.

"Forget it," Adam said in very low, very dangerous tones.

Tucker glared at him over Marlowe's head. "You know, there are a lot of folks here in Frequency who would strongly advise her not to trust anyone connected to the Guild, especially the guy at the top."

Marlowe felt Adam's hand tighten a little around her arm. She looked at Tucker.

"You don't need to worry about my relationship with Adam," she said. "I would trust him with my life. Actually, I've already done that a couple of times, come to think of it."

Adam smiled. "That works both ways."

Tucker's face tightened, but he said nothing. He halted on the top step and knocked twice.

The door opened so quickly Marlowe knew the woman who appeared in the entryway had been watching from behind the closed curtains.

"You must be Charlotte," Marlowe said.

Charlotte stared at her uncertainly and then turned to her brother.

"Tucker?" Charlotte looked past him to Adam. "What's going on? Why is he here?"

"It's a long story, Charlotte," Tucker said, his voice surprisingly gentle. "It's okay, I swear it. Just open the door."

Charlotte did not take her eyes off Adam. "You're the new Guild boss."

Adam smiled his humorless, Guild boss smile.

"Don't mind me," he said. "I'm here to make sure no one gets hurt."

Charlotte flinched. Marlowe opened her talent and looked at the dreamprints on the floor beneath her feet. They seethed with an emotion that bordered on panic.

"It's all right," Marlowe said. "You and your brothers are Arcane. That means you're entitled to J&J's services. In hindsight, perhaps you should have come directly to my office and asked for help, instead of sending your brother to spy on me and the museum."

Charlotte was stunned. "How can you even suggest

that we could have approached J&J as legitimate members of the Society? By now you must know what we are, how we've survived."

"Yes," Marlowe said. "But that doesn't mean I wouldn't have helped you. You're a dreamlight reader. That means you can work up a fairly accurate profile of another person, assuming he isn't a chameleon, of course."

Tucker closed his eyes and looked sad. Marlowe ignored him.

"Your brothers probably rely on your talent to profile a mark and set up the scam, right?" Marlowe continued.

Charlotte's lips thinned, but she did not say anything.

"Take a look at my prints," Marlowe said. "See for yourself if I'm here with the intention of doing any of you harm."

Energy flared. Marlowe sensed that Charlotte had heightened her own talent. Whatever she saw must have convinced her that it was safe to open the door. With a sigh, she stepped back into the hall.

"Keith is in the living room," she said. "Follow me."

She led the way down the short entry hall and into a room furnished in warm, neutral hues. The drapes were pulled across the windows, creating deep shadows.

Keith Deene was curled into a fetal position on the sofa. There was a pitcher of ice water and a half-filled glass on the end table. The room was uncomfortably warm, but Marlowe could tell that he was shivering beneath the heavy quilt. When she got closer, she saw that he was soaked with perspiration.

Gibson mumbled a little.

"Hello, Keith," Marlowe said very softly. She crouched beside the sofa. "What have you done to yourself?"

Gibson hopped out of her arms onto the sofa and chattered softly, ready to go to work.

Keith opened psi-fevered eyes. He seemed bewildered by the sight of Gibson. He switched his attention to Marlowe.

"Who are you?" he rasped.

"Marlowe Jones. I hear you've been fooling around with a very old alchemical recipe for crystals."

"I'm a crystal talent. Thought I could handle any kind of hot stone." He clutched the edge of the blanket with a hand knotted into a fist. "Hell, I forged the damned crystals, myself, using my own energy. I should have been able to control them."

Adam looked at him from across the room. "Your brother said that you were working from a copy of some instructions from one of Nicholas Winters's early notebooks. The old bastard was still perfecting his theory of crystals in those days. He forged a couple of them and ran some experiments, but he realized immediately that they were flawed and potentially dangerous. He eventually abandoned that first engineering design altogether."

Keith stared at him. "Your name is Winters. Guess that's not exactly a coincidence under the circumstances, is it?"

"No," Adam said.

Marlowe looked at Keith. "Unfortunately for you and a few other people over the years who found copies of those early notes, Nicholas never went back and put a warning in his early journals. It was only in his later notebooks that he mentioned the failed experiments of his youth and how they had set him on a different path."

"So, I'm going to die?" Keith asked. "Sort of figured that."

Marlowe braced herself and touched his hot forehead. The shock of hot nightmare energy rattled her senses. It was bad but not nearly as bad as what she and Adam had gone through together in the maze. It wasn't even as jarring as what she had experienced with Vickie Winters.

"How long have you been using the crystals?" she asked.

It was Charlotte who answered. "He made the first one a few months ago. I noticed the changes in his prints about six weeks later. But he didn't believe me at first when I told him that I thought the crystals were responsible."

"Thought the changes meant that I was getting stronger," Keith said, teeth chattering.

"No," Marlowe said gently. "That's not what the distortions in your dreamlight patterns meant."

Keith's nightmare images were coming at her on a storm of chaos. She caught fleeting glimpses of tsunami waves that threatened to drown the dreamer. Scalding flashes of dreamlight burned her. But, as always, it was the sense of helplessness, the realization that the out-come could not be altered or evaded that was the most devastating aspect. In nightmares there was no hope, only desperation, fear, and panic.

The question was not whether she could endure Keith's dreamscape. She had dealt with worse. The issue was the nature of the damage that had been done to his para-senses. As she had explained to Adam, not every kind of dreamlight trauma could be healed.

"You can pet Gibson," she said to Keith.

"Huh?" Keith frowned. "Why?"

"It helps sometimes," she explained. "He has a very calming effect."

Keith eyed Gibson warily. "I heard they bite."

Gibson fluffed up his fur a little more and chattered encouragingly.

"Gibson won't bite you," Marlowe said. "I promise. He's a therapy dust bunny."

"Never heard of a therapy dust bunny."

"Gibson is one of a kind."

She picked up Keith's too-hot hand and placed it lightly on top of Gibson. Gibson mumbled reassuringly and crowded closer to the fevered man. Reflexively, Keith shut his eyes and exhaled heavily. His fingers sank into Gibson's fur.

Marlowe studied the dissonance in Keith's pattern. When she tracked the distorted waves back to their source on the spectrum, she saw that the originating pulses were still strong. The chaos that was gnawing on his aura had not yet reached the point of origin.

"You're in luck," she said. "There's still time to adjust the bad vibes. Your talent for crystals provided you with some natural resistance to the damage. Anyone else who had warped his own patterns this badly would have been either dead or in an institution by now."

Behind her Charlotte gave a soft, half-swallowed cry of relief.

Marlowe pulsed energy into the distorted patterns, urging them gently back into a stable rhythm. Gradually Keith's breathing grew less labored. His fevered body cooled to a more normal temperature. The hand he had clenched in Gibson's fur loosened and relaxed.

Marlowe finished correcting the warped oscillations. She waited quietly for a moment to make sure the patterns were steady and strong once again.

Keith looked at her, his eyes no longer hot. "Thank you."

He went to sleep, exhausted.

Satisfied that his dreamlight currents had been restored to their normal rhythms, Marlowe got to her feet and turned to look at Charlotte and Tucker.

"He'll be all right," she said. "But he's going to sleep for a while, probably several hours. That's normal. When he wakes up, he should be fine."

"I don't know how to thank you," Charlotte whispered. Tears welled up in her eyes. She crossed the room and threw her arms around Marlowe. "I'm sorry for what we did. All I can say is that we were absolutely desperate."

Marlowe patted her shoulder. "Next time try walking in the front door of J&J and asking politely for help. You'd be surprised how that tactic works. Besides, I need the business."

Tucker looked at her. "We owe you, Marlowe. If there's ever anything this family can do for you, all you have to do is ask. We always pay our debts."

"Anything," Charlotte said. She raised her head, released Marlowe, and stepped back, smiling a little through her tears. "Like Tucker said, all you have to do is ask."

"I appreciate that," Marlowe said briskly. "How about returning the fake lamp? I know it's not the real artifact, but it's a pretty good reproduction. The museum staff will be glad to get it back."

"I'll get it," Charlotte said.

She rushed away down a hall. A short time later, she returned with a canvas bag in her hand.

"Here."

"Thanks." Marlowe unzipped the bag and peeked inside. Dull gold-colored metal and the fake crystals gleamed in the darkness. "Yes, this matches the description I was given by the staff." She zipped the bag.

Adam checked his watch. "Time's getting short. Are we done here?"

"We're done," Marlowe said. She tucked Gibson under her arm.

Charlotte's eyes widened. "I forgot. This is the night of the big reception for the new Guild boss. That's you, Mr. Winters."

"So they tell me." Adam's cell phone rang. He

checked the number and took the call. "Winters." There was a short silence while he listened to the person on the other end of the connection. "Keep looking."

He closed the phone.

"What?" Marlowe asked.

"Joey the broker has disappeared," Adam said. "He's either gone to ground or else someone got to him."

Tucker snorted softly. "Joey is a survivor. Trust me, his instincts are excellent. He's gone into hiding."

"In that case, we'll find him," Adam said.

Charlotte glanced at him and then looked at Marlowe. "The opening ceremonies will be starting any time now. You'll be late."

"It's called making a fashionable entrance," Marlowe said.

Chapter 35

AT EIGHT THIRTY-SIX THAT EVENING, ADAM STOPPED with Marlowe at the top of the amber and green carpeted staircase that led down into the glittering ballroom of the Grand Hotel.

As if some mass psychic announcement had been made, a wave of murmurs swept over the crowd. A hush fell. Everyone turned toward the staircase.

At the bottom of the stairs, an honor guard composed of twelve ghost hunters in full dress uniforms formed two rows facing each other. A reception line composed of high-ranking city dignitaries took shape. The representatives of the media surged forward, video cameras held high.

The very elderly Marcus Spearman, one of the few remaining Councilmen, stepped forward to make the official announcement.

"Ladies and gentlemen, the Frequency City Guild of Dissonance-Energy Para-resonators is pleased to present our new director, Mr. Adam Winters. He is accompanied tonight by Miss Marlowe Jones."

The band surged to life, playing the soaring, triumphant music of the traditional "Guild March." The crowd burst into wild applause.

Adam smiled at Marlowe, savoring the knowledge that she was the woman who was here at his side tonight, sharing the moment with him. She looked amazing, he thought. Her hair was pulled back into an elegant twist. Delicate amber and gold earrings cascaded from her ears. Her gown was a column of black silk that discreetly displayed her lithe, feminine body and fine shoulders to perfection.

You would never know that a few hours ago she had nearly been run down by some bastard in a Guild car or that just a short time after that she had been confronted with a mag-rez pistol and then gone on to save the life and sanity of a cheap con artist, he thought. And only a day before that, she had helped him save the underworld.

He smiled.

She gave him an inquiring look. "What?"

"Like I keep telling you, it's no wonder they put you in charge of J&J."

"And no wonder they put you in charge of cleaning up the Frequency Guild."

"Ready to do this?"

"Certainly," she said. "Hey, we saved the under-world, didn't we?"

"We did. If we can do that, we can handle this crowd."

She put on a serene smile and surveyed the sea of expectant faces at the bottom of the stairs. "Besides, what else could possibly go wrong today?"

He laughed and tightened his grip on her arm. To-gether they went down the staircase to greet the wait-ing crowd.

"SO, YOU TWO SAVED THE UNDERWORLD," LYRA DORE said an hour later. "That sounds like an unusual date. Some kind of Guild boss thing?"

"I'm not sure," Marlowe said. "Adam is the only Guild boss I've ever dated."

Both women looked at Adam, who stood a short distance away, talking quietly to Cruz Sweetwater. The two men had a lot in common, Marlowe thought. Both were strong talents, and each, in his own right, wielded a lot of power. The Sweetwaters owned Amber Inc., a major amber mining and production company that con-trolled a huge chunk of the amber market. The firm's only major competition was the RezStone corporation. Wilson Revere, CEO of the company, was also present tonight. At the moment he was on the far side of the room talking to the mayor of Frequency and a Guild Councilman.

"Cruz tells me that Adam Winters will be a little different from his predecessors," Lyra said. "The betting was that Douglas Drake was going to get the CEO's job."

"Who told you that?"

"One of my best customers. She's Hubert O'Conner's girlfriend at the moment, although the last time she came to my shop, I got the feeling she was thinking of bailing. Gloria has very good intuition. Wonder if she has left town yet."

"It's no secret that the Sweetwaters would have preferred just about anyone other than Drake at the top of the Guild," Marlowe said.

Lyra smiled. "They have a major stake in Guild politics. They do a lot of business underground, and whoever controls the Guild controls the underworld. The Sweetwaters, bless their hearts, are very pragmatic about that kind of thing, though. They worked with the former head of the Guild, and they would have worked with Drake if it had been necessary. But between you and me, I think they went a little out of their way to make sure it wouldn't be necessary."

"That doesn't surprise me," Marlowe said. "Although I didn't know until tonight that Cruz and Adam were friends."

"I think they have some connection through the Bureau," Lyra said vaguely.

"Ah, yes, that explains it."

So the Sweetwaters had done a little work for the Bureau. That was a very interesting tidbit, Marlowe thought. She filed it away for future reference. You never knew when that kind of information might be useful in the private eye business.

Lyra Dore was marrying into a family of strong talents, one that possessed a long history with Arcane. Although not officially registered with the Society, the Sweetwaters had, for centuries, maintained what could only be called a nuanced association with Jones & Jones.

For generations the Sweetwaters had made their living as extremely discreet, highly professional assassins. On those rare occasions when J&J had found itself confronting an extraordinarily dangerous rogue psychic who could not be handled in-house, it had called in the Sweetwaters.

The official line from the Sweetwaters maintained that the reclusive, tightly knit clan was no longer in the traditional family business. The clan was, instead, wholly dedicated to its thriving amber empire. But on her first day on the job at J&J, Marlowe had learned that was not entirely true. Uncle Zeke had explained that, while the Sweetwaters now made their living in security work and a number of amber-related enterprises, J&J could still turn to the family when there was no other alternative. She hoped it would never be necessary to pick up the phone and call in the Sweetwaters.

"How are the wedding plans coming?" Marlowe asked.

"To tell you the truth, I'm not sure," Lyra admitted. "I've turned the entire project over to my friend, Nancy

Halifax. She's in the art world, you know. Owns a gallery in the Quarter. She did tell me that this year's wedding colors are blue and pink, which is unfortunate,
because I'm not fond of either one."

"Neither am I."

"Well, you won't have to worry about it," Lyra said.
"Everyone knows that a high-ranking Guild Covenant
Marriage has a whole different set of rules. It will be
a lot of amber and psi green for you, I'm afraid." She
waved a hand. "Sort of like this ballroom."

Shocked, Marlowe almost spilled her champagne.
"Adam and I have never talked about marriage."

"Really?" Lyra appeared surprised.

"We've never even dated. Unless you count this
reception."

Lyra frowned. "Are you sure? According to the papers, you two are an item."

"The press got it all wrong, as usual."

Lyra's expression became thoughtful. "Hmm."

Time to change the subject, Marlowe decided. "I've
got a professional question for you."

"Great." Lyra brightened. "I don't get a lot of questions of a professional nature. Seems like very few
people take a serious interest in amber tuning. Being
a tuner is a lot like being an auto mechanic. Customers don't really want to know about the psi-physics of
flash-rock, they just want the car fixed."

"I understand that those with your kind of talent can
tune amber, but can you reverse the process?"

"Sure. Anyone who can tune amber can untune it."

"How?"

"You're serious about this, aren't you?"

"Yes."

"Well, the process would be exactly the same. You focus on the stone, rez a little talent, and channel energy in a way that would distort the tuned currents."

"Like working dreamlight," Marlowe said.

"I don't know anything about dreamlight," Lyra said, "but energy is energy, regardless of where it comes from on the spectrum. I'm sure there are similarities when it comes to channeling it."

"Whenever I've seen an amber tuner at work, he or she holds the stone in one hand."

"That's right. There has to be physical contact." Lyra paused. "Something I should know? Does this involve one of your cases?"

Adam and Cruz were walking toward them now, moving through the crowd with the easy assurance of a couple of very well-bred, very well-dressed, top-of-the-line predators.

"As a matter of fact, it does," Marlowe said.

"Oh, wow, I get to consult for J&J. This is so exciting."

Adam and Cruz were upon them. Cruz moved in close to Lyra, his arm brushing hers in a subtle act of intimacy. Marlowe opened her senses a tiny bit and glanced at their prints. The energy that burned between the two was clear and strong and radiant, powerful enough to send the ages-old message to everyone else in the room. *We are a mated pair, bonded by love, bonded for life.*

I want that feeling, Marlowe thought, oddly shaken. *I want it with Adam.* She looked at him and saw the heat in his eyes. It stirred her senses in the most intimate way. It would never be the same with anyone else. She did not want to be with anyone else.

He looked at her, eyes watchful. "Something wrong?"

"No," she said quickly. "Lyra and I were just discussing how someone might de-rez tuned amber."

Adam got it at once. "That is a very good question. And the answer?"

"The answer," Marlowe said, "is that someone would have to have a talent for tuning. In addition, he would have to have physical contact with the stone that he wanted to de-rez."

"Well," Lyra said, hesitant, "there is one other possibility. Very unlikely, but technically feasible."

They all looked at her.

"There is a rare kind of quartz that gives off energy that can disrupt standard rez amber. It's called vortex quartz for obvious reasons."

"Because it acts like a vortex down in the catacombs?" Marlowe said.

"Right. Vortex quartz can warp the currents in a tuned stone. But as I said, it's quite rare."

Adam looked at Lyra. "Would it take a special kind of talent to rez it?"

"No, but it would take a lot of power," Lyra said. "I think any strong talent could probably do it. But the stuff is almost impossible to obtain. I don't know any shop that sells it. There's no market for it, really. Even if you got hold of some, you'd have to find a specialist who could tune it for you."

Adam looked at Marlowe. "Got a hunch that when we finally track down Joey the broker, he'll be able to tell us how to buy vortex quartz and locate a tuner who could handle it."

Cruz looked from Adam to Marlowe and back again. "Anything you want to tell us? Or is this Guild business?"

Marlowe answered at the same time that Adam did.

"Actually, its J&J business," she said.

"Guild business," Adam said.

Cruz and Lyra smiled.

Marlowe cleared her throat. "But under the circumstances, I think we can tell you." She paused a beat, glancing at Adam. "Unless the new Guild boss has some objection?"

He shrugged. "Nope, the new Guild boss is wide-open to suggestions tonight."

He told Cruz and Lyra about the crystals and described how his amber had been subtly warped a few days earlier.

There was a short silence while Lyra considered the problem, frowning a little.

"You're absolutely certain no one physically handled your tuned amber?" she said finally.

"I'm certain," Adam said.

"Well, it sure sounds like someone got close enough to you to use vortex quartz on your good amber."

"How close would he have to be?" Cruz asked.

Lyra thought about it. "If he is very strong, he could probably do it from a distance of ten, maybe fifteen feet."

"Which means it could have happened anywhere," Marlowe said to Adam. "Anyone passing you on the street could have destroyed your good amber."

Cruz got what struck Marlowe as an expression that could only be labeled professional.

"Interesting way to get rid of a Guild boss, when you think about it," he said. "De-rez his amber just enough to warp it but not enough to be obvious. Then make sure he goes underground. Tactically speaking, it's brilliant."

Adam looked at Marlowe, amusement gleaming in his eyes. "Works even better if you make sure he goes underground in a region where there's an active vortex."

Marlowe winced. "Just seemed like a good idea at the time."

"I've got an even better idea," Adam said. He took her hand. "Let's dance."

He led her toward the dance floor. The crowd parted magically, making a path for them. The bandleader saw what was happening and immediately struck the opening chords of the famous "Amber Waltz."

The other couples on the floor stopped dancing and

moved to the side to allow the new Guild chief to dance with his lady.

Marlowe went into Adam's arms. His eyes heated and he smiled at her, an intimate, sensual smile that stirred all of her senses.

In that moment she was only distantly aware of the applause from the throng that surrounded them. The music somehow became interwoven with the energy resonating between Adam and her. Unconsciously, she rezzed all of her senses.

It was a mistake, of course. Opening her other vision in a crowded room was always unpleasant. Sure enough, murky layers of dreamlight covered the dance floor. It was as if she and Adam were dancing through a fog of psi.

She was about to close down her talent when she saw the hot, warped prints.

"Adam."

His arms tightened around her. "Are you all right?"

"Yes. Sorry. Just got a good look at the floor."

"Whatever you do, keep smiling."

"Right." She managed to keep her glowing smile in place while speaking through her teeth. "There are a couple of people here tonight who must have been using Keith Deene's crystals. Whoever they are, they've been handling them a lot. The damage in both sets of prints looks bad."

"Can you track the prints without being too obvious?"

"Yes, I think so. One set leads toward the southern corner of the floor. Over there by the flags."

Adam drew her into another long, gliding turn that gave him a clear view of the crowd of guests standing near the flags.

"Hubert O'Conner," he said. "That certainly fits. The second set will probably lead straight to the buffet table."

"How did you know?" She followed his glance and saw a familiar figure. "Douglas Drake. I've seen him on the evening news. I wonder if he or his buddy, O'Conner, was driving the SUV that tried to run me down today."

"Good question."

"I still can't figure out why they would risk coming after me, though. I'm what you all in the Guild call a civilian."

"I've been wondering the same thing. There's only one reason they would take that kind of risk."

"And the reason is?"

"They think I'm going to marry you."

"What?" She was so stunned that she knew she would have lost her balance in her extremely high heels if Adam hadn't been holding her.

"Keep smiling," he said.

"But why would either of them care if you, uh, married me?"

"Remember back at the start of this thing you asked me why the heads of the Guilds are almost always married?"

"You said something about tradition. But you never really answered the question."

"There is an old tradition in the Guilds that allows any member to challenge the chief to a ghost light duel. The duels are fought underground in the tunnels."

"Good grief," Marlowe said. "You could kill someone with the kind of energy that a ghost hunter can pull underground, or at the very least, permanently fry his brains. At best, the loser would probably spend the rest of his life in a parapsych ward. You say this is an old Guild tradition?"

"The right of challenge is incorporated in old Guild law. It's rarely used."

"I can certainly understand why," she said. "What a ridiculous, primitive, idiotic, macho tradition. Dueling is positively archaic, for heaven's sake."

"Got a hunch that, having failed to kill me, Drake is planning to challenge me. I'm stronger than he is, but he may have concluded that he can take me now."

Shock slammed through her a second time. "Because he plans to use one of those crystal flashlights that Keith made?"

"It would be like bringing a mag-rez gun to an old-style amber-rez pistol duel."

"What does marriage have to do with this dumb-ass tradition?"

He smiled. "The wife of a Guild boss has a few exclusive privileges. One of them is the right to go before the Council and block a challenge to her husband."

She caught her breath. "In other words, if you marry me, I can make sure that Drake can't challenge you to a duel?"

"Now do you understand why Guild bosses usually get married?"

"I think so, yes. But I can't believe that they are still conducting duels within the Guilds."

"You're Arcane. When it comes to traditions, you've got very little room to criticize."

Chapter 36

"ADAM, I'VE BEEN THINKING," MARLOWE SAID. "WE should get married. Now. Tonight."

"No."

She ignored him to unlock her front door. "We can go to one of those twenty-four-hour MC places. There's one a few blocks from here. I pass it every day on my way to the office."

"No," he repeated. He reached around her to open the door. He had known this subject was going to come up, he reminded himself. He had to stand firm. The truth was, part of him wanted to jump at any excuse to tie her to him. Even a Marriage of Convenience seemed like a good idea right now.

She moved into the darkened foyer and turned to confront him. "Give me one good reason."

"Because marrying you would make you even more

of a target." He closed the door. "I appreciate the offer, but it's not necessary. Now that I know for certain that Drake and O'Conner are using the crystals, I'll take care of the problem."

She looked at him very steadily. "The Guild polices its own?"

"That's how it works, Marlowe."

"But what will you do with them?"

"The first step is to confiscate the crystals. Once those rocks are all accounted for, Drake and O'Conner will get the same option the others did. Take early retirement or face a Chamber tribunal."

"I see." She sighed and walked into the shadowed living room. "You know, this has all been very exciting for me."

"Yeah?" He followed her, stripping off his jacket and loosening his tie.

"When Uncle Zeke gave me the keys to the office, he warned me that J&J was just a small-time psychic private investigation agency these days. He said it only handled routine cases for members of the Society, and not a lot of those came through the door anymore. Too much competition, he said. Lots of psychic detectives around now. Not like the old days, he said."

"Right. The old days." He tossed the jacket over the back of a chair.

She stepped out of her heels. "Back on the Old World, J&J must have been a very exciting business. Arcane was always busy hunting down conspiracies of rogue talents and mad scientists. They took down dangerous conspiracies like the Order of the Emerald Tablet and Nightshade. Thrilling stuff."

"Sounds like it."

"Then, here on Harmony, during the Era of Discord, J&J helped to defeat Vance's rebels. The records from that time detail all sorts of intelligence operations including the one that John Cabot Winters and Jeremiah Jones conducted against the lab that was turning out the crystal guns."

"Good times."

"Great times. I thought I'd never be lucky enough to get involved in a major case like one of those in the old files, but thanks to you, I've had a taste of what the business must have been like for some of J&J's legendary directors like Caleb Jones and Fallon Jones. Sometimes I almost wish—" She broke off. "Oh, geez. Look. Out on the balcony."

He realized she was staring through the darkened windows at the far end of the room. He walked to where she had come to an abrupt halt and studied the scene.

In the glow of the green psi emanating from the ruins he saw a couple of dozen furry blobs. The dust bunnies perched on the railing and the loungers and the small table, eyes glinting in the eerie light.

"Looks like Gibson invited a few friends over while you were out," he said.

Two dozen pairs of dust bunny eyes abruptly stared back at them through the windows. For an instant no creature on either side of the glass doors moved. Then there was a great deal of mad scurrying on the balcony. The fluffy blobs tumbled and fluttered away into the night. Within seconds the dust bunnies had all disappeared save one.

Gibson dashed through the small door set into the living room next to the glass doors and gave a cheery greeting.

"You threw a party while I was out?" Marlowe scooped him up and continued on into the kitchen. "I'll bet you really impressed your friends with the story of how you helped save the underworld."

Gibson chattered enthusiastically. He bounded out of her arms and up onto the top of the refrigerator. Marlowe turned toward the cookie jar. She stopped short and stared down at the floor. "Good grief."

Adam went to the counter and looked over the edge. The remains of the shattered cookie jar littered the tile floor. There was no sign of any energy bars.

"Must have been a wild party," he said. "A kegger."

"Guess Gibson gave up trying to figure out how to open the wire lock and took the Gordian knot approach to accessing the cookie jar," Marlowe said.

She started to collect the broken shards.

"I'll do that," Adam said. "You're in bare feet. You'll cut yourself."

He went around the corner, hoisted Marlowe by the waist, and carried her out of the scene of the wreckage. He set her on the carpet and went back to pick up the pieces of broken jar.

Marlowe looked sternly at Gibson. "I hope your friends enjoyed themselves."

Gibson chortled and bounced up and down a few times.

Adam dumped the pottery shards and a handful of crumbs into the trash. "You know, what with one thing and another this evening, neither of us got any dinner tonight. Don't know about you, but I'm starving."

Marlowe glanced at the clock. "It's a little late, but we could order out."

"It will take too long. Let's see what you've got on hand."

"Not much," she warned.

He opened the door of the refrigerator and contemplated the sparse contents. Gibson leaned over, watching with great interest.

"No offense, but the cupboard looks bare," Adam said. "Don't you ever eat?"

"As often as possible," Marlowe said. "It's one of my favorite hobbies. But for some inexplicable reason, I don't seem to have had time to go grocery shopping lately."

"No problem. I'm good when it comes to working with the basics."

He took out a package of sharp cheddar, the half-empty jar of dill pickles, mayonnaise, and mustard. He set everything down on the counter and returned to the refrigerator. "You keep your bread in the fridge?"

"I live alone, remember? I can't get through an entire loaf before it starts to mold. It lasts longer in the refrigerator."

"I'll have to remember that trick. I have the same problem." He put the bread on the counter, undid the wrapper, and removed four very dry slices. "Now all I need is a toaster."

"Behind you. I'll open some wine."

"Sounds like a plan."

A short time later they sat side by side at the counter, munching on toasted cheddar and dill pickle sandwiches and drinking a little of the good red that Marlowe had poured.

"You know," Marlowe said, "I would never have thought to put pickles and cheddar together in a sandwich."

"Guild bosses are known for their creativity in the kitchen."

"Really? I hadn't heard that."

They finished the sandwiches in a companionable silence and carried their glasses of wine out onto the balcony. They stood together, leaning on the railing, drinking in the psi-bright night. Gibson crouched next to Marlowe, munching a pickle.

Adam drank some of the wine. It was good to be out here sharing the night with Marlowe. The sense of intimacy and the heady energy that surrounded her felt right. *This is the woman I was born to be with.*

"What happens now?" she asked after a while.

He contemplated the glowing ruins. "You mean, when do I move on Drake and O'Conner?

"Yes. I know what you said earlier about giving them the option of retirement or facing a tribunal. But I don't think it's going to work, Adam. Not with those two. They won't go quietly like the others did."

"I know." He drank a little more wine.

When he did not offer anything further, Marlowe turned her head to look down at his feet. He felt her open her senses and knew that she was reading his dreamprints.

"You're going to have to kill them, aren't you?" she whispered.

"Maybe." He finished his wine and cradled the glass in his hands. "Maybe not. Depends."

"On what?"

He thought about his options. "How long do you think it will take the crystals to do the job?"

"A couple of months, maybe, before they start showing physical signs of the damage. They're powerful, Adam."

He set his empty glass down on the nearby patio table. "Well, one thing's for sure. Can't let O'Conner and Drake run around Frequency stirring up trouble for the next couple of months while I wait for them to get sick. Not now."

She turned away and very deliberately set her glass down next to his. "You mean because they might come after me again?"

He said nothing.

"I don't want you to have to do this," she whispered, her back to him.

"Won't be the first time."

"I know that, too." She turned slowly around to face him. In the glowing green night her eyes were hot with the sheen of tears. "Doesn't make it any easier. Not for a man like you."

"I can handle it," he said.

"I know. That doesn't change a thing."

He said nothing. There was nothing he could say to that. She came to him. He opened his arms. She pressed her damp face into his shoulder. He pulled her close and tight. For a few minutes they stood quietly together, enveloped in the gentle heat that was always there between them.

After a while he raised her chin and kissed her.

He had intended it to be a gentle, reassuring kiss, but within seconds she was clutching at his shoulders, fierce and desperate. He knew it was because she had accepted that she could not protect him from whatever lay ahead; she accepted it but didn't like it.

His senses flashed, igniting his blood and the night.

After a while he picked her up in his arms and carried her back into the dimly lit condo. In the shadows of the bedroom he stripped off the black silk gown and the lacy scraps of underwear beneath it. He clawed the pins from her hair, his hands shaking with the force of his need. She fumbled with the buttons of his shirt and unbuckled his belt.

He got out of his boots, trousers, and briefs, picked her up, and fell with her across the bed.

The lovemaking seared his senses. They rolled together across the quilt. She ended up astride his thighs and watched him through the veil of hair falling in front of her face as she rode him to her climax. Her eyes burned with passion and psi. It was the most erotic sight he had ever seen.

He put her on her back before she had stopped shivering and sank himself deep into her body. She tightened around him, cried out, and convulsed again.

This time he came with her. Endlessly.

THE INSISTENT RINGING OF HIS PHONE WOKE HIM. HE discovered that he and Marlowe had fallen asleep lying across the bed. Automatically, he glanced at his watch. Three in the morning.

Beside him, Marlowe stirred and opened her eyes. "What's that racket?"

"Phone," he explained. He sat up, trying to orient himself. "Don't know where I left it."

"On the floor, I think."

"Oh, yeah. It all comes back to me now."

He extricated himself from her warm body, crawled to the edge of the bed, and reached over the side. He found the phone and got it open.

"Winters."

"This is Galendez. Fifteen minutes ago Drake and O'Conner went into their Old Quarter office. They didn't come back out. Couple of minutes ago there was an explosion inside. The building is in flames."

"I'll be there in ten."

He closed the phone and reached for his trousers.

Marlowe levered herself up on one elbow. "What happened?"

"I've got a team watching the building in the Quarter that Drake and O'Conner use as an office. One of the men just called. Said there'd been an explosion and a fire."

"I'm coming with you."

"Had a feeling you were going to say that."

Chapter 37

"THAT WAS ONE EXTREMELY HOT FIRE," MARLOWE said. "I doubt very much that the arson investigators will call it accidental."

"No," Adam agreed. "Probably won't find much in the way of evidence, though. The question is, how did it start?"

They stood on the sidewalk across from the charred and blackened building. The two Bureau agents who had been assigned to watch the office were with them. Adam had introduced them only as Galendez and Treiger.

The power in the agents' dreamprints was impressive, but you'd never know that they were high-rez talents to look at them, Marlowe thought. Both were dressed in the shabby clothes of homeless men. Their hair was scruffy and untrimmed. They reeked of alcohol, but she knew that neither of them had been drinking. Undercover.

The flashing globes of the fire trucks and emergency vehicles added a disorienting, strobelike aspect to the natural illumination from the Dead City wall. There was a lot of water and foam in the street. Smoke still billowed, and Marlowe could see flames deep inside the three-story building, but the fire department had things under control. The outer walls still stood, although the windows had all shattered.

Most of the two-hundred-year-old structures in the Quarter had been built of high-tech, fireproof materials imported from Earth. But the majority had been remodeled a number of times over the years after the closing of the Curtain. Later architects and contractors had been obliged to use far less exotic materials. The result was that, in the case of major fires in the Quarter, the walls survived, but the interiors were often totally destroyed.

That was the case tonight, Marlowe thought.

"The firemen are assuming some kind of accelerant was used," Galendez said. "When things cool down in a few days, they'll go in to look for it."

"They won't find anything," Treiger warned. "That was ghost fire."

"Go through it again for me," Adam ordered.

"Right," Galendez said. "Not much to tell, though. I was at my post." He angled his chin up toward a broken window in the abandoned warehouse behind Marlowe.

"Treiger was in the alley. Drake and O'Conner entered through the front door."

"No one came through the alley," Treiger said. "No one left that way, either. Drake and O'Conner didn't rez the office lights."

"Is that part of their pattern?" Marlowe asked.

"Yes, ma'am," Galendez said. "Don't really need lights here in the Quarter this close to the wall unless you're trying to read a newspaper."

"That's true," she said.

"Figured it was just another late-night meeting," Treiger said. "But naturally we didn't hear anything because there aren't any bugs inside."

Marlowe understood. "Sophisticated listening devices don't work well in the Quarter, especially this close to the wall. The psi levels cause too much interference."

Treiger nodded. "Next thing we know, we hear the explosion. The fire started immediately."

"The blinds covering the office windows went fast," Galendez said. "I had a clear view into the room, but I couldn't see much. The place was engulfed in ghost fire. I could feel the energy of it all the way across the street. Didn't last long, but by the time it de-rezzed, the whole building was in flames."

"Figure O'Conner and Drake set the fire and got out of the building through their hole-in-the-wall." Treiger said. "That's the only other exit, and it's the one place we can't post a watch."

"Looks like O'Conner and Drake decided to close down the office," Adam said. "They wanted to make sure that there was nothing left in the way of evidence."

"Fire like that will do the trick," Galendez said. "But who could pull that much alien psi? I know Drake and O'Conner are both strong, but I've never heard of any ghost hunter who is that powerful, not outside the tunnels."

Adam exchanged a glance with Marlowe. She knew what he was thinking. A couple of strong Guild men like O'Conner and Drake, working with the crystals, could have generated the kind of psi required to ignite a fire aboveground.

"We can't go into the building," Adam said. "But we can check out the hole-in-the-wall. Doubt if we'll find anything useful, but you never know."

They used the rip in the wall beneath the empty warehouse to enter the catacombs. Although their goal was just across the street, the journey underground was, as always, convoluted. They walked for a good fifteen minutes through the tunnels before arriving at another jagged hole in the quartz.

"This is it," Galendez said.

Adam looked through the opening. "Fire's still smoldering in the basement. It's going to stay hot for a while, probably a lot longer than a couple of days."

Marlowe studied the view through the ripped quartz. She could see only a profound darkness lit here and there by flames. She could not smell the thick smoke on the other side of the tunnel entrance, but no ash drifted into the catacombs. The heavy psi prevented the tainted air from drifting into the underworld.

Adam turned toward her. "What do you see?"

She rezzed her senses cautiously and examined the layers of strong dreamprints that seethed on the floor near the hole-in-the-wall.

"O'Conner and Drake have used this entrance on several occasions over the years. Both sets of tracks show signs of crystal use."

"They knew that the Bureau was closing in on them," Adam said. "They came here tonight to destroy the place to make sure that there was no evidence left that could be turned over to a Chamber tribunal."

"Not exactly," she said, examining the prints very closely.

"What do you mean?" he asked.

"They have certainly come and gone this way many times," she said. "But they did not leave through this exit tonight."

There was a moment of sharp silence.

Adam cast a speculative glance at the portion of smoldering basement that could be seen through the ripped quartz.

"Well, that's interesting," he said.

Galendez frowned. "No offense, but are you sure they both didn't get out of the building through this hole, Miss Jones?"

"Positive," she said quietly. "I think that when the fire investigators are finally able to access the scene, they're going to find the bodies of both O'Conner and Drake in the rubble."

Adam looked at her. "See any other prints?"

"Yes," she said. "A couple of other people besides Drake and O'Conner have come this way recently, but one set of prints in particular worries me. They're only a day or two old. They belong to a woman."

"One of O'Conner's mistresses," Treiger offered. "Or maybe one of Drake's women."

Marlowe hesitated. "Whoever she was, she was terrified."

"Maybe she saw something she shouldn't have seen," Adam said.

"There was someone with her." Marlowe tracked the prints around the corner. "Not O'Conner or Drake. Whoever he was, he took her this way."

Adam and the two Bureau agents followed her. Marlowe kept walking, following the trail of seething dreamlight.

"This stuff is boiling," she said. "I think he meant to kill her. That's why she was so scared. It also explains why his prints are so hot. He was anticipating the kill. There is a return set of prints, as well. His, but not hers."

"Probably didn't murder her outright," Adam said. "More likely, he stripped her of her amber and sent her into the tunnels."

"She wouldn't be the first inconvenient Councilman's mistress to disappear that way," Treiger said.

"If they sent her into the rain forest, I'll never find

her," Marlowe said. "It's impossible to track dream-light in the jungle."

"O'Conner and Drake are old-school," Adam said. "Traditionalists. They aren't comfortable in the rain forest. They don't know the rules there. They would have stuck with the tunnels for this kind of business."

The flat certainty in his words sent a shiver through her. She remembered what he had said about keeping his enemies close. He had studied Drake and O'Conner. He knew them well enough to predict their actions.

She paused to take another look at some of the pooling dreamlight. "She's alone now. He left her here and went back to the office. She was still alive at this point. Maybe we're not too late."

"She probably started running," Galendez warned. "People always run when they end up underground without good amber. They panic. Start to hallucinate. Sooner or later, they blunder into a ghost or a trap, and it's all over."

Marlowe stopped in front of a vaulted opening and looked into the vast rotunda beyond. A dozen glowing passageways opened off the circular space.

There was a woman on the floor in the center of the rotunda. She sat with her arms wrapped tightly around her knees, her head down, rocking gently. The dream-light on the floor around her shimmered with despair.

"Gloria Ray," Treiger said. "Drake's latest mistress."

Marlowe hurried forward. "It's all right, Gloria. You're safe now."

Gloria raised her head. Disbelief and uncertainty flashed across her tear-stained face. "Are you real?"

"Yes," Marlowe said. She reached down and helped Gloria to her feet. "We're real."

"I started seeing things," Gloria whispered. Her voice shook. "They say that happens down here in the tunnels when your amber doesn't work and you're all alone and you know you can't find your way out. The psi gets to you. They say first you start seeing things, and then you panic and you start running."

"You didn't panic, and you didn't run," Marlowe said.

"I almost did," Gloria said. "Lost count of how many times I thought about doing that."

"What stopped you?" Adam asked.

Gloria turned to look at him. "You're the new Guild boss."

"Yes," he said.

"I didn't run because I didn't freak out completely," Gloria said. "Even without amber, I've still got a little talent. I'm intuitive, you see. Had a feeling that if I just stayed put, someone might find me."

Chapter 38

"GLORIA IS STILL FRACTURED," ADAM SAID ON THE other end of the phone. "She was down there in that green hell for nearly two days."

"Long enough to fray anyone's nerves." Marlowe lounged back in the big desk chair and absently swiveled from side to side. The springs squeaked rhythmically.

Gibson left his box of toys on the window bench, fluttered down to the floor and over to the desk. He bounced up onto the arm of the chair and from there to the high back above Marlowe's head. He clung to his perch with his hind paws, chortling in delight as the chair swung back and forth in a slow semicircle.

"She told me she found out that O'Conner and Drake were planning to get rid of me," Adam said. "She decided it was time to disappear. Says she intended to

call and warn me about their plot when she was safely
out of town."

"How did she end up in Drake's and O'Conner's office the other night?"

"She went there to get some insurance. She knew
they kept incriminating financial information in a
wall safe in the office. Somewhere along the line she
discovered the combination. She took a camera with
her and photographed several pages of a journal. She
was planning to use it as blackmail material in case
O'Conner sent someone after her."

"But he found her there in the office photographing
the journal?"

"No," Adam said, sounding very satisfied. "He
found her *after* she had photographed the journal and
hidden the camera in her bra."

"Wait a second." Marlowe sat forward abruptly.
Gibson almost fell off the back of the chair. "Are you
telling me Drake didn't search her and find the camera
before he sent her into the tunnels?"

"All Drake cared about was making sure she didn't
have any good amber. She says he aimed some kind of
weird flashlight at her and then told her that her amber
was dead."

"He used vortex quartz on her."

"Sounds like it. The story checks out. The lab techs
tell me that the one piece of concealed amber that Ray
had on her was warped."

"But now you've got her camera?"

"Better than that. The pages she photographed have

been developed and printed out. It's definitely a financial journal of some kind, but it's coded. Shouldn't be
too hard to crack the code, though."

"You're sure?"

"Trust me, Drake's and O'Conner's minds didn't
work that way. I've got a couple of Bureau forensic
accountants going through the data now. Should have
something soon."

"But now you're looking for a third man," she
said. "The one who set the fire that killed Drake and
O'Conner."

"Someone is pulling the plug on an operation and
snipping off loose ends. You said you saw other prints
leading away from the bolt-hole and that they were
fresh."

"Yes. But there was very little heat in them. I don't
doubt but that whoever set the fire is a cold-blooded
killer, but even cold-blooded killers get hot when they
kill."

"The adrenaline," Adam said quietly.

"After rezzing all that ghost light and killing two
people, there should have been a lot of heat in those
prints."

"Another chameleon like Tucker Deene?"

She thought about it. "Theoretically possible, I
guess."

"You're the one who said that kind of talent is extremely rare. What are the odds that two chameleons
would turn up in this case?"

"Slim to none," she admitted.

"So, odds are we've actually got one chameleon: Tucker Deene. I told you I didn't trust that guy."

"The thing is, he's a con artist, Adam. Not a killer."

"How do you know? He's a chameleon. He's probably never let you see his real prints."

"I saw them when he pulled that mag-rez on me in the stairwell at the condo. But say you're right. Say Tucker was involved in some kind of conspiracy with Drake and O'Conner. What's in this for him?"

"Revenge on the two men who encouraged his brother to forge the crystal guns that nearly killed him? Or maybe he's just trying to make sure there's no trail of conspiracy that leads from O'Conner and Drake back to the Deene family."

"I keep telling you, Tucker is a con artist, not a cold-blooded killer."

"He and his brother and sister were doing business with O'Conner and Drake, who were up to their necks in everything from antiquities smuggling to drugs, not to mention money laundering, fraud, gambling, and extortion. Shall I go on?"

"Okay, I understand that there was a lot of money involved."

"The Deenes have good reason to worry that any serious investigation of O'Conner and Drake would inevitably involve them."

"But you more or less let them off the hook. You didn't threaten them."

"That still leaves the Frequency City Police for them to worry about," Adam said.

She swallowed hard. "You're right. Sometimes I forget that there are regular law enforcement agencies in this town."

Adam was quiet for a time. Marlowe tapped her pen against the desktop. Gibson got bored and bopped down to the floor. He fluttered out the door. Marlowe heard Rick lift the lid of the cookie jar.

"About that real date that we've never had," Adam said.

Marlowe froze. "What about it?"

"Would you be interested in going out to dinner with me? To an actual restaurant?"

She drew a breath and let it out slowly. "Yes. Yes, I'd like that."

"Good. Thanks."

Silence hummed again.

It was as if they had both just made it safely across a fragile bridge strung above a very deep gorge, she thought. The case that had brought them together was winding down rapidly. Soon there would be no more excuses for a partnership. Soon they would be on their own, facing the complications of their relationship, trying to get back to normal, always assuming that there was such a state.

"One piece of good news on this end," Adam said after a while.

"What's that?"

"Got a lead on Joey the broker. I sent Galendez and Treiger to check it out. If they find him, I may be able to get some answers."

"Good luck."

"I'll call you later."

He ended the connection.

Marlowe sat quietly for a few minutes, studying the genealogy file that she had pulled up on her computer just before Adam had called.

After a while she got to her feet and went into the front office. Rick looked at her.

"Going somewhere?" he asked.

"Yes," she said. She took her leather jacket and helmet off the hook. "I'll be at the Arcane genealogical library. Ready to ride, Gibson?"

Gibson did not need a second invitation. He hopped off the desk and dashed across the room toward her. She picked him up and tucked him under her arm.

"What's happening with genealogy?" Rick asked.

"I want to talk to one of the librarians." She opened the door. "Call me if anything comes up."

"Are you kidding? The phone has been ringing all morning. Business is starting to pour in, boss. I told you all that publicity was going to do J&J a lot of good."

"Try to weed out the crank calls, okay? I refuse to do haunted houses."

"Got it. No haunted house cases."

Chapter 39

THE LIBRARIAN'S NAME WAS BEATRICE RAMSEY. SHE was in her early sixties, but she looked like a very stylish forty-five. She was trim, athletic, and passionate about genealogy.

She led Marlowe down a long aisle of floor-to-ceiling bookshelves crammed with thick, heavy volumes. The interior of the Society's Bureau of Genealogy was not unlike the catacombs, Marlowe reflected. A person could get lost in the maze of bookshelves. The windowless, atmosphere-controlled environment added to the disorientation.

"The Society's files are maintained on computers, of course," Beatrice explained. "But we also keep original, hard copy records. The advanced preservation techniques back on Earth made it possible to conserve even the oldest journals before they were brought through the Curtain. Some of these volumes date back to the founding of the Society."

"Yes, I know," Marlowe said. She had learned long ago that once you started talking to a member of the genealogy staff, it was best to just shut up and listen.

"It's not often we get a request for a hard copy original, however," Beatrice said. "It's so much easier to access the information on the computer."

And so much easier to hack into the database, Marlowe thought. But she did not say that out loud.

"Ah, here we go." Beatrice stopped. She studied the labels on the spines of the books and then plucked one volume off the shelf. "I think you'll find what you're looking for in this. Renquist's research has rarely been equaled."

"Renquist?"

"Grace Renquist. She was a brilliant Arcane genealogist who lived back in the twenty-first century on Earth. Over the years, there has been a lot of very fine work done in the field of psychical inheritance traits, but Renquist's analysis is still considered a foundation text. It is often consulted by the experts, even today."

"Sounds like the right place to start." Marlowe opened the volume and read the title page aloud. "*A Study of the Inheritance Patterns of Rare Paranormal Characteristics in Families Registered with the Arcane Society.*" She looked up. "Yes, this will be very helpful."

"There are a few other texts that I think will also answer some of your questions," Beatrice said. "Follow me, please."

"One more thing. I'm going to need the hard copy version of the records of a family named Deene."

"Sure you don't want to use the computer for that? So much easier to search family trees that way."

"No," Marlowe said. "I used the computer the last time. That did not work out well for me. I want to examine the original."

AN HOUR LATER SHE COMPARED RENQUIST'S ANALYSIS of the extremely complicated inheritance patterns of the rare paranormal ability known as chameleon talent with the Deene family tree. A cold chill slithered through her. She closed both volumes and headed toward the door.

Gibson was waiting for her at the receptionist's desk. He was playing with a ruler and flirting outrageously with the receptionist. When Marlowe reached the desk, however, he sensed her urgency. He dropped the ruler and scrambled up onto her shoulder.

"Time to go," Marlowe said. She nodded at the receptionist. "Thanks for keeping him entertained."

"Any time," the woman said. "He's so adorable."

"Yes, and he certainly knows it."

Outside, she discovered that twilight had fallen on the Quarter. She went to where she had parked Dream, dropped Gibson into the saddlebag, and took out her phone. She entered Adam's private code. There was no answer.

"This is not good, Gibson."

She needed to get to Adam, but she had to make one stop first. It was time to retrieve Uncle Zeke's mag-rez from the floor safe at the office.

She swung one leg over the bike and ignited the flash-rock engine. Dream roared to life. She drove swiftly through the Quarter, taking all the shortcuts. She could hear Gibson chortling when she zipped through an alley and turned into the narrow lane outside the offices of Jones & Jones.

She braked to an abrupt halt, cut the engine, dismounted, and ran up the steps to the door. Gibson scrambled out of the saddlebag.

"Stay here," she said over her shoulder. "I'll be right back."

He ignored her to scamper up the steps after her.

The Closed sign was turned over in the window. It was five thirty. Rick had gone home half an hour ago.

She opened the door into the darkened front office. When she heard Gibson's low growl of warning, she glanced down and saw that he had gone into full hunting mode. All four eyes were open.

Instinctively she heightened her own talent. But it was too late. The wave of darkness came out of nowhere, washing over her, dragging her down into the depths. She had time to sense the primordial demons and monsters that moved in the featureless void of dreams, time to know that she had failed to save Adam.

And then she knew nothing at all.

Chapter 40

SHE WAS LOST IN A MAZE OF MIRRORS. AN INFINITY OF *reflections surrounded her on all sides. She saw her parents and Uncle Zeke watching her from one wall. Her brothers looked out from another corridor of mirrors. They did not speak, but there was no need for words. In the Jones family, you always knew when you had failed to meet expectations. You knew it before anyone else in the clan did, because you sensed the failure first deep inside yourself.*

"Next time put a real chaos-theory talent in charge of J&J," she said to the reflections.

She heard Gibson chittering anxiously, but when she turned, searching for him in the endless forest of images, she could not see him.

She saw Adam, though. He watched her from the

brilliant darkness of the chamber in which they had fixed the defective currents. Grief and helplessness brought tears to her eyes.

"I couldn't save you," she whispered.

He reached his hand out to her. "Come back to the surface with me now."

"No," she said. "I can't go back. I don't want to go back."

"Why not?"

"Because I screwed up. I found the answer, but I couldn't contact you. You didn't answer your phone. Why didn't you answer your phone? And now he'll kill you because I failed."

"I'm not dead yet."

She was not sure how to take that. "Are you sure?"

"I'm sure. Come back to the surface, my love. I'm waiting for you."

She heard Gibson chittering again and thought she caught a brief glimpse of him moving about among the myriad images. Then he was gone.

"They should never have put me in charge of J&J," she explained to Adam.

"You can't quit now. You need to do your job."

He certainly sounded confident. That was Adam for you, the man in charge. But he was right. She was in charge of J&J. At least for a while. They hadn't had time to choose a replacement.

Maybe Adam wasn't dead yet. Maybe there was still time to warn him.

She had to get back to the surface. She was a dreamlight talent. She could control the energy of any dream.

She rode the currents up through the darkness toward the light of a midnight sun . . .

. . . AND CAME AWAKE TO THE GLOW OF GREEN QUARTZ. For a few seconds she stared, bleary-eyed and disoriented, at an empty doorway that opened onto another green corridor. No mirrors, she thought. She was in the catacombs, not the maze. She wondered if she had simply exchanged one dreamscape for another that featured the same themes.

She sat up slowly. The quartz she had been lying on was hard to the touch. The small chamber was empty. She was still wearing her amber stud earrings. Cautiously she pulsed a little psi through the stones. There was no response.

Dumped in the tunnels in the traditional Guild style. It was an extremely embarrassing way for the head of J&J to disappear. Should have seen it coming, as Uncle Zeke would no doubt be the first to tell her. But then, Uncle Zeke was a true chaos-theory talent. She was only a dreamlight reader.

You're a Jones. You're alive. Those are huge pluses at the moment. Stop whining and try to think.

Thinking took effort, but it raised the obvious question. Why was she still alive? Why hadn't he made certain that she was dead?

The answer came immediately. *He isn't finished. He needs something from you. He'll be back.*

As if on cue, her captor appeared in the doorway.

She rolled to her feet. "You must be Elliott Fortner."

Chapter 41

FORTNER'S GRAY EYES WERE COLD, BUT THE DREAM-light pooling around his feet was fever-hot. He frowned, clearly annoyed by her observation.

"How did you know my name?" he asked.

"Spent a little time in the Arcane genealogy library today. Where's Adam?"

"Still alive, if that's what's worrying you. He has one last job to do for his old boss at the Bureau."

Adam was alive. She took a deep breath. "What happened to Gibson?"

"That ratlike creature that came into the office with you? A dust bunny, wasn't it? He went down when you did. Given his small size and the fact that he's just an animal, I assume he's dead. Frankly, I didn't bother to check."

Rage flashed through her. She had to fight to keep her voice steady.

"You killed Gibson?"

"I had to use a considerable amount of energy to take you down. Too much of my talent can kill. The rat probably caught some of the backwash."

She folded her arms beneath her breasts. She had to get control. She had to stay focused.

"You want the Burning Lamp," she said.

"Brilliant deduction, Miss Jones. No wonder they gave you the job." His eyes got a little hotter. "Yes, I want the lamp."

She looked down at the oily sheen of iridescent dreamlight on the quartz floor.

"Because you are a true, natural-born Cerberus," she said quietly. "Like most of the handful of other multitalents in the Arcane records, you're going mad and you're dying, but you're doing it far more slowly than the others."

His face hardened with rage. "You can see that in my prints?"

"Yes. I know you're a chameleon, and you've obviously got the ability to do some kind of killing mind blast. In addition, you're a legend in the Guild. That means you can also work alien psi. Three distinct talents, all originating from different points on the spectrum. Did I miss any?"

"No. You're right, I've survived far longer than any Cerberus talent I was able to locate in the Arcane records."

"Probably because you were born on Harmony and so were several generations of your ancestors. The environment here made a difference."

"It made me stronger."

"Yes, but your psi patterns are fundamentally fragile. You might have actually managed to stay sane and maybe even make it through a normal life span, though, if you hadn't started using the crystals. They triggered the sudden deterioration that you're undergoing. You'll be dead in a month or two."

"I'm going to live, Marlowe Jones. You will see to that."

"No one knows that you're a for-real Cerberus, do they?"

"I have kept the secret all of my life since I came into my second and third talents. I was only nineteen at the time, but I knew all about Arcane's theories. I also knew the legends. Your damn experts are convinced that a person endowed with powers like mine is bound to go insane and turn rogue sooner or later. The Society would have sent someone to hunt me down and destroy me."

"I can't help you. I don't have the Burning Lamp."

"Of course not. Winters would never have given it to Arcane. But he has been notified that the only way to keep you alive is to bring the lamp to a certain location in the tunnels."

"Why would he do that?" she asked. "He'll know that you're going to try to kill him."

"He'll bring the lamp to me because he'll have no choice. I've known Adam Winters for a long time. I know how he thinks. He will sacrifice himself in a desperate effort to save you."

"In a heartbeat," she agreed. "Unless he can think of another option. Trust me, he will find another option. And when he does, you'll be a dead man."

"I have left him no alternative. He'll bring me the artifact. I will kill him, and then you will work the lamp for me."

"No."

"Yes, Marlowe Jones. You will work the lamp because if you refuse, I will start killing people. One by one. Innocent people walking on the street. Think about how it will feel to be responsible for the deaths of however many people you choose to sacrifice."

Energy shivered in the atmosphere. On the floor, tainted currents of dreamlight roiled and coiled like a den of snakes.

"You're not thinking clearly here," she said, keeping her voice as calm and professional as possible. "Only a man with the blood of Nicholas Winters running in his veins can handle the energy of the lamp."

"I'm a Cerberus. I can control the power." He started to turn away.

"Out of curiosity, did you buy the vortex quartz from Joey the broker?"

He paused, expression darkening again. "Yes. I see you know about the go-between."

"Sure. You also used Joey to commission the enhancing crystals from your son, Keith."

Fortner flinched as if he'd touched hot flash-rock.

"How did you discover that?" he rasped. "No one knows."

"That you are the father of Tucker, Charlotte, and Keith? Give me a break. Of course people know. Or they soon will."

He took a step toward her. A searing wave of energy slammed at her senses.

She had to rattle him a little more, she thought. He was already teetering on some inner psychic ledge. She had to push him over the edge, make him lose his control, make him stop thinking rationally, make him put his hands on her. She needed physical contact in order to dampen his dreamlight patterns.

"Better be careful," she said, barely able to speak through the hurricane forces pounding silently at her senses. "I won't be any good to you if you destroy my talent."

The energy blast ceased, but Fortner's rage did not diminish.

"How did you find out?" he demanded. "How did you discover that the triplets are my offspring?"

"Plain, old-fashioned detective work, as Uncle Zeke would say. I spent a couple of hours in the Society's genealogical library. Your three children were born to a woman named Tracy Darnell who registered them with the Society."

"Tracy. That bitch. I swear, she haunts me."

"At the age of nineteen you began an affair with her. It didn't last long, but by the end of it she was pregnant with the triplets."

Fortner's face contorted with fury. "I didn't even know about the triplets until after they were born."

"I'll bet Tracy didn't tell you because she knew that you would try to force her to have an abortion. She wanted marriage, a real marriage, not just an MC."

"You know how the marriage laws work. Tracy and I were in an MC for a while. I ended it when I left her. But under the law, the birth of the triplets changed everything. I knew that if she went to the authorities with proof that I had fathered the bastards, I would have been forced into a permanent Covenant Marriage."

"Which was the last thing you wanted."

"I had my whole life in front of me. I had every intention of marrying into one of the major Guild families. I wasn't about to shackle myself to a low-end stripper and three squalling brats."

"You murdered Tracy and abandoned your three children to an orphanage in order to get where you are today. You know what I'm thinking? I'm thinking that the Arcane experts are right. You haven't been slowly going rogue all these years. You've been a rogue from the start, a full-blown para-sociopath with multiple talents. You are the very definition of a crazy Cerberus."

"That's a lie, damn you." He was almost screaming now. "I'm a survivor."

"You're a murdering maniac."

Energy heated the atmosphere again. Fortner took a step closer.

"Tell me exactly how you found out about my connection to the triplets," he said.

"I explained that. They're registered with Arcane."

"You're lying. When I discovered that Tracy had registered them under my name in the Society's genealogical files, I went into the database immediately and deleted everything that connected them to me. Every last link. I gave them a different father, a hunter who died in the tunnels years ago."

"You only altered the computer files."

He stared at her, uncomprehending. "What do you mean?"

"Obviously you're not aware that the librarians in genealogy keep a backup in the form of old-fashioned bound volumes."

Fortner was shaken to the core, horrified. It was all there to see in his pooling dreamlight.

"I don't believe you," he hissed. "Why would they do that?"

She shrugged. "Arcane tradition. Besides, between you and me, I don't think librarians really trust technology. They still remember what happened two hundred years ago after the Curtain closed. All of the computers started to fail within weeks. If Arcane hadn't brought its hard copy records with them through the Curtain, the Society would have lost all of its history. The librarians have never forgotten the lesson."

"What made you think that I was connected to the triplets in the first place?"

"I had no reason to think that you were," she said. "I wasn't looking for a connection this afternoon. I went there to research chameleon talent genetics. There appeared to be two chameleons involved in this case, and that didn't seem likely, given the rarity of the talent. Once I got the genetics sorted out, I realized that there was no way Tucker could have been fathered by a standard ghost hunter. So I pulled the hard copy files of the Deene family records, and there you were."

"You're lying," he shouted. "You're just like Tracy, trying to destroy me."

He rushed at her, primitive rage overcoming all other emotion. In that moment he was maddened with fury, longing only to strangle her with his bare hands.

She moved slightly so that he missed her throat on the first pass. Instead, he grabbed her arm and yanked her back against him. This time his hands went around her throat. His fingers tightened. She could no longer breathe. She gripped his wrists, fighting to stay conscious long enough to use her talent.

But he was astonishingly strong, not just physically but psychically as well. A true Cerberus, she thought. What had made her think that she might be able to suppress his dreamlight patterns long enough to escape?

She fought desperately, sending wave after wave of energy into the storm of power that Fortner was generating, trying to disrupt the pattern. But it was like pounding her fists against a green quartz wall.

She pulled more energy from the depths of her being and reached up, clawing for Fortner's eyes.

Fortner screamed and released her. She staggered toward the entrance of the chamber.

"Bitch." He followed her. "I'll kill you this time."

Her only chance was to get lost in the catacombs. He had destroyed her amber. That meant he would not be able to track her. All she had to do was get through the doorway. Two more steps.

But she knew she was not going to make it. He was reaching out to grab her again.

A wave of nightmare energy slammed into the room, shocking her senses. But it was not focused on her. She was getting slapped by the backwash.

Adam had arrived.

He moved into the room, riding a powerful crest of psi that Marlowe knew must have crashed against Fortner's senses with the force of an explosion.

Gibson shot through the doorway, going for Fortner's leg. Fortner lashed out with one booted foot, forcing Gibson to dodge. The savage kick was accompanied by a small shock wave of energy. It probably amounted to little more than a swat as far as Fortner was concerned, but Gibson reeled from the blow.

"No." Marlowe scooped up Gibson and clutched him tightly against her chest. "He's too strong."

Fortner ignored them both. He whirled to confront Adam.

"I knew that someday I'd have to kill you," he said. "Should have done it a long time ago."

"You couldn't because you needed me," Adam said. "I made you look good at the Bureau."

"I sure as hell don't need you any longer," Fortner roared.

Blue ghost fire blazed in the emerald chamber, a

whirlpool of violent sapphire energy that forced Adam to retreat toward the back wall. The Cerberus had unleashed another one of his three talents.

Marlowe had never seen blue ghost light before, but she recognized it from the descriptions in the old files. It was deadly. Stronger and more easily manipulated that standard ghost energy, it could be wielded like some demonic flaming sword. In certain quarters it was called assassin's fire.

Adam responded with a second wave of raw power. The whirlpool of blue ghost light weakened, but it did not disappear. Infuriated, Fortner forged sapphire lightning bolts and sent them hurtling toward Adam.

The bolts splintered and sparked against the invisible barrier of dreamlight that Adam had erected around himself. Marlowe knew that the self-defense tactic, while astonishingly effective, had cost him dearly in terms of energy.

When the last shaft of lightning disintegrated against the dreamlight shield, Adam did not even try to pull another wave of power from the ultradark end of the spectrum. Instead, he launched himself across the chamber.

It was clear immediately that a straightforward physical attack was the last thing Fortner had expected. He had relied on his paranormal talents for so long that he had forgotten there were other, more primitive ways that a man could be attacked, Marlowe thought.

"Stay away from me," Fortner shouted.

He scrambled to evade Adam's rush. Marlowe realized that the shock of the assault had distracted him for a couple of precious seconds. Before he could pull himself together and concentrate hard enough to focus his talent, Adam slammed into him.

Both men fell hard on the unforgiving quartz. Fierce energy flared again in the atmosphere. Marlowe knew that by now the men had to be pulling on the last of their reserves. The pair rolled across the floor of the chamber and came up hard against the wall. Fortner landed on top, but he suddenly stiffened.

His eyes opened wide. He stared down at Adam with an unholy mix of fury and disbelief.

"Not you," he got out. "No. I'm the true Cerberus."

He screamed once. The horrifying sound ended abruptly. He crumpled. Marlowe watched his dream-light fade to a weak glow. It winked out altogether.

A crystalline silence gripped the chamber.

Adam moved, pushing the body aside. He got to his feet. The knife in his hand dripped blood on the psi green floor.

He leaned down to check for a pulse. Marlowe knew that he would not find one.

He stood and turned to her, his eyes still hot with psi.

"Marlowe," he said.

He did not say anything else. There was no need. It was all there in that one word, her name. She sensed the anguished fear and the rage that had driven him; sensed, too, the mag-steel control he had used to focus and channel his energy so that he could get to her.

She managed a shaky smile. "I love you, too. Why didn't you answer your phone? You said you always answer your private line."

"I didn't get your call because I was underground interrogating Joey the broker when you tried to get hold of me. No reception in the tunnels. Joey told me the identity of the client who had commissioned the crystal guns."

Marlowe glanced at the body on the floor. "Did the news come as a big surprise?"

"No. I'd come to the conclusion that Fortner had to be involved. It was the only explanation for the leaks. When I got back to the surface, Fortner called me himself, telling me that he had you."

"How did you find me? Gibson?"

"When I got to your office, Gibson was still unconscious," Adam said. "He didn't wake up until a few minutes ago. I couldn't afford to wait. I knew where Fortner's bolt-hole was. It gave me a starting point. So I called in backup to help track the two of you through the tunnels."

"Backup?"

Adam looked toward the doorway. Marlowe turned and saw Charlotte Deene. Tucker and Keith were with her.

"Of course," Marlowe said. "You called in a strong dreamlight talent. Good thinking, Guild boss."

"This family owed you," Charlotte said. "You may not approve of the way we make our living, but we have our rules, just like the Joneses and the Winters do. We always pay our debts."

"You know," Marlowe said, "the more I think about it, the more I'm convinced that J&J really could use the three of you. Why don't you come to my office soon? We'll talk."

Charlotte, Tucker, and Keith looked at each other. None of them spoke, but they seemed to come to a silent consensus.

"We'll think about it," Charlotte said.

Chapter 42

THEY GATHERED IN MARLOWE'S OFFICE THE FOLLOW-
ing afternoon. She sat behind her desk, Gibson perched
on the back of her chair. The Burning Lamp stood on
the desk in front of her.

Adam lounged against the window ledge, arms folded
across his chest. The others occupied the two office chairs
and the folding chairs that Rick had magically produced.

They had all come to the debriefing: her parents,
Ben and Elizabeth; her uncle Zeke; together with
Diana and Sam Winters. Vickie Winters was also pres-
ent. She looked surprisingly rested, given what she had
been through, Marlowe thought. Like the Joneses, the
Winters family was resilient.

Marlowe sat forward. The chair squeaked. She
folded her hands on her desk and tried to look like a
professional investigator.

"Everything started to go wrong for Elliott Fortner after the Chamber voted to put Adam in charge of cleaning up the Frequency Guild," she said. "As the head of the Bureau, Fortner could have argued against the decision, but he didn't dare."

"Adam was the obvious choice," Sam said. "Fortner knew that if he made any objection, there would be too many questions from the powerful Guild chiefs who rule the Chamber."

"Yes," she agreed. "Fortner had a very good reason for not wanting the Frequency Guild cleaned up. He was raking in a fortune from various illegal operations, all Guild-related, all managed by Hubert O'Conner and Douglas Drake."

Adam looked at the group. "Afraid of having his business activities exposed by the kind of sweeping investigation he knew I would conduct, Fortner devised a plan with Drake and O'Conner to get rid of me. But just as it was all coming together, I discovered the mirror maze."

"Adam went straight to Fortner with the news, of course," Marlowe said. "He also told Fortner that he thought the artifact known as the Burning Lamp might be the key to fixing the dissonance energy in the maze. But first he had to find the lamp."

Ben frowned. "Fortner must have been stunned."

"He knew the legend," Elizabeth said. "The lamp is said to have the power to save a man who was in danger of becoming a true Cerberus."

"And as it happened," Marlowe continued, "Fortner

had just begun to fear that he might be deteriorating psychically. He had been able to handle his three talents surprisingly well until recently, thanks to the genetic advantages of having been born on Harmony. But his condition had always been extremely fragile."

Vickie looked thoughtful. "Using the crystal guns that Keith had forged was probably what pushed him over the edge."

"Yes," Marlowe said.

"He hadn't made the connection with the crystal guns," Adam said. "But he was starting to realize that he was failing. He was getting scared. When I told him that I was going after the Burning Lamp, it dawned on him that if I found it, he might be able to use it to save himself."

. There was a squeak as Marlowe leaned back in her chair. Gibson fluttered briefly, adjusting to the lurch.

"Fortner tried to call off O'Conner and Drake, but that proved impossible," Marlowe said. "In the end, he took care of both of them, himself. Among other things, Fortner was a chameleon talent. He left the prints of one of O'Conner's men at the scene of the fire."

"Did he know that the lamp in the Arcane Museum was a fake?" Ben asked.

"Yes," Adam said. "Because I told him."

"But no one told the Deene triplets," Marlowe added. "So when Keith became seriously ill a few weeks ago, Charlotte and Tucker hatched the idea to find and steal the lamp. They located the fake and went after it."

Zeke got a knowing expression. "That, of course,

set you on a collision course with Adam. Once you two teamed up, you were able to find the lamp and work it."

Marlowe cleared her throat. "To save the underworld," she said very deliberately. "We were able to work it to save the underworld."

Diana smiled. "And to fix Adam's little dreamlight pattern problems. We understand."

"Just to clarify, Adam didn't have any serious dreamlight issues," Marlowe said.

Adam was amused. "It's all right, Marlowe. My family knows, and yours, obviously, has figured it out as well. No need to play any games."

Marlowe glared at her small audience. "Adam does not possess multiple talents. I have reviewed the historical archives and his dreamlight patterns. He has a single, very powerful talent that developed in stages."

Zeke snorted. "The Cerberus part of the Burning Lamp legend is just another Arcane Society myth, along with that nonsense about Nicholas having somehow infused the Midnight Crystal with a dangerous hypnotic command."

Ben nodded. "Obviously, the fact that Adam brought Marlowe safely out of the mirror maze and we are all sitting around chatting is proof that he was not overcome with a sudden urge to kill off the entire Jones line."

Zeke made a face. "I'm a chaos-theory talent. Hell, I was born to see conspiracies everywhere, and even I never believed that part of the legend."

Adam looked at Marlowe. "You see? No need for any secrets in this room."

Jayne Castle

"That's good to know," she said. She returned his smile.

In that moment she knew that neither of them was ever going to mention that the psychical hypnotic command infused in the Midnight Crystal had functioned precisely as Nicholas Winters had intended.

"No one is concerned with the Midnight Crystal," Elizabeth said. "But what about the Deenes' decision to steal the fake lamp, the action that we all agree threw you and Adam together so that you could save the underworld? Was that pure coincidence?"

Zeke scowled. "There are no coincidences. I've told Marlowe that a thousand times."

"Hmm," Marlowe said.

Everyone looked at her.

Marlowe looked at the Burning Lamp. "I'm no crystal talent expert, and for obvious reasons I won't be handing the lamp over to the Arcane labs. But it's clear that the artifact has a long history of drawing together the Winters male who needs it and a dreamlight talent strong enough to work the energy in it."

"Surely you don't believe that the artifact has some supernatural influence," Vickie scoffed. "No one in Arcane believes in magic."

"No magic involved here," Marlowe said. "Just the laws of para-physics. I think that when a man of the Winters bloodline starts to develop the second stage of his talent, the violent energy of the change activates the lamp."

"You're talking about the nightmares and hallucinations?" Adam asked.

"Right," she said. "It takes a lot of extremely powerful energy from the dark end of the spectrum to produce severe nightmares and visions for weeks on end."

"Makes sense," Vickie agreed. "But humans can't project psychic energy much beyond a radius of fifteen or twenty feet."

Sam grew very thoughtful. "That doesn't mean the psi currents don't keep going."

Marlowe sat forward again in her chair. There was another squeak. Gibson chortled, struggling to keep his balance.

"Exactly," Marlowe said. "Psychic energy waves obey the laws of physics just like radio waves or light waves or sound waves. They come from a different end of the spectrum, that's all. We can't hear sound or see light beyond a certain range, but various kinds of instruments and machines can pick up that kind of energy at great distances. They can also transmit it."

Her father nodded. "Radios, cell phones, and rez-screens do it all the time."

"When you think about it," Marlowe said, "the Burning Lamp is just a machine that generates dreamlight. I think that it was originally tuned to detect a very unique frequency of psi, the precise frequency produced by the Winters male who inherited Nicholas's type of talent. The powerful energy of the nightmares and hallucinations activate the device, even over long distances."

Vickie looked intrigued. "Once activated, the machine responds by sending out a signal to any dreamlight reader who is strong enough to sense it unconsciously."

"Meanwhile, the Winters male who is going through the change wisely starts looking for said dreamlight reader," Adam said. "I'd identified half a dozen in the Arcane computer files, but none of them were strong enough. Marlowe, of course, was not listed." He smiled politely. "Being a Jones and all."

"But I had begun to sense the lamp's pull," Marlowe said. "There was no giant red psychic sign, just a general sense of restlessness. I was searching for something, but I didn't know what. I assumed that what I was experiencing was nothing more than the normal reaction anyone would have after taking over a legendary firm with the kind of history that J&J has."

"And the self-doubts that plagued you after you discovered that you had been deceived by Tucker Deene didn't help," Elizabeth added gently.

"No," Marlowe said. "But here's the really interesting part. I don't think that I was the only one who sensed the lamp's energy unconsciously. I think Charlotte Deene picked up some of the vibes, as well."

They all looked a bit startled.

"Really?" Vickie asked.

"Yes," Marlowe continued. "Like I said, the lamp is a machine. The signal it sends out is designed to attract a powerful dreamlight talent, any powerful talent. Charlotte wasn't quite strong enough to locate the lamp or to work it, even if she had found it, but because she was looking for a way to save her brother, she focused on the artifact much sooner than I did."

"That resulted in the theft of the fake," Zeke said. "Which, in turn, caused you to focus on the lamp. Once that happened, you and Adam found each other almost immediately."

Marlowe tapped the end of her pen on the desk. "I'm certain that Adam and I would have connected sooner or later, because his search for the lamp had created rumors among the antiquities dealers in the Quarter. Some of those rumors had reached this office, and I was intrigued by them. I was planning to investigate. But, yes, I think it's safe to say that Charlotte's search and the theft of the lamp speeded up the process."

Diana looked at Adam. "In other words, you and Marlowe would have been drawn together one way or another, regardless of the triggering incident."

Adam smiled at Marlowe, energy shimmering in the atmosphere around him. "No question about it."

Mischief sparkled in Vickie's eyes. "In other words, any powerful dreamlight reader could have done the job?"

"No," Adam said. Absolute certainty rang in the single word. "Only Marlowe."

Marlowe pursed her lips, "Well, as long as there was a strong bond between—"

He stopped her with a look. "Only you."

She smiled. "Okay."

Sam's brows bunched together. "Something else

I've been wondering about. How did those early notes of Nicholas Winters fall into Keith Deene's hands?"

"I found a journal in Fortner's office," Adam said. "He had kept an eye on the triplets over the years because he was curious to see if any of them would inherit his Cerberus talent. He was well aware that Keith was a strong crystal talent. He arranged for his son to find the notes, guessing that Keith would be unable to resist the challenge of trying to forge the enhancing crystals."

Ben looked at Marlowe. "But how did Fortner come across Nicholas's notes in the first place?"

"He inherited them," Marlowe said.

"How, for heaven's sake?" Elizabeth asked.

"The usual way," Marlowe said. "They came down through his family. When I discovered that Fortner was the Deenes' father, I did a little more research and found out that Fortner is a descendant of Samuel Lodge."

"That name rings a bell," Zeke said. He snapped his fingers. "Now I remember. Lodge figured in a very old case that involved the lamp and a nineteenth-century crime lord, Griffin Winters."

"Lodge had some of Nicholas's notes," Adam said. "They descended down through his family."

"Amazing how difficult it is to keep secrets in the Society," Zeke mused.

Diana looked at Marlowe. "Are you going to tell the Deenes the truth about their father?"

"I did that last night after we got out of the tunnels,"

Marlowe said quietly. "I felt they had a right to know the truth. They were shocked but not totally surprised. Charlotte told me that she and her brothers had suspected for years that the ghost hunter named as their father in the Society's files was probably not their real father."

Zeke looked thoughtful. "Think they'll show up here to talk about becoming J&J agents?"

"Yes," Marlowe said. "I think they will."

Vickie frowned. "Why would they do that?"

"Because I made it clear that as far as Arcane is concerned, they are full-fledged members of the Society," Marlowe said. "The Deenes have never had a family. Arcane can provide them with a sense of connection."

Elizabeth smiled. "You may be right."

"At the very least, J&J will be able to keep an eye on them," Zeke said.

Marlowe smiled. "That thought did occur to me." She got to her feet and crossed the room to pick up the coffeepot. "Being the head of J&J, I don't believe in coincidence, of course. But at times like this, I do sort of wonder about karma." She poured coffee into a cup. "The old reap-what-you-sow thing."

Vickie understood. "What goes around, comes around," she said softly.

Diana frowned. "What are you two talking about?"

Marlowe put the pot back down on the burner. "In the end, it was using the crystals that pushed Fortner to the crisis point. Even though he was a true Cerberus, he probably would have lived several more years if he hadn't started using the crystals."

Adam's eyes got very cold. "And the reason those crystals existed in the first place was because Fortner made certain that his son, Keith, got hold of Nicholas Winters's notes."

"Elliott Fortner wielded three talents, but he was insatiable," Marlowe said. "He wanted more power. He became obsessed by the possibility of enhancing his abilities with the crystals."

"In other words," Elizabeth said, "the children that Elliott Fortner abandoned all those years ago had their revenge, although they didn't know it at the time. They forged the very crystals that accelerated his psychical deterioration. And it was Fortner himself who gave them the key."

"Karma," Zeke said. He smiled, satisfied. "Like I said, no such thing as coincidence."

"But you're okay with karma?" Marlowe asked.

"If you look hard enough, far enough, and deep enough, you will find that there is always some kind of balance in the universe," Zeke said. "For want of a better word, I like karma."

Chapter 43

ADAM PICKED UP THE BOTTLE OF AMBER DEW AND followed Marlowe out onto the balcony of her condo. The balmy, psi-lit night stirred his senses. So did Marlowe. She was still wearing the sexy little dark violet dress that she had worn to dinner earlier. Her hair was pinned up in a sleek knot.

She went to lean against the railing and looked out at the glowing ruins. Gibson fluttered through the open doors and bounded up to perch nearby. He had an energy bar clutched in one paw.

"Been a fast week," Adam said. He set the glasses down on the small table. "Not a lot of time for us to talk."

She smiled at him from the shadows.

"No," she said. "Not a lot of time at all."

He filled the glasses and handed one to Marlowe.

Energy and intimacy shimmered in the atmosphere around them. He touched his glass to hers.

"Here's to our first real date," he said. "I thought it went well. No one tried to kill us. We didn't run into any stray Cerberus talents. I don't recall any odd artifacts infused with hypnotic commands."

"I hope you weren't bored."

"Not for a second." He brushed his mouth against hers. "You?"

"No," she said. "Never. Not with you."

She sipped some of the Amber Dew. He swallowed some, too. Gibson chortled and munched his energy bar.

Adam touched Marlowe's cheek. "I love you. The first time I saw you, I knew that you were the woman I'd been waiting for."

"I love *you*, Adam. I had given up. I thought there would never be anyone for me. When I first met you, I was afraid to hope, afraid to believe that you might really be the one."

"But you're not afraid anymore, are you? After all, you're the head of Jones & Jones. Takes more than the thought of a Covenant Marriage to scare the daylights out of you."

"Is that what we're talking about?" she asked. "A Covenant Marriage?"

"When it comes to marriage, the Winters family holds the same traditional views as the Jones family. We consider Marriages of Convenience tacky."

"Well, that settles it, then," she said. "Wouldn't

want anyone to think that the man who was hand-picked to clean up the Guild would get involved in a tacky MC."

He took the glass from her fingers and set it down beside his. "The Winters family has a couple of other traditions in common with the Jones family." He drew her into his arms. "When we fall in love, we fall all the way and forever."

"Yes." She put her arms around his neck. Her eyes were deep and filled with dreams. "All the way. Forever."

He kissed her for a long time. After a while, he picked her up and carried her inside, all the way to the bedroom.

OUT ON THE BALCONY GIBSON WAITED UNTIL THE bedroom went dark. Then he dashed through the small door and headed for the kitchen.

He hopped up onto the counter. The new cookie jar was filled with High-Rez Energy Bars, and there was no lock yet. He got the lid off and reached inside with his two front paws.

By the time he got the first load out to the balcony, half a dozen guests had already arrived. They helped him carry out the rest of the hors d'oeuvres. By then there were nearly a dozen dust bunnies present.

The night was young, the energy was good, and it was safe to go back into the rain forest again. Time to party.

Mr. Gibson
Jones & Jones Investigations
12 East Wall Lane
Frequency City

Dear Mr. Gibson:

Welcome to the High-Rez Energy Bars of the Month
Club!

    Your admirers at the headquarters of the Frequency
City Ghost Hunter Guild have purchased a year's sup-
ply of our finest energy bars just for you. Each month
you will receive a case of these premium gourmet treats
delivered to your doorstep.

    We hope you enjoy them and tell a friend.

            Sincerely,
            R. J. Calhoun
            CEO, High-Rez Energy Bar Corp.

TURN THE PAGE FOR A LOOK AT

FIRED UP

by Jayne Ann Krentz

Available now from Piatkus.

Dear Reader:

The Arcane Society was founded on secrets. Few of those secrets are more dangerous than those kept by the descendants of the alchemist Nicholas Winters, fierce rival of Sylvester Jones.

The legend of the Burning Lamp goes back to the earliest days of the Society. Nicholas Winters and Sylvester Jones started out as friends and eventually became deadly adversaries. Each sought the same goal: a way to enhance psychic talents. Sylvester chose the path of chemistry and plunged into illicit experiments with strange herbs and plants. Ultimately he concocted the flawed formula that bedevils the Society to this day.

Nicholas took the engineering approach and forged the Burning Lamp, a device with unknown powers. The radiation from the lamp produced a twist in his DNA, creating a psychic genetic "curse" destined to be passed down through the males of his bloodline.

The Winters Curse strikes very rarely, but when

it does the Arcane Society has good reason for grave concern. It is said that the Winters man who inherits Nicholas's genetically altered talent is destined to become a Cerberus—Arcane slang for an insane psychic who possesses multiple lethal abilities. Jones & Jones and the Governing Council are convinced that such human monsters must be hunted down and terminated as swiftly as possible.

There is only one hope for the men of the Burning Lamp. Each must find the artifact and a woman who can work the dreamlight energy that the device produces in order to reverse the changes brought on by the curse.

In the Dreamlight Trilogy you will meet the three men of the Burning Lamp, past, present, and future. These are the passionate descendants of Nicholas Winters. Each will discover some of the deadly secrets of the lamp. Each will encounter the woman with the power to shape his destiny.

And ultimately, far in the future, on a world called Harmony, one of them will unravel the lamp's final and most dangerous mystery, the secret of the midnight crystal.

I hope you will enjoy the trilogy.

Sincerely,
Jayne

Prologue

Capitol Hill neighborhood, Seattle

THE TWO-BLOCK WALK FROM THE BUS STOP ON BROAD-
way to her apartment was a terrifying ordeal late at night.
Reluctantly she left the small island of light cast by the
streetlamp and started the treacherous journey into the
darkness. At least it had stopped raining. She clamped
her purse tightly to her side and clutched her keys the way
she had been taught in the two-hour self-defense class the
hospital had offered to its staff. The small jagged bits of
metal protruded between her fingers like claws.

Should never have agreed to take the night shift,
she thought. But the extra pay had been too tantalizing
to resist. Six months from now she would have enough
saved up to buy a used car. No more lonely, late-night
rides on the bus.

She was a block and a half from her apartment when she heard the footsteps behind her. She thought her heart would stop. She fought her instincts and forced herself to turn around and look. A man emerged from a nearly empty parking lot. For a few seconds the streetlight gleamed on his shaved head. He had the bulky form of a bodybuilder on steroids. She relaxed a little. She did not know him but she knew where he was going.

The big man disappeared through the glass doors of the gym. The small neon sign in the window announced that it was open twenty-four hours a day. It was the only establishment on the street that was still illuminated. The bookstore with its window full of occult books and Goth jewelry, the pawn shop, the tiny hair salon, and the payday loan operation had been closed for hours.

The gym was not one of the upscale fitness clubs that catered to the spandex-and-yoga crowd. It was the kind of facility frequented by dedicated bodybuilders. The beefy men who came and left the premises did not know it but she sometimes thought of them as her guardian angels. If anything ever happened to her on the long walk home, her only hope was that someone inside the gym would hear her scream and come to help.

She was almost at the intersection when she caught the shift of shadows in a doorway across the street. A man waited there. Was he watching her? Something about the way he moved told her that he was not one of the men from the gym. He wasn't pumped up on steroids and weights. There was instead a lean, sleek, almost predatory air about him.

Her pulse, already beating much too quickly, started to pound as the fight-or-flight response kicked in. There was a terrible prickling on the nape of her neck. The urge to run was almost overwhelming but she could hardly breathe now. In any event she had no hope of outrunning a man. The only refuge was the gym, but the dark silhouette on the other side of the street stood between her and the entrance. Maybe she should scream. But what if her imagination had gotten the better of her? The man across the street did not seem to be paying any attention to her. He was intent on the entrance of the gym.

She froze, unable to make a decision. She watched the figure on the other side of the street the way a baby rabbit watches a snake.

She never heard the killer come out of the shadows behind her. A sweaty, masculine hand clamped across her mouth. A sharp blade pricked her throat. She heard a clatter of metal on the sidewalk and realized that she had just dropped her only weapon, the keys.

"Quiet or you die now," a hoarse voice muttered in her ear. "Be a shame if we didn't have time to play."

She was going to die anyway, she thought. She had nothing to lose. She dropped her purse and tried to struggle but it was useless. The man had an arm around her throat. He dragged her into the alley, choking her. She reached up and managed to rake her fingernails across the back of his hand. She would not survive the night but she could damn well collect some of the bastard's DNA for the cops.

"I warned you, bitch. I'm really going to take my time with you. I want to hear you beg."

She could not breathe and the hand across her mouth made it impossible to scream. To think that her fallback had always been the plan to yell for help from the gym.

The alley was drenched in night but there was another kind of darkness enveloping her. With luck she would suffocate from the pressure of his arm on her throat before he could use the knife, she thought. She'd worked in the trauma center at Harborview. She knew what knives could do.

A figure loomed at the entrance of the alley, silhouetted by the weak streetlight behind him. She knew it was the man she had seen in the doorway across the street. Two killers working as a team? She had sunk so far into panic and despair that she wondered if she was hallucinating.

"Let her go," the newcomer said, coming down the alley. His voice promised death as clearly as the knife at her throat.

Her captor stopped. "Get out of here or I'll slit her throat. I swear I will."

"Too late." The stranger walked forward. He was not rushing in, but there was something lethal and relentless about his approach; a predator who knows the prey is trapped. "You're already dead."

She felt something then, something she could not explain. It was as if she was caught in the center of an electrical storm. Currents of energy flooded her senses.

"No," her captor shouted. "She's mine."

And then he was screaming, horror and shock mingling in a nerve-shattering shriek.

"Get away from me," he shouted.

Suddenly she was free; falling. She landed with a jolt on the damp pavement. The man with the knife reeled back and fetched up against the alley wall.

The unnerving energy evaporated as swiftly and mysteriously as it had appeared.

The killer came away from the wall as though he had been released from a cage.

"No," he hissed, madness and rage vibrating in the single word.

He lurched toward the other man. Light glinted on the knife he still clutched.

More energy shivered in a heavy wave through the alley.

The killer screamed again, a shrill, sharp screech that ended with stunning abruptness. He dropped the knife, clutched at his chest, and dropped to the pavement.

The dark figure loomed over the killer for a moment. She saw him lean down and realized that he was checking for a pulse. She knew that he would not find one. She recognized death when she saw it.

The man straightened and turned toward her. Fear

held her immobile. There was something wrong with his face. It was too dark to make out his features but she thought she could see a smoldering energy in the dark spheres where his eyes should have been.

Another wave of panic slammed through her, bringing with it a fresh dose of adrenaline. She scrambled to her feet and fled toward the street, knowing, even as she ran, that it was hopeless. The creature with the burning eyes would cut her down as easily as he had the killer with the knife.

But the monster did not pursue her. A block away she finally stopped to catch her breath. When she looked back she saw nothing. The street was empty.

She had always hoped that if the worst happened on the way home she might get some help from the men in the gym. But in the end it was a demon that had saved her.

Chapter 1

DREAMLIGHT GLOWED FAINTLY ON THE SMALL STATUE of the Egyptian queen. The prints were murky and thickly layered. A lot of people had handled the object over the decades but none of the prints went back any further than the late eighteen hundreds, Chloe Harper concluded. Certainly none dated from the Eighteenth Dynasty.

"I'm afraid it's a fake." She lowered her senses, turned away from the small statue, and looked at Bernard Paddon. "A very fine fake, but a fake nonetheless."

"Damn it, are you absolutely certain?" Paddon's bushy silver brows scrunched together. His face reddened in annoyance and disbelief. "I bought it from Crofton. He's always been reliable."

The Paddon collection of antiquities put a lot of big city museums to shame but it was not open to the public. Paddon was a secretive, obsessive collector who hoarded his treasures in a vault like some cranky troll guarding his gold. He dealt almost exclusively in the notoriously gray world of the underground antiquities market, preferring to avoid the troublesome paperwork, customs requirements, and other assorted legal authorizations required to buy and sell in the aboveground, more legitimate end of the trade.

He was, in fact, just the sort of client that Harper Investigations liked to cultivate, the kind that paid the bills. She did not relish having to tell him that his statue was a fake. On the other hand, the client she was representing in this deal would no doubt be suitably grateful.

Paddon had inherited a large number of the Egyptian, Roman, and Greek artifacts in the vault from his father, a wealthy industrialist who had built the family fortune in a very different era. Bernard was now in his seventies. Sadly, while he had continued the family traditions of collecting, he had not done such a great job when it came to investing. The result was that these days he was reduced to selling items from his collection in order to finance new acquisitions. He had been counting on the sale of the statue to pay for some other relic he craved.

Chloe was very careful never to get involved with the actual financial end of the transactions. That was an excellent way to draw the attention not only of the police and Interpol but, in her case, the extremely irritating self-appointed psychic cops from Jones & Jones.

Her job, as she saw it, was to track down items of interest and then put buyers and sellers in touch with each other. She collected a fee for her service and then she got the heck out of Dodge, as Aunt Phyllis put it.

She glanced over her shoulder at the statue. "Nineteenth century, I'd say. Victorian era. It was a period of remarkably brilliant fakes."

"Stop calling it a fake," Paddon sputtered. "I know fakes when I see them."

"Don't feel bad, sir. A lot of major institutions like the British Museum and the Met, not to mention a host of serious collectors such as yourself, have been deceived by fakes and forgeries from that era."

"*Don't feel bad?* I paid a fortune for that statue. The provenance is pristine."

"I'm sure Crofton will refund your money. As you say, he has a very good reputation. He was no doubt taken in, as well. It's safe to say that piece has been floating around undetected since the eighteen-eighties." Actually, she was sure of it. "But under the circumstances, I really can't advise my client to buy it."

Paddon's expression would have been better suited to a bulldog. "Just look at those exquisite hieroglyphs."

"Yes, they are very well done."

"Because they were done in the Eighteenth Dynasty," Paddon gritted. "I'm going to get a second opinion."

"Of course. If you'll excuse me, I'll be on my way."
She picked up her black leather satchel. "No need to
show me out."

She went briskly toward the door.

"Hold on, here." Paddon rushed after her. "Are you
going to tell your client about this?"

"Well, he is paying me for my expert opinion."

"I can come up with any number of experts who
will give him a different opinion, including Crofton."

"I'm sure you can." She did not doubt that. The little
statue had passed for the real thing since it had been
created. Along the way any number of experts had
probably declared it to be an original.

"This is your way of negotiating for an additional
fee from me, isn't it, Miss Harper?" Paddon snorted.
"I have no problem with that. What number did you
have in mind? If it's reasonable I'm sure we can come
to some agreement."

"I'm sorry, Mr. Paddon. I don't work that way. That
sort of arrangement would be very damaging to my
professional reputation."

"You call yourself a professional? You're nothing but a two-bit private investigator who happens to
dabble in the antiquities market. If I'd known that you
were so unknowledgeable I would never have agreed
to let you examine the piece. Furthermore, you can bet
I'll never hire you to consult for me."

"I'm sorry you feel that way, of course, but maybe
you should consider one thing."

"What's that?" he called after her.

She paused in the doorway and looked back at him. "If you ever did hire me you could rest assured that you would be getting an honest appraisal. You would know for certain that I could not be bought."

She did not wait for a response. She walked out of the gallery and went down the hall to the foyer of the large house. A woman in a housekeeper's uniform handed her the still-damp trench coat and floppy brimmed hat.

Chloe put on the coat. The trench was a gift from her aunt Phyllis. Phyllis had spent her working years in Hollywood. She claimed she knew how private investigators were supposed to dress because she'd known so many stars who played those kinds of roles. Chloe wasn't so sure about the style statement but she liked the convenience of the numerous pockets in the coat.

Outside on the front steps she paused to pull the hat down low over her eyes. It was raining again and although it was only a quarter to five, it was almost full dark. This was the Pacific Northwest and it was early December. Darkness and rain came with the territory at this time of year. Some people considered it atmospheric. They didn't mind the short days because they knew that a kind of karmic balance would kick in come summer when there would be daylight until nearly ten o'clock at night.

Those who weren't into the yin-yang thing went out and bought special light boxes designed to treat the depressive condition known as SAD, seasonal affective disorder.

She was okay with darkness and rain. But maybe that was because of her talent for reading dreamlight. Dreams and darkness went together.

She went down the steps and crossed the vast, circular drive to where her small, nondescript car was parked. The dog sitting patiently in the passenger seat watched her intently as she came toward him. She knew that he had been fixated on the front door of the house, waiting for her to reappear, since she had vanished inside forty minutes ago. The dog's name was Hector and he had abandonment issues.

When she opened the car door he got excited, just as if she had been gone for a week. She rubbed his ears and let him lick her hand.

"Mr. Paddon is not a happy man, Hector." The greeting ritual finished, she got behind the wheel. "I don't think we'll be seeing him as a client of Harper Investigations anytime soon."

Hector was not interested in clients. Satisfied that she was back, he resumed his customary position, riding shotgun in the passenger seat.

She fired up the engine. She had told Paddon the truth about the little Egyptian queen. It was a fake and it had been floating around in the private market since the Victorian period. She was certain of that for three reasons, none of which she could explain to Paddon. The first reason was that her talent allowed her to date objects quite accurately. Reason number two was that she came from a long line of art and antiquities experts. She had been raised in the business.

Reason number three was also straightforward. She had recognized the workmanship and the telltale dreamlight the moment she saw the statue.

"You can't rat out your own several times great-grandfather, Hector, even if he has been dead since the first quarter of the twentieth century. Family is family."

Norwood Harper had been a master. His work was on display in some of the finest museums in the Western world, albeit not under his own name. And now one of his most charmingly brilliant fakes was sitting in Paddon's private collection.

It wasn't the first time she had stumbled onto a Harper fake. Her extensive family tree boasted a number of branches that specialized in fakes, forgeries, and assorted art frauds. Other limbs featured individuals with a remarkable talent for deception, illusion, and sleight of hand. Her relatives all had what could only be described as a true talent for less-than-legal activities.

Her own paranormal ability had taken a different and far less marketable form. She had inherited the ability to read dreamlight from Aunt Phyllis's side of the tree. There were few practical applications—although Phyllis had managed to make it pay very well—and one really huge downside. Because of that downside, the odds were overwhelming that she would never marry.

Sex wasn't the problem. But over the course of the past year or two she had begun to lose interest in it. Perhaps that was because she had finally accepted that she would never have a relationship that lasted longer than a few months. Somehow, that realization had removed what little pleasure was left in short-term affairs. In the wake of the fiasco with Fletcher Monroe a few months ago, she had settled into celibacy with a sense of enormous relief.

"There is a kind of freedom in the celibate lifestyle," she explained to Hector.

Hector twitched his ears but otherwise showed no interest in the subject.

She left the street of elegant homes on Queen Anne Hill and drove back downtown through the rain, heading toward her office and apartment in Pioneer Square.

TURN THE PAGE FOR A LOOK AT

BURNING LAMP

by Amanda Quick

Available now from Piatkus.

London, late in the reign of Queen Victoria . . .

IT TOOK ADELAIDE PYNE ALMOST FORTY-EIGHT HOURS to realize that the Rosestead Academy was not an exclusive school for orphaned young ladies. It was a brothel. By then it was too late. She had been sold to the frightening man known only as Mr. Smith.

The Chamber of Pleasure was in deep shadow, lit only by a single candle. The flame sparked and flared on the cream-colored satin drapery that billowed down from the wrought-iron frame above the canopied bed. In the pale glow the crimson rose petals scattered across the snowy white quilt looked like small pools of blood.

Adelaide huddled in the darkened confines of the wardrobe, all her senses heightened by dread and panic. Through the crack between the doors she could see only a narrow slice of the room.

Smith entered the chamber. He barely glanced at the heavily draped bed. Locking the door immediately, he set his hat and a black satchel on the table, for all the world as though he were a doctor who had been summoned to attend a patient.

In spite of her heart-pounding fear, something about the satchel distracted Adelaide, riveting her attention. Dreamlight leaked out of the black bag. She could scarcely believe her senses. Great powerful currents of ominous energy seeped through the leather. She had the unnerving impression that it was calling to her in a thousand different ways. But that was impossible.

There was no time to contemplate the mystery. Her circumstances had just become far more desperate. Her plan, such as it was, had hinged on the assumption that she would be dealing with one of Mrs. Rosser's usual clients, an inebriated gentleman in a state of lust who possessed no significant degree of psychical talent. It had become obvious to her during the past two days that sexual desire tended to refocus the average gentleman's brain in a way that, temporarily at least, obliterated his common sense and reduced the level of his intelligence. She had intended to take advantage of that observation tonight to make her escape.

But Smith was most certainly not an average brothel client. Adelaide was horrified to see the seething energy in the dreamprints he had tracked into the room.

His hot paranormal fingerprints were all over the satchel as well.

Everyone left some residue of dreamlight behind on the objects with which they came in contact. The currents seeped easily through shoe leather and gloves. Her talent allowed her to perceive the traces of such energy.

In general, dreamprints were faint and murky. But there were exceptions. Individuals in a state of intense emotion or excitement generated very distinct, very perceptible prints. So did those with strong psychical abilities. Mr. Smith fit into both categories. He was aroused and he was a powerful talent. That was a very dangerous combination.

Even more unnerving was the realization that there was something wrong with his dreamlight patterns. The oily, iridescent currents of his tracks and prints were ever so faintly warped.

Smith turned toward the wardrobe. The pale glow of the candle gleamed on the black silk mask that concealed the upper half of his face. Whatever he intended to do in this room was of such a dreadful nature that he did not wish to take the chance of being recognized by anyone on the premises.

He moved like a man in his prime. He was tall and slender. His clothes looked expensive and he carried himself with the bred-in-the-cradle arrogance of a man accustomed to the privileges of wealth and high social rank.

He stripped off his leather gloves and unfastened the metal buckles of the satchel with a feverish haste that, in another man, might have indicated lust. She had not yet had any practical experience of such matters. Mrs. Rosser, the manager of the brothel, had informed her that Smith would be her first client. But during the past two days she had seen the tracks the gentlemen left on the stairs when they followed the girls to their rooms. She now knew what desire looked like when it burned in a man.

What she saw in Smith's eerily luminous prints was different. There was most certainly a dark hunger pulsing in him, but it did not seem related to sexual excitement. The dark ultralight indicated that it was another kind of passion that consumed Smith tonight and it was a terrifying thing to behold.

Adelaide held her breath when he opened the satchel and reached inside. She did not know what to expect. Some of the girls whispered about the bizarre, unnatural games many clients savored.

But it was not a whip or a chain or leather manacles that Smith took out of the satchel. Rather, it was a strange, vase-shaped artifact. The object was made of some metal that glinted gold in the flickering candlelight. It rose about eighteen inches from a heavy base, flaring outward toward the top. Large, colorless crystals were set in a circle around the rim.

The waves of dark power whispering from the artifact stirred the hair on the nape of her neck. The object was infused with a storm of dreamlight that seemed to be trapped in a state of suspension. *Like a machine,* she thought, astonished—*a device designed to generate dreamlight.*

Even as she told herself that such a paranormal engine could not possibly exist, the memory of a tale her father had told her, an old Arcane legend, drifted, phantomlike through her thoughts.

Smith set the artifact on the table next to the candle. Then he went swiftly toward the bed.

"Let us get on with the business," he commanded. Tension and impatience thickened the words.

He yanked aside the satin hangings. For a few seconds he stared at the empty sheets, evidently baffled. An instant later, rage stiffened his body. He crushed a handful of the drapery in one fist and spun around, searching the shadows.

"Stupid girl. Where are you? I don't know what Rosser told you, but I am not one of her regular clients. I do not make a habit of sleeping with whores and I certainly did not come here tonight to play games."

His voice was low and reptilian cold now. The words slithered down her spine. At the same time, the temperature in the chamber seemed to drop several degrees. She started to shiver, not just with terror, but with the new chill in the atmosphere.

He'll check under the bed first, she thought.

He seized the candle off the table and crouched to peer into the shadows beneath the iron bed frame.

She knew that he would open the wardrobe as soon as he realized that she was not hiding under the bed. It was the only other piece of furniture in the room that was large enough to conceal a person.

"Bloody hell." Smith shot to his feet so swiftly that the candle in his hand flickered and nearly died. "Come out, you foolish girl. I'll be quick about it, I promise. Trust me when I tell you that I have no plans to linger over this aspect of the thing."

He stilled when he saw the wardrobe.

"Did you think I wouldn't find you? Brainless female."

She could not even breathe now. There was nowhere to run.

The wardrobe door opened abruptly. Candlelight spilled into the darkness. Smith's eyes glittered behind the slits in the black mask.

"Silly whore."

He seized her arm to haul her out of the wardrobe. Her talent was flaring wildly, higher than it ever had since she had come into it a year ago. The result was predictable. She reacted to the physical contact as though she had been struck by invisible lightning. The shock was such that she could not even scream.

Frantically, she dampened her talent. She hated to be touched when her senses were elevated. The experience of brushing up against the shadows and remnants of another person's dreams was horribly, gut-wrenchingly intimate and disturbing in the extreme.

Before she could catch her breath, she heard a key in a lock. The door of the chamber slammed open. Mrs. Rosser loomed in the entrance. Her bony frame was darkly silhouetted against the low glare of the gaslight that illuminated the hallway behind her. She bore a striking resemblance to the nickname that the women of the brothel had bestowed upon her: the Vulture.

"I'm afraid there's been a change of plans, sir," Rosser said. Her voice was as stern and rigid as the rest of her. "You must leave the premises immediately."

"What the devil are you talking about?" Smith demanded. He tightened his grip on Adelaide's arm. "I paid an exorbitant price for this girl."

"I just received a message informing me that this establishment is now under new ownership," Rosser said. "It is my understanding that the former owner has recently expired. Heart attack. His business enterprises have been taken over by another. Don't worry, your money will be refunded."

"I don't want a refund," Smith said. "I want this girl."

"Plenty more where she came from. I've got two downstairs right now who are younger and prettier. Never been touched. This one's fifteen if she's a day. Doubt if you'd be the first to bed her."

"Bah. Do you think I give a damn about the girl's virginity?"

Rosser was clearly startled. "But that's what you're paying for."

"Stupid woman. This concerns a vastly more important attribute. I made a bargain with your employer. I intend to hold him to it."

"I just told you, he's no longer among the living. I've got a new employer."

"The business affairs of crime lords are of no interest to me. The girl is now my property. I'm taking her out of here tonight, assuming the experiment is completed to my satisfaction."

"What's this about an experiment?" Mrs. Rosser was outraged. "I never heard of such a thing. This is a brothel, not a laboratory. In any event, you can't have the girl, and that's final."

"It appears that the test will have to be conducted elsewhere," Smith said to Adelaide. "Come along."

He jerked her out of the wardrobe. She tumbled to the floor at his feet.

"Get up." He used his grip on her arm to haul her erect. "We're leaving this place immediately. Never fear, if it transpires that you are of no use to me, you'll be quite free to return to this establishment."

"You're not taking her away." Rosser reached for the bellpull just inside the door. "I'm going to summon the guards."

"You'll do nothing of the kind," Smith said. "I've had quite enough of this nonsense."

He removed a fist-sized crystal from the pocket of his coat. The object glowed blood-red. The temperature dropped another few degrees. Adelaide sensed invisible, ice-cold energy blazing in the chamber.

Mrs. Rosser opened her mouth, but no sound emerged. She raised her arms as though she really were a great bird trying to take wing. Her head fell back. A violent spasm shot through her. She collapsed in the doorway and lay very still.

Adelaide was too stunned to speak. The Vulture was dead.

"Just as well," Smith said. "She is no great loss to anyone."

He was right, Adelaide thought. Heaven knew that she'd had no fondness for the brothel keeper, but watching Rosser die in such a fashion was a horrifying, entirely unnerving experience.

Belatedly, the full impact of what had just happened jolted through her. *Smith had used his talent and the crystal to commit murder.* She had never known that such a thing was possible.

"What did you do to her?" Adelaide whispered.

"The same thing I will do to you if you do not obey me." The ruby crystal had gone dark. He dropped it back into his pocket. "Come along. There is no time to waste. We must get out of here at once."

He drew her toward the table where he had left the artifact. She could feel the euphoric excitement flooding through him. He had just murdered a woman and he had enjoyed doing it—no, he had *rejoiced* in the experience.

She sensed something else as well. Whatever Smith had done with the crystal had required a great deal of energy. The psychical senses required time to recover when one drew heavily on them. Smith would no doubt soon regain the full force of his great power, but at that moment he was probably at least somewhat weakened.

"I'm not going anywhere with you," she said.

He did not bother to respond with words. The next

thing she knew, icy-cold pain washed through her in searing waves.

She gasped, doubled over, and sank to her knees beneath the weight of the chilling agony.

"Now you know what I did to Rosser," Smith said. "But in her case I used far more power. Such intense cold shatters the senses and then stops the heart. Behave yourself or you will get more of the same."

The pain stopped as abruptly as it had begun, leaving her dazed and breathless. Surely he had used the last of his reserves to punish her. She had to act quickly. Fortunately he was still gripping her arm. She required physical contact to manipulate another individual's dreamlight energy.

She raised her talent again, gritting her teeth against the dreadful sensations, and focused every ounce of energy she possessed on the currents of Smith's dreamlight. In the past year she had occasionally manipulated the wavelengths of other people's nightmares, but she had never before attempted what she was about to try now.

For an instant Smith did not seem to realize that he was under attack. He stared at her, mouth partially open in confusion. Fury quickly tightened his expression.

"What are you doing?" he demanded. "You will pay for this. I will make you freeze in your own private hell for daring to defy me. *Stop*."

He raised his other arm, perhaps to reach back into his pocket for the crystal. But it was too late. He was already sliding into a deep sleep. He started to crumple. At the last second, he tried to grab the edge of the table. His flailing arm knocked the candle off the stand and onto the floor.

The taper rolled across the wooden floorboards toward the bed. There was a soft whoosh when the flame caught the trailing edge of the satin drapery.

Adelaide rushed back to the wardrobe and took out the cloak and shoes that she had stashed inside earlier in preparation for her escape. By the time she was dressed, the bed skirt was fully ablaze, the flames licking at the white quilt. Smoke was drifting out into the hall. Soon someone would sound the alarm.

She pulled the hood of the cloak up over her head and went toward the door. But something made her stop. She turned reluctantly and looked back at the artifact. Smith had called it a lamp, but it did not look like any lamp that she had ever seen.

She knew then that she had to take the artifact with her. It was a foolish notion. It would only slow her down. But she could not leave it behind.

She stuffed the lamp into the black satchel, fastened the buckles, and started once more toward the door. She paused a second time over Smith's motionless figure and quickly searched his pockets. There was money in one of them. The dark ruby-colored crystal was in another. She took the money but when she touched the crystal, she got an uneasy feeling. Heeding her intuition, she left it where it was.

Straightening, she stepped over Rosser's dead body and moved out into the corridor.

Behind her the white satin bed was now engulfed in crackling, snapping flames. Down the hall someone started screaming. Men and women in various stages of dress and undress burst out of nearby doorways, seeking the closest exits.

No one paid any attention to Adelaide when she joined the frantic crush on the staircase.

Minutes later, she was outside on the street. Clutching the satchel, she fled into the night, running for her life.